~NED~ CIRCUS OF MARVELS

JUSTIN FISHER has been a designer, illustrator and animator for both film and television. He has designed title sequences for several Hollywood films, branded music TV channels and has worked extensively in advertising. But after many years of helping to tell other people's stories, he is now following a lifelong passion and writing his own. Justin lives with his wife and three young children in London. He has never worked in a circus but he can juggle. Sort of.

First published in Great Britain by HarperCollins *Children's Books* 2016
HarperCollins *Children's Books* is a division of HarperCollins*Publishers* Ltd,
HarperCollins *Publishers*,
1 London Bridge Street,
London SE1 9GF

The HarperCollins *Children's Books* website address is
www.harpercollins.co.uk

1

Text © Justin Fisher 2016
Justin Fisher asserts the moral right to be identified as the author of this work.

ISBN 978-0-00-821239-1

Printed and bound in the United States of America by
LSC Communications.

Find out more about HarperCollins and the environment at
www.harpercollins.co.uk/green

NED'S CIRCUS OF MARVELS

JUSTIN FISHER

HarperCollins *Children's Books*

For C,
the glue that binds my pages

And for L, G and L,
my tiny pots of Ink

PROLOGUE

The building work at Battersea Power Station had been abandoned without warning. 'Site under new management' billboards had been hurriedly put up years ago, with a small logo stamped across their tops, 'Oublier and Co'. The army of cranes, bulldozers and diggers lay silenced, their only visitors an occasional seagull and deepening bouts of rust. It was late and London was asleep. As always, the River Thames flowed quietly by, disturbed only by the odd houseboat and the occasional taxi making a final drop off before heading home.

It started as it usually did. Deep in the bowels of the old power station, the air began to move. Behind a half-cracked mirror, water pipes trembled, inexplicably flowing backwards, inexplicably flowing at all. If anything could have lived down there, which it couldn't, it would have run. Only the building's four vast chimneys could see how the shadows turned and twisted, before revealing a mud-splattered, silver-haired nun.

Sister Clementine was tired, tired of running, tired of

always being afraid. Ever since she'd agreed to carry the message, they'd had her scent. No matter how well she'd hidden, no matter what tricks she'd used, they'd always found her. Her chest was tight and her legs ached from the chase. She had to think fast; any minute now and they'd be on her. She couldn't outrun them, especially not the little one. By the time she made it to the fence, they'd have her, and if they had her, there was no hope of keeping quiet. No one ever kept quiet.

Looking out towards the river, she saw a sliver of hope. If she could make the crane in time, she might get high enough to go unnoticed. She climbed the ladder quickly and quietly, her robes perfect cover under the pitch-black sky.

But Sister Clementine did not go unnoticed. Finally at the crane's arm she slowed enough to hear them. The same two men that had tracked her since the beginning, one short and barrel-chested, the other impossibly tall. They were studying their new surroundings carefully. The shorter man sniffed at the air's unique aroma, while the tall man's pin-sharp eyes scanned the horizon. Their kind might usually have been nervous, afraid even of being on land owned by Oublier and Co. But not these men. It was not their job to fear, but to be feared. They were the things that went *bump* in the night.

In no time they had zeroed in on their target. They moved fast, the tall one climbing with all the skill of a spider while the other charged with the excitable brute strength of a predator nearing its prey.

Sister Clementine moved further down the crane arm as her assailants reached the top.

"Gimme the co-ordinates, Clementine. Jus' two sets o' numbers and you go free," said the tall man, in a thick American accent.

Clementine's foot slipped, finding only air instead of metal. There was nowhere else to run. The tall American pulled a revolver from his hip, aiming it squarely at the woman's head.

"Don't kill her, just wound her; she's worth nothing if she can't talk," snarled the barrel, edging down the crane's arm towards her.

The nun looked down at the void of black, before closing her eyes for one last prayer.

"He wants the child, Clementine," said the American.

But the nun's mind was already made up.

"Lord, make me an instrument of your peace.

Where there is hatred, let me sow love…"

Where there is darkness, joy…"

"WHERE IS SHE?" barked the barrel, almost upon her now.

Sister Clementine opened her eyes and smiled.

"Go to hell."

She stretched out her arms like wings and pushed hard on the crane beneath her, launching herself into the air. There was no hard crunch of concrete below, only a splash as she landed in the River Thames's waters. The tall American waited, peering into the darkness, before firing a single perfect round.

"Did you get her?" asked the barrel.

"Have I eva missed?"

CHAPTER 1

A Birthday Wish

"**H**inks?" said Mr Wilkinson.

"Yes, sir."

"Well done. A plus. Johnston?"

"Sir."

"Not a bad B, Johnston. Widdlewort?"

"It's Waddlesworth, sir."

"Yes, yes of course it is. C *again*, Widdlewort."

The subject didn't matter. Ned Waddlesworth always got a C. Not a C plus or minus, nothing with any particular character, just your average, everyday C. He was an unremarkable-looking boy too, with light brownish sort of eyes, and hair that was neither long nor short, styled nor loose, brown nor blonde. His hair was, quite simply, there. Ned wasn't tall or short, chunky or particularly thin. At school Ned wasn't in the clever classes, nor did he slouch at the back. Ned, like his hair, was just: there.

Teachers barely noticed him arrive at his new schools, or leave again a few months later. He never got to try out for any of the teams and, until recently, was never around long enough to make any friends. Unnoticeable Ned slipped through the cracks, again and again and again.

His father, Terry Waddlesworth, had once been an engineer. He'd retired from that profession before Ned was born and now sold specialist screws for a company called Fidgit and Sons. "Best in the business", according to Terry. The job had them move around the country often, sometimes with little or no warning, and was, as far as Ned was concerned, the reason for all his woes. But that wasn't the only issue Ned had with his father. Terry Waddlesworth had a profound dislike for anything risky or "dangerous", which meant he rarely left the house unless going to work. He was interested in only three things: amateur mechanics, watching quiz shows on the telly, and Ned's safety. It did not make for an environment that let growing boys … 'grow'.

They lived at Number 222 Oak Tree Lane, in Grittlesby, a suburb south of London, famed for its lack of traffic, quiet streets and generally being entirely unremarkable. It was the longest they'd stayed in any one place though, and

Ned was just happy to have finally managed to make some friends, Archie Hinks and George Johnston from across the road. Despite his father's best efforts Ned was growing roots.

"So, last day of term," said Archie as they all headed home from school.

"Yup," agreed Ned happily.

"And it's your birthday," said George. "Major event, Ned, major event. We'll need to meet up tomorrow for the ceremonial exchanging of presents, of course."

It would be Ned's first birthday with the added bonus of friends. The fact that they'd even thought of gifts came as a genuine shock.

"You got me presents? Actual presents?"

"Well, I wouldn't get too excited. Arch got me batteries last year, wrapped up in old newspaper."

"They still had a little juice left in them," grinned Archie.

"Your dad got anything planned?"

Ned's face darkened.

"My dad? Doubt it. He's not great with stuff like that. Last year we stayed in watching cartoons. I mean, *cartoons*! We never go anywhere. It's like I'm made of glass or something, like he thinks the world was made to break me."

"Cheer up, Widdler, least he cares, right?" said George.

"I know, I know…" sighed Ned.

At Ned's gate they said their goodbyes and agreed to meet up after lunch the following day.

Ned opened the door of Number 222 and headed for the kitchen, weighing up the choice between another one of his dad's microwave meals, or a jam sandwich. The sandwich won.

"Hi, Dad," he called as he passed the living room.

"And the answer is – Eidelweiss," chimed the TV.

"Dad?"

"Ned, is that you?"

"No, Dad, it's one of the millions of visitors you get every day."

Terry Waddlesworth walked into the kitchen, wearing the kind of tank top you could only find in a charity shop and looking unusually dishevelled.

"Neddles, I was starting to get worried."

"Oh come on Dad, you've got to stop. I sent you the obligatory 'I'm alive' text message fifteen minutes ago and I came straight home because of tonight…"

"Because of…?" Terry was now staring through the kitchen window, and out on to the street.

Ned's heart sank. His dad was like a satellite link when

it came to knowing where his son was, but remembering anything else was often problematic. He had a habit of getting… 'distracted'.

"You didn't forget… did you?"

"Forget what?" asked Terry, his focus now back in the room.

"The large pile of presents and the party you've planned, you know, the one OUTSIDE the house, FOR MY BIRTHDAY?" said Ned, now certain that there'd be neither.

Terry's eyes started to go a little watery and he pulled Ned in for a large hug.

"You all right, Dad? You're not thinking about her again, are you? You know it only makes you sad."

"Not this time, Ned, I promise. She would have loved it though. Our little boy, thirteen years old. Who'd believe it?"

"We said we wouldn't talk about her today, Dad… and I'm not a little boy, not any more!"

"So you keep telling me."

"I wouldn't have to if you just let me… be," muttered Ned, through gritted teeth and a faceful of his dad's shirt.

"I know."

"Dad?"

"Yes, son?"

"You can let go now." And Ned didn't just mean with his arms.

Ned's dad released him at last. "I didn't forget, son," he said, producing an envelope and a badly wrapped present no bigger than the end of his thumb and handing them over.

Ned smiled, turning over the tiny package in his hands. "Please tell me this isn't, like, really rare Lego. Because we've built just about everything you can with the stuff and I am *seriously*, like *totally* too old for it now."

"No, Ned, it's actually a bit rarer than that, but you'll have to wait till tonight to open it. I do have a surprise for you though. We're going to the circus. It's on the green; the tickets are in the envelope."

Ned would have loved the circus a few years ago, but he was thirteen now, and thirteen-year-olds had the internet, and cable TV and, more recently, friends. Still, any Waddlesworth outing outside the house was worth encouraging.

"Great... I love the circus," he managed, with all the enthusiasm of a boy that still loves his father just a little bit more than the truth.

"Put them in your pocket, son. I've got a bit of a work

crisis on. An old colleague of mine... she's... she's in a pickle, and I have to go and help her out, but I'll be back later. We need to have ourselves a little talk before the show. Stay indoors till then, OK? You'll love the circus, Ned. There's nothing quite like it."

Terry Waddlesworth didn't usually mention "colleagues" and had never had a work crisis, at least not as far as Ned could remember. What worried him more were his dad's shaking hands, as he went to pick up the keys.

"Dad, are you sure you're OK? I hope this isn't about moving again, because..."

But his father was already out the door, double-locking it behind him before marching off down the drive, and Ned was talking to himself.

Ned took his sandwich up to his room and looked around him. Everywhere a mess of abandoned projects lay scattered. Things he and his dad had started building, or were in the process of taking apart. The largest by far was a scale model of the solar system, every planet recreated from a mass of tiny metal parts and their corresponding screws. What made it different from more ordinary construction sets was that the planets actually orbited the sun, or at least they would, when Ned finally got round to finishing it. However, Ned's new friends, all two of them, meant that he had less time for the compulsory Waddlesworth hobby, besides he was rarely challenged now by the things his dad wanted them to make. Plus he was starting to think that maybe building model sets with your dad was a little geeky anyway.

He didn't have the heart to tell his dad though. It had always been their thing, but as Ned had got older he'd come to realise that Terry had a disproportionate obsession with it, as if any problem, any issue that life threw in their direction, might be answered by something found within the folds of some manual.

Ned was fed up with plans, with diagrams and instructions. "Don't do this", "don't go there", "make sure you call or text". Much as he loved his dad, Ned wanted freedom, wanted to try life without a manual or his dad's overprotective ways.

Ned sat down on his bed. Whiskers was lying on his pillow as usual and looked like he might be asleep, though Ned could never really tell. The old rodent had the uncanny habit of sleeping with at least one eye open.

Ned's mouse never slept in a cage, barely moved unless you were looking at him and in all the years they'd had him, Ned couldn't remember ever seeing him eat. According to Terry, he preferred dining alone.

"All right, Whiskers?"

The mouse didn't move.

"Yeah, Happy Birthday to you too."

He lay down beside him and thought about Terry. Something was making him particularly jumpy. And annoying as his dad could be, Ned did not like seeing him upset.

Ned was pretty sure his dad's jumpiness had started on Ned's very first birthday. Olivia Waddlesworth – Ned's mum – had gone out to buy a candle for their son's cake when she'd lost control of her car. In his grief, Ned's dad had destroyed all the photos he'd had of her. Ned didn't have any other relatives so everything he knew about his mother had come from his father's memories. He'd described her in detail so many times over the years; the flecks in her eyes, the tint of rose her cheeks turned when she was embarrassed or cross. But it was who she'd been inside that made Terry's eyes fill with tears. According to Ned's dad, she had been kind and fierce at the same time. She would go out of her way to help a stranger, was passionate about the world around her, and had never told a lie, ever.

Ned stared at the photo frame on his bedside table. It was worn with both love and age, even though it was completely empty. Ned always made a wish on the night of his birthday and though he knew it would never come true, he always wished for the same thing: a photo of his mother.

And so, as he did every year, Ned made his birthday wish and waited for something to happen. But this year, unlike every other, as Ned closed his eyes and for a moment dozed off to sleep, something actually did.

***

Elsewhere, a tracker in a long, wax trench coat looked out across a forest. He had been there before. The beasts he hunted often used the old part of the wood, the part where shadows still moved with a will of their own, the part where one could hide, even from the hidden.

But this beast had grown too greedy, ventured too far, and now it had come under the watchful eyes of the Twelve and Madame Oublier. They would not allow it to continue. The two men stood beside him, with their matching pinstripe suits and carefully combed hair, had been watching this place for some time. When they were quite sure, they had called for the tracker, him and his animals. The hawk was his eyes, the lions his teeth, and the rest the tracker did himself. One of the pinstripes checked his pocketwatch, while the other made notes in a leather-bound book.

They needed to catch the haired one tonight before it could do more harm. In the branches above, the tracker's bird called out to him.

"Lerft, roight… go!" the tracker breathed in a heavy Irish whisper.

His lions padded forward and in a moment were in the darkness and out of sight. The pinstripes nodded and he left them at their posts. His breathing steadied. Out here there was no time to be scared; fear could kill you as quick as claws.

Crack.

A broken branch, somewhere in the distance.

Crack. Crack.

Another and another.

The tracker paced forward, low to the ground. In a clearing in front of him a man sat by his tent and cried.

"Niet, niet," moaned the tourist.

The beast circled him, growling, claws at the ready, saliva dripping from its hideous fangs.

The beasts were never found this far across the border. There were treaties with their kind written in blood, an oath as ancient as the forest it now walked. But something had changed, something had made them bolder, and this one was crazed with a hunger only the tourist and his warm, oozing blood would satisfy.

The boy pulled the silver from his pocket. A delicate chain could be as strong as a cage if handled the right way. He whistled to his lions. The beast was big and he was going to need them.

CHAPTER 2

Surprise

Ned had been having the exact same dream for weeks now. It started with grey. No sound, no texture, just a wall of pure grey. But the grey had a way of turning in on itself, of tumbling and changing, till a shape would emerge, boldly lumbering towards him to the rising *brum brum brum* of a deep bass drum. The shape scared Ned. It was large and indistinct and heavy-breathing. But today the dream was different. Today he could see the shape as it truly was.

The shape was an elephant with pretty white wings. The animal was ancient and also had terrible breath. He knew this because, as the drumming got louder, it started to lick his face.

Ned found that there were moments, between being asleep and awake, when sounds and senses were stretched, altered. The ringing of an alarm clock might become a siren in a dream. Often it was hard to tell what was dream and what reality, and so it was as the licking from the elephant changed to the prodding of Whiskers' snout on his cheek, as if the little rodent were trying to wake him up.

Ned opened his eyes. He must have been asleep for hours because it was now dark outside. So it had all been a dream. And yet, the drumming had not stopped, or at least, had become something else, some other strange sound. A sound that Ned instantly knew was bad before he had any idea what it might be, because the hairs on the back of his neck prickled, and the nails on his fingers felt tight.

It seemed to be coming from downstairs. Short laboured scrapes, one after another, then a pause.

"Dad?"

The scraping continued. Whiskers scampered off the bed and sniffed at Ned's door. Dad had always joked that he made the perfect guard dog. Too small to need a walk, but with the hearing of a bat.

"Dad…" Ned shouted, "if this is a birthday surprise, it's not very funny."

There was no reply. Ned opened his bedroom door

and cautiously crept down the stairs, closely followed by his mouse. The scraping was coming from the sitting room's patio doors. Something outside was trying to claw its way in.

Ned's first reaction was to run, and Whiskers, who was already squeaking noisily by the front door, was clearly of the same mind, but Ned's curiosity had taken a hold. He turned, inching his way towards the sitting room, and was about to flick on the light switch when he saw something that made his blood turn cold. Standing in the glass doorway, lit up in the cold glow of the garden's security lights, was the scariest sight he'd ever seen.

It was a clown, though nothing like the ones he'd seen in books or on the telly. He had the same shrunken hat, oversized boots and orange curly hair one would expect, but he was caked in dirt. His make-up had cracked, like white clay left too long in the sun, and the few teeth he still had were gnarled black stumps.

The horrible scraping sound began again as the clown dragged a claw-like nail across the glass. Then Ned realised – scratched into the glass of the patio doors were four letters.

Y C U L

Ned ducked down out of sight behind the sofa, heart

pounding, speechless with fear.

Suddenly from behind him Ned heard the sound of the front door being thrown open and a rather different Terry Waddlesworth than Ned was used to burst into the house.

"Dad!" Ned managed to croak over his shoulder.

"Ned? Ned!"

"Dad, there's something..." But he was suddenly unable to speak, only point with a shaking finger.

"Thank goodness you're all r..." His father's voice trailed off as his eyes followed Ned's hand. The only sound now was the continued scraping from the clown's fingernails, who seemed not to have heard them through the thick, double-glazed patio doors.

When Ned's dad at last spoke again, he did so in a slow, deliberate whisper. "Ned, it's time to go," he hissed, beckoning him back towards him on all fours then grabbing him by the arm and leading him into the hallway.

Ned was in a daze.

"It's OK, Dad, no need to panic. I've figured it out, I'm still dreaming. I'll probably wake up in a minute and you'll tell me we're staying in Grittlesby for good, because I like it here, and I've got actual friends and they've bought me presents and we're going to start behaving like a normal family and everything's going to be great and…"

Ned's dad ignored his babbling and picked up two black bags from under the stairs, before pausing by the front door. The scratching stopped.

"Give me a minute, son, and don't go back in there. Whatever happens, he mustn't see you."

And in a second he'd pounded up the stairs to Ned's bedroom. On his way back down, Ned's dad was stowing something into one of the black bags. Just as he was dragging Ned out the front door, they heard behind them the sound of shattering glass from the sitting room.

"GET IN!" shouted his dad as he threw open the door of their Morris Minor and revved the engine, and before Ned knew what was happening they were tearing out of the driveway in a cloud of dust.

Slowly Ned started to surface from his stupor. A bank of grey fog had rolled into Grittlesby, just like the one from his dream, and as they sped through their little suburb, Ned wondered whether his dad was using his eyes or his memory to navigate.

"I'm not dreaming, am I? Dad, what's going on? What was that thing?"

"A clown, and a particularly nasty one at that. I just hope he didn't see you."

"See me? I don't understand. Why would that be bad?"

"Because I haven't had enough time!"

"Time? Time for *what?!*"

"To get you to safety, to explain, you see... not everything we see is as we see it. The world is a complicated place. It has layers, Ned, lots of layers. What might be the norm for one person, is not really the same for..."

CRUNCH!

Just then something crashed into the right side of their car, hitting it hard. Through the fog, lit up by the streetlights, Ned saw a bright purple ice-cream van with a sign on it reading, Mo's CHILDREN's PARTIES. Its driver was hideously fat, with the same monstrous grin and cracked make-up as the clown from Ned's home.

"GET DOWN!" ordered his dad, before shoving Ned further into his seat and out of the clown's line of sight.

"Please don't tell me you hired these clowns for my birthday?!"

"Ned, the tickets and present I gave you, do you have them?"

"What?" said Ned, peeking between the seats at the grinning clown tearing after them.

"THE PRESENT! THE TICKETS! DO YOU HAVE THEM?"

Ned had never seen his father quite so crazed. Fumbling through his pockets he found both envelope and package, and pulled them out.

"OPEN IT! QUICKLY!" shouted his dad.

Ned tore at the present's paper to reveal a smooth metal box. Just then there was another loud crash at their rear and the box flew from Ned's hands.

"I've dropped it!" he shouted, scrabbling around by his feet. "It's on the floor here somewhere…"

Terry cursed loudly and flicked on the car's reading light, before making a sharp turn.

"Find it, Ned, that box is the key!"

"The key to what?"

"Just do it!"

Something in Ned's dad's voice made Ned do as he was told, and he soon found himself upside down in the passenger seat, scrambling around under the car seat to find his mysterious gift. Their old car wasn't used to being pushed so hard and the engine groaned loudly as Terry hammered on the accelerator. Under his chair, Ned could just make out the glimmer of an edge.

"I think I can see it!" he shouted.

"Hold on, son, it's going to get rough."

"Hold on to what? I'm upside down!"

The car hit something hard, launched into the air and just as Ned's fingers closed around it the box was gone again.

"Ow! What was that?"

"Speed bump... and another coming."

Their car flew over another of the hard, tarmacked lumps, and Ned smacked his head again on the vehicle's dashboard.

"One last bump, have you got it?"

"No I have not, and I won't have a neck if we carry on like—"

The final bump hurt the most, but as they landed, Ned saw the glimmering metal box leap off the ground just before it hit him square in the eye.

"Ow!" he said, grabbing at it before it fell again. "OK. Got it..."

Ned felt his dad's hand reaching for his neck and, in a single hard pull, he'd yanked him up and back into his seat.

"Don't lose sight of it again, Ned. Not now, not ever. Do you understand?"

"Is this... is this what they're after?"

"Only two people in the world know about that box. Those clowns are after me."

"YOU! What could they possibly want with—"

Crash!

A horrible crunching sound rang through the car as Mo's van smashed into the back of them again.

Through the fog, Ned could barely make out the 'NO ENTRY' sign to Grittlesby's pedestrianised shopping arcade and the two metal bollards at its sides.

"Dad, we're not going to make it!"

"Oh yes we are, my boy, oh yes we are!"

Their beloved old car hurtled through the barrier and there was a loud tearing noise as both of the Morris Minor's wing mirrors were ripped off. Ned looked out the rear window to see Mo's van screech to a sudden halt as it crashed into the bollards. At the other end of the arcade, their path was blocked by an even larger barrier, that Ned was sure not even his newly crazed father would try and break through. Terry went quiet, looking left and right, then left again.

"Hold on to your seat, son."

Ned's dad slammed the gearstick into reverse and spun the wheel. The old Morris Minor flew backwards, turning wildly up a narrow one-way street. Faster and faster the car sped, crossing one then two intersections, and then another. Ned now had no doubt that his father had gone mad when the car hit a high kerb and flew into the air.

In that moment of free fall, Ned saw his life flash before him. He saw his school surrounded by a flock of C's, his dad staring at the inner workings of a toaster, Whiskers asleep on his pillow. And Ned did the only thing he could think of.

"Argggggggghhhhhh!"

The car landed with a loud crunch. Its boot popped open sending their bags flying as smoke poured out of the engine.

It took a good thirty seconds of his dad shaking him before Ned felt ready to stop yelling.

"It's all right, Ned, we made it!"

But Ned's thoughts were somewhere else. "Whiskers… what about Whiskers? Dad! We left him behind!"

"Don't worry about him; he's tougher than he looks. You need to move," said his dad, thrusting one of the black bags into Ned's arms. "Quickly, Ned, they'll be on us in a second."

The thought of the clowns brought him back to the moment with a thump.

"Where am I going? Why?"

"I was going to explain everything before the show, I

wanted to prepare you, but my plans they… just get to the Circus of Marvels, Ned, they'll keep you safe."

Ned couldn't believe what he was hearing.

"We're being chased by homicidal clowns and you want me to hide in a *circus*?"

"I'm sorry, it wasn't supposed to be this way, I've tried to protect you…"

"What wasn't? Dad, you're scaring me. What's happening?"

"Just get to the circus – they're waiting for you. Take one of the tickets, you won't find them without it. Don't worry, Neddles, just give Benissimo the box, he'll know what to do."

Terry grabbed the remaining ticket, tore it into shreds and started swallowing the pieces.

"What is going on, Dad?? How do you know these people? Where are you going? When can I come home?"

Ned could feel the tears welling in his eyes.

"You're going to need to be brave, son, and grown up, more grown up than I've ever let you be before… but I will find you, Ned, I promise. Trust only Benissimo and Kitty, and don't lose sight of that box."

"But what does it do? What's it for?"

From back the way they'd come, still hidden in the

fog, came the honk of a horn and somewhere beyond it another.

"The clowns... they're coming," said his dad, now peering into the darkness. "They've found me."

"T E R R Y," called a rasping voice, that was both ugly and near.

"Run, boy, just run!"

CHAPTER 3

The Greatest Show on Earth

Ned held onto his dad, tears beginning to flow down his face. How could he leave him to those monsters, with their cracked make up and glass cutting nails? It was the strength of his dad's push that gave him his answer. Ned had no choice..

He ran in the direction he was pushed, through the thick fog, only stopping when he could run no more. He looked down at the ticket clutched in his hands. Gold letters spelled out **'BENISSIMO'S CIRCUS OF MARVELS'** and underneath the words was something he recognised. A picture of an elephant with tiny wings. It was just like the one from his dream. Nothing in his little world made sense any more. How could a travelling salesman obsessed with safety be mixed up in all this, whatever 'all this' actually was? Who were those clowns and what was the first one scratching into the glass?

When he had caught his breath, Ned set off again, half running, half stumbling deeper into the wall of fog, until suddenly he hit something hard. When he looked up, in place of the tree he was expecting was a mountainous, red-cheeked man, who looked every bit as terrifying as the clowns. Ned was too dazed to try and escape, and was still catching his breath when the mountain spoke.

"You are boy, no?" he said, sounding decidedly Russian.

"Err, yeah…" At least, he thought he was. Though the last half hour had left him unsure of… well, almost everything.

"I am Rocky. You are safe now, no one mek passing. De Circus has you."

There was a gust of wind and within a few seconds the surrounding fog started to form shapes. It swirled and rolled over itself, revealing lights and an echo of music. The mountain stepped aside to reveal his father's birthday surprise: **BENISSIMO'S CIRCUS OF MARVELS.**

It had an old, hand-carved wooden entrance, with angels at its top and pitchfork-bearing devils at its bottom. Miniature red and yellow hot-air balloons with little lanterns at their bases floated above the sign, welcoming in their visitors.

Ned's father – safe, sensible Terry Waddlesworth – was in serious trouble, Ned was in the hands of a Russian mountain, and yet somehow, as they approached the entrance, Ned couldn't help the faintest of smiles.

A team of three, white-moustached emperor monkeys worked the crowd. They wore smart red outfits, with bellboy hats cocked to one side, one taking the admissions at the front desk, while another checked people's tickets. The third monkey cranked the handle of a strange-looking machine. From its mass of brass pipes, percussion instruments and what looked to be part of a violin, came the most bizarre music. It sort of wheezed out a tune that was both fast and slow, light-hearted and melancholy.

Ned followed Rocky past the queue and into the packed grounds. His head was a riot of adrenaline, of both horror and wonder, as he took in the sights while his father's name and the way the clown had snarled it still throbbed in his ears.

There seemed to be three main strips or streets, formed by gypsy caravans and painted lorries, strung together by a web of fairy lights. He could see palm readers, tests of strength, a mechanical Punch and Judy show and a hall of mirrors, outside of which, according to the sign, stood Ignatius P Littleton the third, 'the Glimmerman', who was a portly old gentleman covered from head to toe in tiny, rectangular mirrors.

"Roll up! Roll up!" he yelled, his suit and hat alive with reflections. "See yourself as never before! I guarantee you'll wish you hadn't, or your money back!"

The circus folk were dressed in a mix of old styles and new. A top hat with a leather coat, gypsy bracelets and ruffled shirts under military jackets and bowler hats. Their faces were all decorated in one way or another, some with glitter, others with white face paint and a few were covered in tattoos. 'CANDY MONGER'S' sold sweets and the biggest popcorn buckets he'd ever seen, while 'the Rubbermen' passed out helium balloons of every conceivable size and shape.

But as much as Ned marvelled at the sights and sounds, he couldn't stop thinking about the clowns out in the fog, and his dad out there with them.

"Rocky, my dad said I should talk to Benissimo, do you know where he is? Can you take me to him?"

"Everyone see Benissimo, Benissimo is boss," answered Rocky, motioning beyond the sea of faces and over to the big top.

Ned had the sense that Rocky had been waiting for him and knew at least something of his predicament, though the urgency of the situation seemed to be going over his head. He hoped that, for all Rocky's enigmatic comments, he was taking Ned where he needed to be. As they waded through the crowd, Ned had an odd sensation. It wasn't that anyone was looking straight at him, but it felt like there was someone out there watching from the shadows, from the nooks and crannies of the tents and trailers. Then just as suddenly as the feeling had started, it stopped. It was then that Ned noticed something else. He didn't recognise anyone in the crowd, not a single soul, and yet they all seemed to know each other, giving the occasional nod or stopping to shake hands. Ned realised that he hadn't seen a single circus poster or ad in any of the usual spots around town. In a place like Grittlesby, a visiting circus was news, so why weren't they publicised? Where had they all come from and who *were* they?

Suddenly a crescendo of horns, trumpets and drums all blared at once as a dozen men on stilts appeared, towering over the crowd.

"Your circus awaits!" they shouted, as they began ushering people to the big top.

Some juggled fire, others plucked violins or blew

trumpets. They worked like a team of cow hands, coaxing their herd to the mouth of the big top. Ned followed, too much in the moment to notice himself take his seat: front row and centre.

"Watch show. After, I find you," announced Rocky, and with that he was gone.

"But…"

Ned tried to protest but at that moment the shouting stopped and the lights dimmed and Ned found himself surrounded by many, but completely alone. He'd just have to sit it out and wait for Rocky to return.

A beat later, the big top's main spotlight fired up, casting its beam on the centre of the ring. There was an almighty crack, as a pile of sawdust was kicked up off the floor by a coiled leather whip and in strode the Circus of Marvels' Ringmaster. He was an imposing figure, at least six-foot-three with a thick moustache and eyebrows to match. He wore a red military jacket with tarnished gold buttons and tatty braiding, faded striped trousers and a waistcoat that had seen better days. Even his top hat was crooked and a thin scar ran down the left side of his face, giving the impression of a man part gypsy, part rogue. Was this who Rocky had meant by the boss? Was the Ringmaster Benissimo? He paced around the ring almost leering at the audience; this was clearly his ring and his circus. If anyone under the big top was going to help, Ned hoped that it was going to be him. That was, until he started to speak, and as he did so Ned noticed the strangest thing: the Ringmaster's whip was moving on its own. It was hard to see at first, but it seemed to twist slightly, like a coiled snake writhing in his hand. Ned blinked and it stopped. Who were these people and why did his father trust them so much that he'd left Ned here alone with them?

"My Lords, Ladies and layabouts, welcome to the Circus of Marvels!" the great man barked. "I, Benissimo, am your Ringmaster and guide. From the mountains of China, the deserts of Africa and the jungles of South America, I have brought you the most miraculous and strange. Tonight you will see and hear things that will blind your ears and deafen your eyes! Let the show begin!"

The band burst into action and in strode seven of the cheeriest men Ned had ever seen, with 'THE FLYING TORTELLINIS' emblazoned on their shirts.

"Hey! How you doing, whad-a ya know, where ya been, whad-a ya say?" they chorused.

Boys with overprotective fathers have little in the world to be scared of, apart perhaps from homicidal clowns. But ever since he could remember, Ned had had an overwhelming fear of heights. He felt his stomach lurch as the Tortellinis flipped, lunged and somersaulted through the air. Up on the trapeze and high-wire they moved like mountain goats, as happy a hundred feet up as they were on the sawdust below.

The next act – 'Mystero the Magnificent' – came as a welcome relief to Ned. He wore a dinner jacket with a bow tie and was a slight, ill-looking man with pale, clammy skin and a serious disposition. How he managed to escape from the inside of a safe, without so much as a rattle, was completely beyond Ned. Ned knew more than most boys his age about how intricate a locking mechanism actually was. He pictured it in his mind, how the chained and padlocked escape artist might move in the cramped space of a safe, how he might try to unlock it. His father would have had an idea, Ned thought with a twinge. He always had an idea when it came to puzzles and plans. Again Ned felt restless in his seat, wishing he could talk to Benissimo.

But there was no time for that, as the next act took to the stage – a Frenchman who called himself Monsieur Couteau, and announced himself to be the finest blade in all of Europe. He was also wearing a blindfold. There were screams from the crowd as his razor-sharp sword cut a series of crossbow bolts from the air, each and every one of which had been aimed directly at his head. When the lights came up, only sawdust and matchsticks remained of his would-be assassins.

The acts went on and on. The Guffstavson brothers lit bulbs by placing them in their mouths. The Glimmerman walked through one mirror only to emerge through another, more than thirty feet away. Ned imagined an elaborate trap door and tunnel, hidden beneath the sawdust, but the Glimmerman had seemed to disappear and reappear in an instant.

As much as it made his head hurt, the final act was the strangest and most unsettling of all.

"Now," announced Benissimo, "do not be alarmed. Though our next act has a terrifying aspect, I assure you, you are in no danger. Even so, our youngest members of the audience may wish to look away. Found as a small baby by my own hand, he is the largest gorilla in recorded history. I present to you, George the Mighty!"

Benissimo stepped back into the shadows. For a long time nothing happened. And then it came. A long drawn out wailing – a grunt – and then a deep thundering roar that silenced the big top. Curtains were pulled back to reveal a huge gorilla, at least twice the size of an ordinary ape. He snarled and bellowed at the audience, his mouth curling back over his gums angrily. Ned had never seen such real or ferocious rage.

There were several displays of George's incredible strength. Metal pipes were bent, huge weights lifted and members of the audience duly terrified. And then it happened. As the ape snapped his last metal chair into countless broken pieces, he stopped moving, peered across the ring, and fixed his great dark eyes front row and centre, on Ned's own. He grunted softly and then... smiled, a smile that seemed to be aimed directly at Ned.

Ned's body tensed. He looked about him to see if he was mistaken and the giant gorilla was in fact looking at someone else, but at that moment the big top's lights flared up. The crowd clapped and cheered. The show was over.

And then there it was again, that feeling, that from somewhere in the shadows, from way beyond the now empty stage, someone was watching him.

***

Outside the big top, the sky was a deep black. All the stalls had closed and just a few fairy lights pointed the way to the exit. Ned had no idea what he was supposed to do now. He had to find Benissimo, the Ringmaster was sure to be backstage somewhere and Ned's head physically hurt with questions. When would he see his dad? Who were those clowns? What was the Circus of Marvels and was Ned really safe with them?

Happy Birthday, Ned, he thought to himself as the rest of the crowd walked off into the fog, chatting happily, back to their ordinary, clown-less homes. He turned back to the big top, ready to go and look for the Ringmaster, and came face to face with Rocky.

"Boy, come. Sleep," announced his surly bodyguard.

"Erm, I… I still need to see Benissimo. It's urgent. My dad sent me, Terry Waddlesworth, do you know him? Is he safe?"

"Niet niet. Now tomorrow you meet boss, mek questions."

Ned protested as Rocky shepherded him towards a clearing surrounded by cages, with one large container at its centre. The cages were empty and around the entrance to the central container, which was apparently his new bedroom, were multiple signs – 'NO ENTRY', 'KEEP OUT' and 'DANGER', each one larger than the next.

"Are you sure this is right? This is where I'm sleeping?"

asked Ned spinning round, but Rocky had gone. Ned's sense of humour was beginning to wear thin. His phone still had half a bar of batteries; it was time to try Dad.

"Hello, Dad?" he blurted out as soon as the phone stopped ringing, "I'm not having a very good time here! This place is really weird and I still don't know what's going o—"

"The number you are calling is no longer in service."

Ned's heart skipped a beat, then another. What had happened to his dad's phone?

"Just come and get me, Dad…" he whispered.

But the recording at the other end of the line had nothing left to say. It wasn't fair. You couldn't treat someone like a rare piece of china for years then abandon them to some freakshow without the slightest explanation. Ned had wanted to be free, but not like this.

He reached for the metal box in his pocket and was about to hurl it away angrily, when he heard what sounded like soft scratchy music being played on an old gramophone. He followed its trail to the door of the container and stepped through. What he found inside was something between a library and a home. In place of plain walls, were row after row of leather-bound books, with strange titles like, *Tales from Beyond the Veil, What*

Hides from the Hidden, and *From Shalazaar to Karakoum — A Traveller's Compendium.*

The back of the room was shrouded in shadows, but when Ned stepped further in he could make out a huge leather armchair, and, peering closer, to Ned's horror, sat in the chair was… George the Mighty. And yet, the terrifying ape looked quite calm. He was chewing a banana and reading from an old book through delicate, steel-rimmed spectacles.

Ned blinked, and wondered for the millionth time that day if this could all still be a dream. At that moment the ape turned his head towards Ned, laid his book to one side and got up from the chair. Ned could feel his legs starting to tremble. George lumbered closer and closer, with each pace the container rocked back and forth, till they were only inches apart and Ned could feel the hot air from the gorilla's nostrils on his skin.

Very suddenly, George narrowed his eyes and opened his jaws wide, revealing large yellow fangs, as thick as Ned's wrists. Was this it? Was this the end? Was Ned about to be eaten by a bookish monkey? But George the Mighty, George the Ferocious, George the Terrible, only yawned, and said in the queen's best English: "My dear boy, are you lost?"

That was it, the final straw. The room started to spin and a blackness came over Ned. As he fell to the floor, the last thing he saw was the metal box slipping through his fingers and tumbling away.

CHAPTER 4

Kitty

When he eventually crossed over from deep slumber to the first glimmers of being awake, Ned was smiling. There was a gentle hand patting him on the head. Dad hadn't woken him like that for years. It didn't matter, he'd either dreamt the whole circus thing up, or his dad had come to get him. Life was going to go back to normal, or at least the Waddlesworth version of normal.

"Hi Dad, I had the weirdest dream…" he said groggily.

There was no answer, which wasn't the only thing that was strange. Dad's skin felt rough and clammy. It also smelt horrible.

"Now, Alice, come on girl, we talked about this. You can't go pestering the boy, he's trying to sleep."

Ned opened his eyes abruptly. An elephant, oddly like the one in his dreams and apparently called Alice, had opened a window from the outside, reached in to his room and was stroking him with her trunk. A man, who Ned couldn't see but assumed was her trainer, was clearly trying desperately to move her away.

"Morning, Mr Waddlewats," wheezed the man, poking his head round the door, "I'm Norman, sir, Alice's trainer. So sorry about this, but I think she likes you."

Ned could see from looking around that he was no longer in George's container. He seemed to be on the ground floor of a huge, pink, multi-storey bus. Judging by the beds and the equipment he could see, he guessed it must be the circus infirmary – the perfect place to recover from the shock of the last twenty-four hours. At least it would have been without an elephant trying to break in through the window, or the three emperor monkeys he now saw approaching his bedside, finishing off the remains of his breakfast.

"No, no, no, this won't do at all!" squeaked an elderly lady, as she hobbled in through the infirmary's entrance. "How many times have I told you to leave the newlings alone. He's a josser, for goodness' sake! Julius, Nero, Caligula... out of here this instant!"

The three emperors stuck out their tongues and leapt out of the window, sliding down Alice's trunk, which disappeared seconds after them.

"Name's Kitty," warbled the elderly woman, holding her hand out to Ned for shaking, which he did. Her skin was old-lady soft. Ned guessed she must be in her late eighties at least. She had grey-white hair, but, somewhat strangely, she was carrying a pink plastic schoolbag, which Ned noticed had a Hello Kitty label on it. In fact, she was dressed from head to toe in Hello Kitty merchandise. She wore Hello Kitty shoes, badges, bracelets, and even Hello Kitty hair clips.

"So, here we are, my little gum-drop," she said, breaking into a beautiful smile.

"I'm Ned, Ned Waddlesw—"

"Yes, I think you probably are. But how are you, dearie? That's the question."

Ned had plenty to say on that subject.

"Honestly? Well, let me see... The most safety-conscious dad on the planet has abandoned me to a bunch of —" Ned paused for a second — "a bunch of *weirdos,* no one will tell me why I'm here, I've been chased by homicidal clowns, and last night I walked in on a giant talking gorilla. It talked, you know? Actually talked. And Dad is somewhere—"

"Tea, dear?"

"Oh, err, yes that would be nice, thanks. But—"

"Now. That wasn't really what I meant, Ned. What I want to know is how you are *inside,* what it is exactly that you're made up of. Whether it's snips, snails or puppy dogs' tails. Benissimo needs to know about you before he can tell you about us. I'm the circus's Farseer. It's my job to see where our new arrivals are heading and where they aren't."

Ned had no idea what she was talking about.

"I'm not really sure what you mea— oi!"

The old woman had taken an alarmingly large pair of scissors and cut a strand of hair from the side of his head.

"Jossers always yelp the first time!"

Kitty giggled like a small schoolgirl, before busily tying his hair with a knot of old lace. Job done, she locked the bundle in a tiny safe nearby.

"Wha… why, why did you just do that?"

"Well, to make a spirit-knot, dearie, why else? All the newlings get them. They're quite dangerous in the wrong hands, but only one can exist at a time. Now I have yours, you'll be quite safe from any of that sort of mischief."

It was at this point that Ned realised Kitty was as mad as a box of frogs.

"Why don't I show you?"

The old lady reopened the safe and reached into a tray of tiny containers, pulling out a bundled curl of elephant hair, tied together with grey ribbon.

"What goes around comes around," she announced, before chanting something under her breath and stroking the bundle with a small white feather.

Through the bus window, Ned could see Alice the elephant and Norman. As Kitty stroked the knot, Alice's leg started to twitch, before kicking back gently and knocking her trainer into a barrel of water.

"Don't worry, dear, he'll dry out soon enough, and next time he might just stop the old girl from waking up my patients!"

Ned's mouth was hanging open. Where had his dad sent him?

"Umm, I'm sorry, but I think there's been a mistake."

The old woman's face shifted, to clear, cold focus.

"Mistake? I don't think so, my little seedling. Those clowns don't make mistakes, and if they've seen you, things from here on in will be *different*. Your old life may well be over, dear. What we need to find out is where your new one might take you."

Ned suddenly felt very small.

"I don't want a new life, I just want to go home. My

dad sent me here but I haven't heard from him and I don't know if he's—"

"Safe and long gone, dearie, and don't worry, you'll see him again," cut in Kitty.

Ned lit up. It was the first glimmer of hope that he'd had since leaving his father, though he didn't understand how she knew. The last time he'd checked, his dad's phone had been disconnected.

"Are you sure? Did he contact you?"

"In a manner of speaking, yes. You'll be staying with us for a little while, anyway. Now have a sip of that tea and we'll take a wee look at you, shall we?"

The tea tasted strange but was hot, sugary and soothing. It seemed to flow through his body, warming him right to the ends of his eyes. Somehow it managed to make him feel calm.

What happened next did not. Kitty took his hands into her own and gave them a good long squeeze, checking over the length of his fingers one by one.

"Hmmmm," she pondered, then smiled wildly. "Do you play the piano?"

Before he could answer, Kitty drew back her arm and slapped him in the face.

"Owww! What was that for?"

"It's how I do it, my boy. Blindness, you see, has forced me to do my readings by touch and your boney little hands are not giving much away. Sorry, dear, but the only way to get the proper measure of you is through your face."

"What? You're blind? So when you cut my hair just now you—"

SLAP!

The next ten minutes were extremely uncomfortable for Ned. Kitty repeatedly slapped, pinched and prodded his cheeks, nose, ears and neck. Never hard enough to actually hurt, but always enough to shock him. The strange thing was, with every slap, pinch and prod came a squeal of joy from the old woman, even at one point an attack of the giggles that made her snort through her nose.

"I think I want to go home now," Ned scowled as soon as she paused.

"Sorry, dear, I just haven't had such a fun reading in ages, and your skin is so very soft, isn't it? Now let me see," she said, continuing her strange exploration, "interesting, not keen on homework... and not that good with a football either. Face not entirely remarkable, but not by any means plain. Something of a blank canvas on which to paint."

This was the part Ned was dreading. If Kitty really

could read his mind and was hoping to discover anything exciting about him…

"Not really the rising star, are we? Oh yes, I see… a bit cross with dad, but some new friends and a longing to grow roots. Hang on, I sense… Oh dear, a little sadness. We'll have to see if we can't fix that…"

Ned was already feeling increasingly uncomfortable when Kitty's fingers pressed down particularly hard on his forehead.

"Oww!"

"Interesting," she whispered.

"What? What have you seen?" Ned asked, trying to sound casual but secretly praying that she'd found something about him that was worth remarking on. "And if you prod me like that again, I'm leaving, clowns or not."

Kitty smiled. "There's no reason to get all snippy, my little powder-keg. Nearly done, pinky promise," squeaked Kitty. "Just close those eyes and breathe…"

Suddenly he felt a pressure in the back of his mind. It was the same feeling he'd had outside the big top and again at the end of the show. It was as though someone, or something, were in there with him. "Heyyy, you've… bin here… bef… orrrr," he slurred.

"Yes, dear, I did have a little peek or two. Now pipe

down, I'm trying to think."

In the darkness of his mind, Ned saw a pinprick of light a million miles away from his troubles. It was disorientating and strange, as though he were in the room and somewhere else at the same time.

"Kitteee... moy stomach... feeeeels..."

"A minute more... OK, just as I thought. Open your eyes, that's enough for today," said the old woman.

Ned felt strange and very slightly sick, as the room came back into focus.

"What just happened?"

"Yes, Kit-Kat, what did just happen?" came a deeper voice from the bus's doorway.

Ned looked up. There, framed in the doorway, was the huge figure of the Circus of Marvels' Ringmaster – Benissimo.

Ned felt a mix of awe and hope. Perhaps he was finally going to get some answers. This was the man his father trusted, the man who would get Ned's life back in order.

"It's unclear, Bene. On the one hand, something... on the other, most definitely nothing," answered Kitty brightly.

"Hell's teeth, Kit-Kat! What kind of answer is that?"

"It is the only answer you're getting till you mind your

manners and ask the right question," she retorted, now in the deeper voice of an elderly but formidable woman, all traces of giggly girlishness gone.

"I just did!" snapped the Ringmaster, his bushy moustache twitching irritably.

"Not to me, you fool, *to the boy*."

The great tower that was Benissimo changed, his face shifting from irritation, to new-found understanding.

"I see… yes, yes, of course."

He raised one of his large eyebrows, then lowered it and raised the other, before studying his subject more closely.

"So this is him and here he is. Not much to look at and very young, Kit-Kat, too young," said the Ringmaster, now drawing uncomfortably close.

Ned's shoulders tensed again. Benissimo may have seemed saner than the rest of the circus crew but he was also slightly terrifying and he was staring at Ned so closely it was as if he was trying to read the pores of his skin.

"Err, sorry, but too young for what?"

"Too young for *us,* pup," said Benissimo, "for the Circus of Marvels and the road we travel. Tell me, did your father explain anything about what we do here and where it is we come from?"

Ned shrugged. "He garbled a lot of stuff, none of it made much sense though…"

Benissimo did not look impressed.

"Just as I thought. Underaged, unprepared and frankly… underwhelming."

The brutish Ringmaster was intimidating, but he was also rude and Ned had had enough.

"Look, I don't know who you lot are or what my dad's mixed up in, all I know is you're supposed to help me, and right now you're not being very nice, so what I want to do is… call the police, or something, so if I can use your phone…"

"Help you?" said Benissimo with a snort. "That's not it at all. You're here to help us – though I seriously doubt a josser like you will be anything but a hindrance."

Ned didn't know what Benissimo meant by "josser" but by now he was somewhere between the salty welling-up of tears and outright anger. His dad had told him to trust Kitty and Benissimo, and one of them was mad – and clearly a, well, witch – and the other was rude, bordering on foul. What was his dad thinking and how could he possibly help anyone when he didn't actually know what was going on?

"Why don't you tell him about your little box, dearie?"

cut in Kitty's singsong voice.

Ned suddenly remembered the birthday present and how it had slipped through his fingers the night before.

"How do you know about that? Dad said I should give it to you, but I think I lost it last night…"

"Fear not, lamb chop, George found it when he scooped you up off the floor," said Kitty, pulling the box from her pocket and handing it to Ned.

He studied the cube and for the first time noticed a tiny O embossed on to one of its sides.

"Yes, this is it. It's a puzzle box I think. I'm usually pretty good at stuff like this, but I can't figure out how it opens."

Benissimo's eyes grew wide.

"Jupiter's beard! That's no puzzle box, boy, that is something else… *entirely*."

CHAPTER 5

Lots & Lots of Marvels

"If it's not a puzzle box, then what is it?" asked Ned.

"My suspicions will need a pinch or two of verification, but if I'm right, this may well be the second half –" the Ringmaster paused, eyeing Ned up and down – "of a *very* slim chance."

"Chance of what?"

"Of keeping the world's biggest secret a secret, boy. And of keeping your father alive. Come with me, there are some things you need to see."

Ned's chest tightened. "Keeping your father alive" were not words he wanted to hear. Was his dad really in that much trouble?

The Ringmaster stepped off the bus and beckoned Ned to follow. Outside, Ned realised they were nowhere near Grittlesby green. The sun was rising and he could see now that the circus had pitched its tents by the side of a motorway. In front of them was the abandoned building site of a half-constructed shopping mall. A single large sign across its fencing read 'OUBLIER AND CO'. Beyond that, thick untameable forest.

"Where are we?"

"Across the Channel, southern France."

"France! How did we get here so quickly? Did you get the entire circus on the ferry while I was asleep?" gasped Ned.

"Our presence was required to take care of a local disturbance. It's what we do, my troupe and I."

"Disturbance? I thought you like… juggled and stuff?"

"Juggled and *stuff*?" Benissimo sighed. "This is going to take longer than I thought… I'll start at the beginning, shall I? You see, the circus, as you and the rest of the world know it, is a place of harmless fun, but its roots are of a more secretive nature. When the old Roman Empire used to rule, they would scour the world for its best fighters and train them in mortal combat. Back then we fought as gladiators, for money, and for fame. It was barbaric, they were barbaric times, but it was done for a reason – to ready us to manage certain borders, to keep what was in *in*. We're descendants, Ned, of those very same circuses, those very same warriors, the gatekeepers of a border or borders that we collectively call 'the Veil', behind which certain things hide or are kept hidden."

"I still don't understand. What hides? And what's it got to do with me and my dad?" Ned asked.

"What you need, young pup, is a little orientation, a little bit of knowing your up from your down," said Benissimo. "Come with me."

The Ringmaster turned abruptly and marched Ned over to the circus's empty animal cages, then stopped by its smallest.

"Do you believe in fairies, boy?" he asked, without a hint of sarcasm.

"Course not, I'm thirteen."

"That is a shame… but you did? When you were younger, yes?"

"Maybe."

"And at that time, you were probably a little scared of the dark too? Saw things in it when nothing was there?"

Of all the people Ned had met, Benissimo was the very last he'd want to admit that to.

"I… erm…"

"Seeing things in the dark," continued Benissimo, "we call that 'sight'. The gift of it leaves us when we come of age. The less we believe, the less we see. The Veil takes away that sight completely. Do me a favour, pup, and look into that cage."

Ned did not like being referred to as "pup" and he certainly wasn't Benissimo's "boy", that privilege was his dad's alone, though he was starting to wonder if he'd ever forgive his father for leaving him in the Ringmaster's care. Nonetheless, the man had a way of asking that made you feel like you had to say yes. He stared through the bars.

"What do you see?"

"Just the cage, that and a little sunlight, I guess."

"Dusk and dawn are the best times to see them, especially the Darklings that we have caged here. Your youth and Kitty's tea should be enough to break the glamour. Look again."

This time, as Ned stared through the bars, something began to form. In the dance of shadow and light, he saw a shape. Something small and sinewy, something with teeth.

"Wha... what?"

Before him stood a ferocious creature, which snarled and lashed at the cage bars. Its clothing might once have had some colour, but today the creature's threadbare rags were reduced to a grimy mush. It had white clammy skin, orange slits for eyes and a pointy, evil face.

"That, my boy, is a hob-gor-balin, only a level three menace, but quite clearly on the wrong side of the Veil. The effects of Kitty's tea at your age should be permanent, though breaking the strongest glamours needs more aggressive magic…"

Ned's jaw dropped.

"Ned Waddlesworth, son of Terry. Feast your eyes on the truth. Drink it down like a warm cup of honey. This…" said Benissimo as he led him round the corner to where a large troupe of performers were having their lunch, "…is my circus, the *real* Circus of Marvels," announced Benissimo, gesturing in a circle, his chest puffed up with pride.

Ned looked over the troupe and his already dropped jaw gaped wider still. The cook was an unshaven, gruff-looking man who had clearly never washed his apron. He also had tusks hanging down from his mouth, and the snout of a pig. Pretty dancing girls in sparkly make-up laughed, as a red-faced cheery-looking woman sewed sequins and bells on to a pink dress. One of the girls had scales for skin, another short fur and the spots of a leopard, and the third was covered in tiny blue feathers.

Beside them, an excited group was laying down wagers, as Rocky and what Ned could only assume was his wife, despite the beard, went head to head in a playful arm-wrestle. Except that Rocky wasn't Rocky any more. His bulging muscular skin had turned a hard grey and had the texture of rock. Watching the two lovebirds wrestle were Julius, Nero and Caligula, but the breakfast-stealing monkeys were now in their blue-skinned, mischievous pixie form, and the elephant that had ruffled his hair only moments ago had the pretty white wings at the top of her back Ned had seen in his dreams, where there had previously only been cardboard.

Each and every one was different, from the enormous troll that was Rocky, to the dwarven unicyclists delivering food at the food truck's trestle tables.

"The hidden. Marvellous, aren't they? Every myth and legend, every obscure or forgotten tale, they are all, most wonderfully, most stupendously and on numerous occasions, rather dangerously… true."

Ned turned around to take in the other Darklings in their cages. They weren't like George or Rocky or even the clowns. They were monsters, of every possible size and shape.

"That there is a harpy," said Benissimo indicating a brown-winged woman sat scowling in one of the cages, her mouth covered to stop her taunting screams. "Her voice can cause instant paralysis, or madness, or both. Very nasty indeed," explained Benissimo. Behind her, in a far larger cage, were a pair of thin-limbed creatures wearing clothes that looked like they'd been stolen from the dead.

"Nightmongers; the less said about them the better. Look into their eyes and you see your worst fears. Hear them talk and it's already over."

Their faces were covered by wide-brimmed hats, and instead of fingers Ned saw long claws the length of kitchen knives hanging from their wrists.

"Please, please tell me I've gone mad," said Ned, suddenly longing for his dull, safe dad more than ever.

"It's always hard on jossers the first time," said Benissimo dismissively. "That wyvern took ten hands to capture, most of which wound up in the infirmary."

The beast he was talking about was in the largest cage by far. It was about the size of a horse with the features of a dragon. Its leathery wings had to be chained down and it wore a heavy iron muzzle.

"Flammable spit. I've seen them burn bones to ashes in mere seconds."

As still as it was, the briefest look from its glowering grey eyes was enough to chill Ned's bones. The Darklings were nightmares come to life, only worse, only real. Ned didn't care whether he was going mad or not. He was quite beyond that now.

BANG.

An unmarked grey truck backfired beside them. Its rear doors were flung open and out stepped a tracker. He wore a long wax coat to match his long greasy hair and his wild eyes looked entirely feral.

"Lerft! Roight! Heel!" he called in a strong Irish accent.

Ned watched in awe as the tracker's pet lions, Left and Right, bounded out of the truck and fawned over him like obedient puppies. It wasn't so much that he had a power over them, it looked more like he was one of them, a creature of the wild too.

"Aark!" he called next, in a voice only part human.

From somewhere high in the air came a screech and a swoosh of wings as a large black hawk flew down to the man's arm. A large black hawk… with two heads.

It was at this point that Ned lost the power of speech altogether.

Circus hands lowered a covered cage from out of the back of Finn's truck, while two men in matching pinstripe suits interviewed the German tourist who'd been unlucky enough to stumble upon whatever it was the tracker had captured.

"Oh dear, Mr Smalls," said one of the suits.

"Yes, quite, Mr Cook," agreed the other.

The tourist was babbling and in severe shock.

"You see, one moment it was there unt the next, nosink. No beast unt only the forest. You believe me, ja?" pleaded the tourist.

"Yes, sir, actually we do rather. Mr Cook, if you wouldn't mind doing the honours?"

The taller of the two pulled a long silver tube from his breast pocket that looked a little like a flute, only it wasn't. He pointed it at the tourist's face and blew. The two men then dragged the now sleeping backpacker to Kitty's bus.

"You see," Benissimo rumbled, his great eyebrows furrowed, "when the two worlds come crashing together, yours and mine that is, it's the Circus of Marvels and others like her that have to clear up the mess. When things go awry and the shadows bite, it's my troupe that bites them back. Whether you've the teeth for it, pup, remains to be seen."

Ned felt his anger rise up again. Benissimo kept talking to him as though he'd somehow agreed to join their band of travelling monstrosities while in the same breath reminding him that he was not up to the task. And he still hadn't explained how he and his dad were part of all this! He was about to tell his host exactly what he thought of him when there was an almighty howl from inside the truck's cage. As the beast within threw itself at its bars, the cover slipped and fell. In place of the monster Ned was expecting, was a thin, shaking man, clammy with sweat. The man looked at Ned, cocked his head to one side and started to whimper. But despite the timid sound, he watched Ned with the same look of interest a dog gives a cat, before trying to tear its head off.

Benissimo's whip snapped at the cage bars, seemingly without the Ringmaster moving.

"Any more of that and I'll order our boy Finn here to give you a bath with his lions," he warned.

The man cowered at the Ringmaster's glare and the cage was covered up again. Ned was shocked by Benissimo's ferocity. Could they really treat a person like that? Weren't there rules and laws for that kind of thing?

"Don't be fooled by its human form. That's the level fifteen our pinstripes called us in for. Thankfully the threat of soap is usually enough to calm them before it comes to blows. Ours is a dangerous path, boy, and requires a firm hand to keep it straight."

Ned looked at the man in front of him as he strode

on once more, a towering mast in a sea of monsters. One thing seemed certain – the Ringmaster would do anything to keep the shadows, as he'd called them, at bay.

As they passed the big top, the troupe were now going through rigorous training. Though not entirely of the traditional circus kind. Grandpa Tortellini and his seven grandchildren were up on the high-wire, which of course made Ned's stomach churn. At one end of the arena, another group of men and women were scaling a wall in what looked like blindfolds, which was when Ned realised that those in the air also had their eyes completely covered.

Directly in front of them, Monsieur Couteau – the master swordsman – was drilling several troupe members in armed combat using charmed axes, silver swords and even flame-tipped spears. As Ned watched he demonstrated the effectiveness of what he called runes, by throwing a small square of engraved stone at a wooden dummy. A moment later the dummy had turned to a pile of ash. A small group of them, moving together like a well-oiled machine, were children even younger than Ned. It was abundantly clear that safely trapping beasts was not always an option.

"How… how old is she?" Ned stammered, pointing to

one of the smallest.

"Daisy is a smidge over seven. We get them going as early as possible. Without proper training, one's life expectancy around here is practically nil. You, pup, are quite woefully in that category, and if you're to stay safe or be of any use, you'll have to get in there and test your own metal soon enough."

Ned knew screwdrivers not swords and wasn't sure he had any "metal" to be tested.

"This isn't a circus, it's… it's an army," said Ned.

For a moment, the rock-hard swagger slipped from Benissimo's face, and was replaced with the same tinge of disappointment he'd seen in the Ringmaster's eyes on Kitty's bus.

"You need an army to fight a war, boy. Even the ones you have no hope of winning."

CHAPTER 6

Whiskers

Ned's head was spinning when at last they stopped by one of the circus's larger vehicles. Benissimo punched numbers into a keypad and its door slid open.

"I'm going to have our head of R&D – research and development – cast an eye over your box. If my nose is right, you'll need to make a choice. Now, pup, the Tinker is a minutian. Minutians can make most anything from anything, but they're sensitive about their size. DO NOT, by all that is holy, say the word 'gnome' in his presence. There are gadgets in there that could blow up half of Europe if you make him angry."

From the expression on Benissimo's face, it was quite clear that he was not joking.

Inside the lorry, machines whirred and spun, bottles bubbled with strange liquids and every available surface was covered in notes, diagrams and mechanical contraptions. It made Ned's eyes water. His dad would have loved it; every gadget, every blueprint, every complex contraption. This was the kind of place that Terry Waddlesworth would have lost himself in for weeks. And when Ned was younger, he would have sat there with him, copying every move with a wrench or screwdriver. A part of Ned that he had forgotten was still there suddenly longed for his old hobby, and his dad, and the way things had been before.

"Wow!" he breathed. "Look at all this gear! You really could make *anything* in here!"

Ned ran his hand along the nearest machine, a hydraulic press, marvelling at its unique design. Ned noticed that the Ringmaster seemed to be eyeing him curiously.

"Ahem, no touching the equipment, thank you," said a voice.

At the room's centre was a table where a man, no more than four feet tall, was working. On his head were various goggles, glasses and light fittings, and nearly every pocket of his white lab coat was stuffed with tools. He had a smattering of grey bristles that led into the beginnings of a patchy beard. Though Ned had never seen a real one before, he looked exactly the way he thought a gnome should look; small and rather hairy.

"Tinker, this is… the boy."

'The boy' rolled off Benissimo's tongue in much the same way as 'the problem' might have come from a plumber while inspecting a blocked drain.

"Ahhhh, so you're Mr Widdlewats?" the diminutive inventor said, peering up at him through a particularly large lens.

But Ned hadn't heard a word. Lying on the workbench in one of his more stationary positions was an unexpected sight – his pet mouse Whiskers.

"You found him! Whiskers, I've been worried sick!"

Finally, something that made sense, something he recognised. The Waddlesworths' beloved pet mouse was safe and had found him!

But the Tinker did not let him enjoy the moment for long.

"Whiskers? Oh no, Mr Widdlewats, this is no 'Whiskers', this is a Ticker, a Debussy Mark 12, to be exact. Top of the line in its time, or at least was until yesterday."

"Debussy Mark what? That's my mouse, I'd know him anywhere!"

"How old is your mouse, Mr Widdlewats?"

"Not sure, but he's definitely older than me."

"And how many mice do you know that live to be that age, sir?"

"Um, well, Dad always said he was special."

"Indeed he is. This little fella arrived at the green just a short while after you. Would have got there quicker too, if an ice-cream truck hadn't run him over."

The Tinker took a needle-thin screwdriver and twisted it into the mouse's back. He then carefully peeled away some fur, revealing an ornate maze of coiled springs, turning cogs and tiny metal pistons. The rodent's eyes flickered white for a split second, which was followed by a whirring of gears as it moved its head from left to right, before slumping back down again. Ned watched in stunned silence.

"Oh Whiskers, not you too…"

The Tinker fetched him a small stool and he slumped down on to it.

"How long till it's operational?" asked Benissimo.

"Well, boss, it's not quite as bad as it looks. I've pinched some parts off the Punch and Judy show and I should have him up and running by the morning."

"Operational?" said Ned. "What is he… I mean, what's 'it' for?"

"Tickers come in as many forms as you can imagine. They make great pets for the rich, and tireless workers. They make terrifying soldiers too, till that was outlawed. Their greatest use these days is undercover work. This model in particular was very popular for surveillance," explained the Tinker.

Ned couldn't believe his ears. His pet mouse, a full third of his dysfunctional family, was made of metal.

"Magical creatures, clockwork soldiers and... undercover mice? Why hasn't anyone heard of this, of these... things?" asked Ned.

At that the Tinker looked rather surprised.

"Well, because of us, sir. We monitor it all, you see, every creature and every sighting. Anyone outside of our lot who sees anything is immediately visited by our pinstripes."

"Like the two men outside, the ones with the flutes?"

"Precisely, sir, only they're not really flutes."

He pressed a button on an old-fashioned typewriter of sorts and a panel on one of the walls slid away, revealing a large brass monitor. It had little boxes of text, scalable windows and streaming rows of data, just like a regular computer screen, except that everything was made of moving metal parts.

"Our computator gives us up-to-date information on every sighting and everyone who's done the seeing."

The monitor clattered noisily and a map of Europe covered in tiny bulbs slid into view.

"The 'fair-folk', as we call them – creatures human or otherwise with any kind of magical ability or curse – live behind the Veil and they do so for their own protection, to keep them safe from your witch-hunts, scientists and zoos." The Tinker paused until Ned nodded his understanding. "Most of them, like Rocky and our resident pixies, use glamours to stay hidden when outside its borders, while a few can change their appearance at will. There are also those who look completely human and are, well… not. We have to keep tabs on all of them to stop the Veil and the creatures it hides from being discovered. You'd be surprised by how many live on your side, with ordinary lives and jobs. Our little audience last night were all fair-folk. Circuses are a good place for them to catch up on the latest gossip."

Ned peered at Benissimo. He looked eccentric like all the troupe members, but he also looked human. If the Tinker was right, then there was far more to the man than a steely eye and a tough swagger. But what?

"This map is for the *other* kind," continued the Tinker,

"the kind that are strictly forbidden to cross the Veil's boundaries. The ones YOUR kind need protecting FROM. The Darklings outside are just a taste. Yellows are level five and under, oranges six to fifteen, and reds, sixteen to thirty-five. Whites, well… whites are their own thing altogether – the puppeteers, if you will, that pull on the Darklings' strings."

There were literally hundreds of bulbs on the map, only six of them were white.

"Demons, Ned," cut in Benissimo. "Thankfully extremely rare with a profound aversion to light. They mostly dwell underground, safely within Veil-run reservations. The last one to go unchecked was Dra-cul, a particularly vile creature with a soft spot for human blood. He and his Darklings nearly swept the whole of Eastern Europe, bringing their darkness with them. But we fought them back eventually."

Ned gulped – this was a history lesson unlike any other!

"They haven't tried anything on that scale since and the borders have remained manageable. You see, it isn't easy for a Demon to cross. It takes an act of true evil, coupled with pitch-black magic. Or at least… it did. Something is stirring them up."

How any of this fitted in with a safety-obsessed screw

salesman was completely beyond Ned.

"I'm sorry, my brain feels like it's melting. The world was normal when I woke up yesterday, sort of. Whatever this Veil thing is, this secret world of yours, what's it got to do with my dad and this box?"

The Ringmaster leant in closely.

"Maybe nothing, but most probably everything. No one knows why but the Veil is falling, tumbling down around our very ears, and there are those that want to see it that way. If it does, the horror that is Demon-kind will walk freely. And when they do, we will have ourselves a war that can't be won. It will mean the end for all of us, on both sides of the Veil."

Ned swallowed.

"We have one small chance of saving it. Since the beginning, there have always been two people, each generation or so, who have discovered in themselves the rarest and most particular of gifts, gifts that they have used for the most part for good. Because of the nature of their magical abilities they're known as the Medic and the Engineer. There is a prophecy amongst the likes of Kitty and her kind, that in the Veil's greatest hour of need they will combine their powers to save it. If this is indeed that hour then they are the only thing that stands between us and unbridled evil."

Ned shook his head in frustration. "But I still don't know how my dad fits into all this!"

"We've been searching for a girl, Ned. Her name is Lucy Beaumont and she is the last Medic. Her parents were taken from her in a cloud of unspeakable violence and many think her dead. The Engineer, and the one who we believed knew of her whereabouts... is your father."

CHAPTER 7

The Present

Ned could feel the blood draining from his face.

"He told me he was an engineer before I was born, before Mum's accident. But it doesn't make any sense. He's a Waddlesworth. We, I mean he, especially Dad, he doesn't go in for this kind of thing. Telly, screwdrivers, jam sandwiches, that's what Waddlesworths are good at. Dad was always saying it."

"I dare say that's what he's tried to make you and everyone else believe and I dare say he's come fair close to succeeding. But you see that's just it – you're *not* a Waddlesworth. Your father's given name is Terrence Armstrong."

Ned repeated the name in his head over and over again. Terrence Armstrong was somebody else. No one with a name like that would eat jam sandwiches in front of the telly wearing their favourite tank top and slippers. "I'm... Ned *Armstrong*?"

"Indeed you are, and if your box is what I think it is," Benissimo continued, "then you and you alone hold the answer to finding the Medic."

Ned wanted to scream. With every word, the Ringmaster was turning his life, even his name into a lie.

"*Me*? Look, whatever you think Dad is mixed up in, you're wrong. He was an engineer but I don't think he was the kind you're talking about. He likes building stuff... though nowadays mostly he just sits there on his own looking at all the parts. Besides, if, if he were this 'Engineer' you're looking for, he'd have been lying to me, for, like, a really long time and Dad would never..."

"Whrrr, dzt, ching."

Ned stopped mid-sentence at the twitching of his mechanical mouse. It kicked its legs briefly, before shutting itself down again.

"...lie to me," Ned finished lamely.

"All we know is that the last message between your father and Lucy's guardians was intercepted at Battersea Power Station two days ago. That's when he sent for us. The harsh reality is that events now rest on your rather small shoulders, which is as much a concern to me as it is a shock to you."

Benissimo passed the Tinker Ned's birthday present.

"Tinker, what do you make of this?"

The Tinker held the little cube up to the light and adjusted one of his lenses.

"Blimey. Well, boss, the work is unmistakable, a rarity these days. I didn't think they made them any more."

"They don't. I think you'll find it's almost exactly twelve years old," said Benissimo.

"Yes, right you are, sir. Well, the symbol's a bit out of place but there's no doubting it – it's a blood-key."

Their explanation of what a blood-key actually was came in the form of a pin being pushed into Ned's forefinger.

"Ow!"

What proceeded next would have been strange had it happened before his birthday. A drop of Ned's blood was placed on the cube, and the box began to unfold, its microscopic hinges twirling and twisting in the Tinker's hand. Seconds later, it had reformed itself into the unmistakable shape of a key. Ned was speechless as the Tinker placed it in his hand.

"Take a look, sir. It's yours, after all."

"What is it?"

"Blood-keys were fashionable before your time, Mr Widdlewat— I mean, Mr Armstrong. They activate for one person and one person alone, or at least for their fresh blood, that is."

Looking closely at the key's edge, Ned saw it was marked with beautifully inscribed letters: 'FIDGIT AND SONS, EST. 1066, CLASS A DEPOSIT BOX.'

"But… but that's the company Dad works for. They make screws!"

"Among a great many other things. Fidgit and Sons is a shop. It's in one of our oldest trading cities, hidden behind the Veil in the deserts of the Yemen. The men who are after your father have been after him since before you were born. I think he gave you the key for a reason, a way for us to unearth Lucy if he was… *unable*," said Benissimo.

"He's in really serious trouble, isn't he?"

"Until we retrieve what's in your deposit box, you both are."

Ned's breathing quickened. The name Armstrong kept turning over in his mind. If he wasn't who he thought he was, was he even *really* human? Frantically he began searching the Tinker's worktops. Finally exasperated, he grabbed hold of the minutian's head and peered into one of his mirrored lenses.

"Young man! Unhand me this instant!" protested the Tinker.

"I'm me. Why am I still me? If Dad's this Engineer character, then shouldn't he have horns or something, and shouldn't I be like him, you know, like everyone else in this freak show?"

"No, boy, you're both quite human, and that will be the last time you use the word 'freak show' in my presence," said Benissimo with a clear note of warning in his voice. "Being human does not however mean that your dad can't have magic in his blood. Sometimes it happens that someone is just born with magical ability, like your dad, or given it. I was quite human myself once…" At that the Ringmaster paused for a moment, as if in thought. "And Kitty is completely so. Human, minutian, elven or troll, good, bad or somewhere in between, there are all kinds behind our beloved shroud. Now, please let go of the Tinker's head. We have serious matters to discuss. Besides, I need it in one piece almost as much as I need yours."

Ned unclasped his fingers and slumped back on to his stool.

"What is he? I mean, being an Engineer, what does

that mean? Why is it so important?"

"Engineers can control atoms with their minds. With strong enough focus, air can turn to fire, wood to metal, and water to stone. But it doesn't end there. The creations can be shaped to any variety of complex structures. The possibilities are endless. It's a hard concept to grasp, especially for a josser who is new to our ways, but his skills together with the Medic's are unique. Add one to the other, and their combined purpose is to mend, to rebuild and heal. *I need to make that happen.* The Veil is failing and I need them to mend it."

Ned looked up at the Ringmaster. He was torn between the loyalty a boy feels to his past and the almost certain knowledge that his past is not what he had thought it was. More precisely, that his father was not what he had thought he was. What had his life been like as an Engineer? What kinds of things had he seen and done? Why had he never told him? The questions hurt too much to want answers, at least not from anyone except his dad, and for that to happen, he was going to have to trust a man who clearly thought very little of him and join his troupe of oddities.

"So let's just say I'm not mad. You, the Tinker and everything you've told me is all real." Ned paused for a second to gather his thoughts. "If we go to this Fidgit and Sons place, and we find the girl, and she and Dad do whatever it is they're supposed to do... then I get him back for good and life goes back to normal? Like, Grittlesby normal?"

Even as he said it, it surprised him. He wanted his father back just the way he was. Even if it meant being bored, even if it meant being fussed over and forced to stay in. He would do anything for that right now, anything at all.

"I can't promise normal, but with enough wind behind us..." the Ringmaster sighed and looked him up and down yet again, "...and a great deal of luck, yes, you'll get your dad back."

"I'm going to ignore that look you just gave me, if you promise not to do it again."

"I'll do no such thing."

Ned gritted his teeth. "Fine. When can we go?"

Benissimo's mouth turned towards what might have been a smile, though it ended up with just a hint of sadness.

"Perhaps you're more like your father than it first appears... though while you're with us, it'd be for the best if you kept him to yourself. Just a few of the troupe know who you really are – let's keep it that way. Tell me, did the clowns see you?"

"I don't think so, but I can't be sure."

"Well, 'don't think so' will have to do. That said," continued Benissimo, "it does not guarantee that prying ears or eyes won't find out about you. There's a rot in my circus, a spy or spies that are trying to hamper our progress. Until I root them out, you keep your head down, understood?"

"Understood."

"For now we'll say you're a runaway. We get a lot of recruits that way and no one will pay someone like you much heed."

Ned felt another flicker of anger. Why did the man dislike him so much?

"By 'like me' I guess you mean ordinary, right?"

"I had something else in mind, but ordinary will do."

Ned had a pleasing vision of yanking Benissimo's moustache, then setting it on fire with one of the Tinker's gadgets.

"Tinker, a message to Oublier, if you will?"

"Right you are, boss!"

Ned seethed quietly as Benissimo's head of R&D opened two windows at the back of the truck and picked up a large device shaped like a trumpet. Directing one end out of the window, he started to speak in a mixture of slow drawn out tones and revolting nasal snorts, all the while contorting his face and lips horribly.

"N e w ... l e a d ... f o u n d .... F i d g i t ... a n d ... S o n s."

A large gust blew up, swirling leaves into a pillar of spinning greenery, before launching itself over the forest's canopy and away from the truck.

"What's he doing?"

The Ringmaster gave Ned a withering glare. "Hush, boy, it's an air-modulator. He's harnessing the wind to send a message."

"Who is he messaging?" whispered Ned in amazement, but they were too deep in concentration to hear him, or to reply.

The Tinker continued to work the machine, twisting dials and pressing its keys to change pitch. Finally something else happened. A dozen wind chimes, both crystal and wooden, started to sound on the truck's roof. Outside a gust of wind was blowing in over the treetops. And then it came, in soft blowy whispers. A reply.

"H ... U ... R ... R ... Y."

"Well, we'd better get to it then," said Benissimo, "it's time for tear down." And taking Ned's blood-key for safe-keeping, he charged out of the Tinker's vehicle.

Ned followed closely behind, having no idea what he was talking about. But as Benissimo called for the troupe to gather round, he soon found out.

"All right everyone! Pull your tent pegs and fire up the engines…" he called. "We're going home!"

***

Much further than the crow flies but only moments later, a meeting was held between a spy and his master. The master was holding an apple, which he cut carefully, his sharp knife making perfect incisions across its golden skin. He was a great dark hulk of a man, with a deep, unsmiling voice.

"Sister Clementine's 'ending' was unfortunate. She was the closest we've come in years," brooded the master.

"Yes… but now there is the boy," whispered back his spy.

"A lucky turn of events. Tell me, does he know?"

"Not all of it, no. Bene has kept nearly everyone in the dark for fear of your watchful eyes."

"And fear them he should!"

"How shall we proceed?" asked the spy from his shadow.

"Everything depends on the boy's key. I believe it always has. Do you remember the tale of the Parnifer tree?"

"Vaguely."

"You of all creatures should. In the story, the King's son was taken by a terrible affliction and could not be woken. The King cried for a hundred days and a hundred nights, till his tears formed a river. By its banks, a tree sprang up from the ground."

"The Parnifer tree."

"Precisely. They say a single seed from the tree's fruit could cure anything. The girl is like the seed. If she were to meet with the Engineer…"

The master put down his knife, before crushing the apple in his fist, its wet pulpy flesh oozing through his fingers.

"*The seed, must, be, crushed.* I'll send the devil himself if I have to." He gazed for a moment at the fruit falling from his hand. "In the meantime, we'll be needing some leverage. With the boy's spirit-knot and enough time, we could do extraordinary things. I'll leave that up to you.

Watch, observe, slow them down if you can. When the moment is right, we'll make our move."

And with a silent nod, the spy melted into the shadows and returned from where he came.

CHAPTER 8

The Flying Circus

There was all-round whooping and hollering and a happy trumpeting from Alice as the Circus of Marvels readied itself for departure. According to the Tinker, they always did their real travelling at night. When Ned stepped outside, he could see why. The very same fog that had rolled into Grittlesby had followed them again across the sea. Through the layers of rolling grey he saw the circus's big top. Its red and white striped canvas was bulging as if it were about to burst, making it more than twice its normal size.

Even stranger though was the fact that the big top seemed to be floating thirty feet off the ground, as if it were some sort of hot-air balloon… Then Ned saw them through the fog…

Hanging from the big top, suspended in the air, was

a series of buses and caravans that had all been joined together. Some were inside out, and others bent in half, all forming a huge metal gondola more than three storeys high through the middle and four at the back. It was all tethered together with great bars of steel and knots of iron rope. Walkways taken from the big top's inner seating ran all over its hull, and Ned could see crewmen running along the upper deck, checking its rigging and shouting to one another over the roar of the engines. Not for the first time that day, Ned stood wide-eyed and open-mouthed, gawping up at this great metallic beast as against all odds it rose up through the fog. It was the stuff of dreams, a marvel of engineering, and Ned was lost in its every detail.

"Come on, josser, don't just stand there! Wind's about to change!" yelled Benissimo.

Ned's body suddenly drained of blood as he was marched up a narrow walkway and into the airship's belly. Inside were mismatched corridors of old and new. Not even his dad could have made any sense of it. Every room was different, latched together from some metal bus or wooden trailer, and yet it all seemed to fit perfectly, as though it had been built as a whole first and its separate four-wheeled vehicles extrapolated after. But it was dawning on Ned that impressive as it was, it was also uncommonly large; large and extremely heavy, and also extremely high. As he peered over the edge, his heart plummeted to his stomach. Being scared of heights was one thing; flying in an inflatable tent was quite another. He was already dreading Benissimo's reply as the question left his lips…

"This thing, this flying machine… is it… safe?"

The Ringmaster stopped dead in his tracks and began muttering to himself.

"Why me? A blasted child and scared of his own shadow…"

"Oi, I am here, you know?" said Ned crossly.

"For your information, boy, this is not a 'thing', this is the *Marilyn* – the finest airship on either side of the Veil and as safe as a ruby in a crown." Benissimo's moustache was now twitching quite violently. "There are 'things' aplenty where we're going that will offer up more than ample danger. Your fear of heights should be the least of your – or my – concerns."

Ned sensed that it might be a good time to hold his tongue.

"Now, while you're aboard, you need to follow a few simple rules. One – don't touch anything. Two – don't talk to anyone, and if anyone talks to you remember: you're a runaway." The Ringmaster paused to scratch at his chin. "On second thoughts, it might just be better if you stayed in your bunk. Don't leave unless you absolutely must."

Benissimo indicated a door to their immediate right.

"What about permission to breathe? You left that out," Ned grumbled under his breath.

"Veil-bound and right secure on the third!" roared one of the *Marilyn*'s crewmen.

"Nearly home and all aboard on the second!" yelled another below.

The first floor's reply was a loud metallic *clunk* as the circus's captured Darklings were locked into their hold. Benissimo strode away to take his place at the helm from where Ned heard a long blast of the ship's foghorn. From all around the *Marilyn* a chorus of trumpets and what could only have been a cannon replied and Ned realised she was only one floating vessel in a much larger convoy.

He went into his cabin and looked out the window to a wall of fog. It came as a huge relief. Without seeing their take-off, at least he could pretend he was on a bus. A really big, weird bus.

One thing was certain, Benissimo – his protector and only route to finding his father – did not think very highly of him, which was fine because the feeling was entirely mutual. He decided to focus on more pressing matters. There was the girl for one thing, Lucy Beaumont. Did she know they were looking for her? Was she lost? Afraid? Were the clowns after her too? It was then that he remembered the scratched writing on the patio doors of his sitting room.

Y C U L…

Of course! He hadn't thought about it at the time but the clown's writing, seen from the other side of the window, would appear backwards. It was Lucy's name. Was that what his dad had wanted to explain? Did he want to tell him about her? This new world that his father was supposed to be part of was not Ned's. It made him feel like he didn't really belong, even at home with his own dad.

Alone in his swaying bunk, Ned checked on the black bag his dad had given him. He found clothes, a toothbrush and his passport (which had never actually been used). He opened it up and looked at his name. It made him wince because it wasn't really his name after all. Was any of it real? Was anything his father had ever told him actually true?

At the bottom of the bag he found some cash, quite a

lot of cash. But the most surprising item was the empty photo frame Ned kept by his bedside. So that was what his dad had run up the stairs for when they'd made their escape.

This was not the freedom Ned had wanted. This was the kind of bag you prepared if you knew you weren't coming home. It made his eyes prick with tears. He took his phone from his pocket and laid it by the photo frame. A pictureless frame and a powerless phone; even Ned's pet mouse wasn't real. He had never, in all of his life, felt more alone.

"Room for another?" came a polite grunting voice from the doorway. It was George the giant gorilla.

His attempts to fit his enormous bulk into the small cabin made him look rather clumsy and much less intimidating. Despite everything that he'd seen that day, Ned still had no idea what to make of him.

"Err, sure, but I don't think I'm allowed to talk to you. Or anyone else."

"I think that's over-egging it a bit, old bean. I've been fully briefed on your situation along with the rest of our inner circle."

"Oh. Right…"

"And on that note," George rumbled gently, "I made

you some angel cakes. Had a feeling our resident josser might need a smidge of cheering up."

The oversized ape opened a bag and beneath a pile of books and his favourite reading glasses, were four of the ugliest cakes Ned had ever seen.

"Wow, err, George, I don't know what to say. You, err, you really shouldn't have?"

"My pleasure, laddie. Of course, as far as I'm concerned, nothing beats these little gems," said the gorilla, pulling out a banana. "I could write an entire book of sonnets about the joys of this yellow beauty. There's baked banana, creamed banana, puffed, boiled and fried banana. Caramelled, salted, barbecued, even pickled. Of course my favourite is sushied," he added, before gulping it down whole.

Ned couldn't help smiling.

"There now," said George, "a smile, that's more like it." He beamed – revealing his huge teeth – but somehow still managing to look friendly.

"George?" asked Ned. "What's a josser? Only Benissimo's been calling me that a lot, amongst other things, and I don't know what it means. I don't really know what any of this means and the only thing I thought I knew, is, well… not what I knew at all."

"You mustn't take it personally, old chap. The boss has a few rough edges, but he's a decent fellow under all that bluster. Jossers are what we also call outsiders, folk who are unaccustomed to our ways."

Ned was used to being an outsider, but in the Circus of Marvels he was something else, something way beyond average. Half of the troupe weren't even human and even those that were had powers of some sort. Ned was average by tradition, because that's what the Waddlesworths were, or so his father had led him to believe. But being average in the Circus of Marvels did not mean slipping through the cracks – it was like strapping a flashing light to your head and asking people not to look.

"I don't fit in here, George. What if, even without me talking to anyone, someone figures out who I am, or why I'm here?"

"Don't fret, dear boy, I have your back while you're with us, and no one will bat an eyelid. Being lost with nowhere else to turn is something of a requirement before the Circus of Marvels will have you."

"Is that what happened to you? Were you a josser?"

George grinned again. "Between you and me, I think I still am, but then I've got my books and my bananas."

Ned suddenly felt far less alone.

"What about Benissimo? What is he, besides being… well, obnoxious?"

George looked over to the doorway, before lowering his voice.

"We are not all the creatures we become by choice, old bean, and the least said about it the better. When a chap tries as hard as the boss to hide what he is, it's considered rude to ask."

Ned took George's hushed tones as the warning they were meant to be. Whatever Benissimo was or had been was clearly not a topic for discussion.

The towering ape talked late into the night and turned out to be a living encyclopedia on the creatures and places that the Veil kept hidden. He told Ned about the Grand Duke of Albany, Viceroy to St Albertsburg; the last hidden city of Queen Victoria's old empire; the Norwegian library city of Aatol, buried deep underground, which could only be accessed by solving a series of impossible riddles; Gearnish, the city of Tickers where almost everything was run by metal machines; and Shalazaar, the trading city and 'jewel of the desert', where they were currently heading.

Ned listened to George's descriptions in contented silence. To his relief, the angel cakes didn't taste at all how they looked. They were the lightest, fluffiest things he had ever eaten and for just the briefest moment, over-affectionate, winged elephants and talking gorillas didn't seem quite so bad.

Later that night, he was woken by the cabin-shaking snore of his new roommate. The colossal pile of fur lay on his back, his great chest heaving up and down and his nostrils blowing out so much air that the curtains in their cabin actually flapped. The troupe had stopped singing about the joys of returning home hours ago and Ned tiptoed his way to the bathroom quietly. He was breaking Benissimo's in-flight rules, but needing the loo was in his view an acceptable emergency. Aside from George's snoring, the only sound was the gentle groan of rigging being pulled by the wind and the purr of the airship's engines. Being in the air wasn't so bad after all. It was the first time there had been any actual calm since just before his birthday. That was, till he heard a somehow familiar metal clunk.

It was the door to the Darklings' hold.

Two floors below, some 'thing' stirred.

It moved slowly, methodically. Boards creaked and the stairs groaned as the 'thing' began to climb from the first floor to the second, then the second to the third. Ned stood in frozen horror, the smell of wet dog and old meat drifting towards him as the 'thing' appeared at the other end of the passageway.

Somehow Ned knew – maybe it was its smell, or its manner – it was the sickly, shaking man that had been brought in that morning. But it was now transformed to its natural state – a hulking mass of claw and fang. His bottom half was human, but above his waist, grey hair bristled, till his chest, neck and head were completely covered in thick, sweat-stained fur. His face had pushed itself outwards to a slobbering pointed snout and two sharp ears protruded from the top of his head. He was half-man, half-dog, or more accurately... half-wolf.

The wolf-thing eyed Ned, sniffed in his direction, and growled, before baring it's teeth and lunging.

And then it pounced.

CHAPTER 9

Collision Course

Ned scuttled and scrambled over the *Marilyn*'s floorboards, a speck of frightened boy, against a freight train of lashing claw. He felt a fear unlike anything he had ever known. How could nightmares actually come true?

Lights flickered on and those unlucky enough to look out from their cabins were quickly knocked back through splintered doorways. With every pace it drew closer, lashing, biting, howling and raging. Behind it, a trail of broken debris; in front, a thirteen-year-old boy inches from death. Ned nearly broke his fingers as he reached the entrance to *Marilyn*'s flight deck and pulled at the hatch door, desperately trying to prise it open, until he realised with mounting horror – it needed a key.

"What? Not now, please not now!" he cried.

And then he felt it, rasping breath down the back of

his neck and a warm droplet of wolf-spittle. No nightmare had ever come close to this.

"Grrrrr."

And then the hatch flew open and Benissimo's arm yanked him on to the flight deck. He dropped down into a room full of levers and blinking coloured lights. Ned scrambled to his feet as Benissimo tried unsuccessfully to lock the hatch again, but there was no time. The door flew back open.

Ned and the Ringmaster faced the wolf-thing, their backs pressed up against the airship's controls. The creature drew closer, easing its way through the bulkhead's hatch.

"Easy, boy, stay still and steady," said Benissimo, and something in his voice managed to soothe not only Ned, but also the drooling wolf-thing in front of them.

The creature calmed for a moment, cocking its head to one side and sniffing at Ned, its terrible eyes scowling with confusion. Then Benissimo whistled a note through his teeth and the wolf-thing spun in his direction. Ned finally understood why his father might have trusted him, though Ned wondered if he was being protected for his own sake, or for the deposit box that he was supposed to open.

The Ringmaster's hand reached for a switch and he

spoke from the corner of his mouth to a small tube in the wall. As he did so, his whip began to unfurl itself and creep towards the wolf-thing's ankle.

"Benissimo to head of security. You may well have noticed by now but your company is *required*."

The wolf-thing's arm suddenly tore out at him and Benissimo's shirt ripped open. Then the beast became still, but it was not the sight of Benissimo's flesh that sent it into a drooling trance. Its eyes were fixed on the leather pouch around the Ringmaster's neck, the pouch that held Ned's blood-key.

"Get down, boy!" Benissimo ordered, his whip suddenly tightening at the monster's ankle.

As it did so, security arrived in a blur that was Mystero – the escape artist Ned had seen in the show in Grittlesby. Benissimo's number two dived straight through the hatch and flew towards the beast. Though its ankle was pinned, it turned in time to let loose its claws. But where they should have connected with flesh, they found only air and came crashing down on a bank of switches. Mystero meanwhile was reforming himself beside the beast, from wispy tendrils of mist. Even in his terror, Ned could hear the Tinker's words: "There are also those who look completely human and are, well… not." Benissimo's head of security was clearly a "not".

The monster aimed his next attack straight at Benissimo. As he did so, one of his legs swung out fast, smashing the main console violently and knocking Ned into *Marilyn*'s flight stick. The airship veered hard right and a voice came in over the intercom.

"This is the *Leonora*! Watch your starboard! I repeat: WATCH YOUR STARBOARD!"

Ned looked on in horror as the *Marilyn* swayed at pace towards another airship in the convoy.

The beast now had Benissimo by the throat, but the Ringmaster was keeping his calm, as though the claws at his windpipe were just a minor annoyance, but probably more because his able number two was making ready to strike.

"Bring her steady, boy," the Ringmaster managed to gasp.

Ned would have loved to, except...

"Err, HOW?"

"Pull the flight stick to its centre, straighten her up. She won't like it, so pull hard."

Ned shoved with all of his might to bring the *Marilyn* about. She moved slowly, three hundred tonnes of airborne metal fighting both her own momentum and a heavy wind. She wasn't straightening fast enough, they were going to…

Crash!

Ned watched appalled as the *Marilyn*'s starboard side brushed the other ship, leaving her tangled with the *Leonora*'s rigging.

For a second, the fight stopped and Benissimo broke free. His whip was out of his hand and moved with a will all of its own, holding both of the beast's legs together. The wolf-thing struck out wildly. But as fast as the beast was, it was no match for the Circus of Marvels' head of security. It screeched with frustration as its claws lashed out and cut through… nothing, as though he were mist. He was mist. Spinning around the creature, Mystero's face reformed again as a blur of angry tendrils growling at the monster furiously. The creature whimpered, and Benissimo landed a powerful blow. The monster fell to the ground, exhausted and breathless. The two men pounced, quickly grabbing at its arms and pinning them down.

"*Eagle Eye* to *Marilyn*, *Eagle Eye* to *Marilyn*, over!" came another voice over the intercom.

"This had best be of considerable significance, *Eagle Eye*, we're a little tied up at the minute," seethed Benissimo.

"BOEING!" screamed back the lookout.

"BOEEEEEEING!"

Which was when they saw a large white shape ahead of them, its red lights blinking.

"Someone must have messed with the flight plans! The red button, boy… hit the red button," yelled Benissimo, his composure broken for the first time that day.

Ned was still battling *Marilyn's* flight stick, trying to keep them on course.

"Red button or bring her steady?" he yelped.

"BUTTON!"

The main console had been significantly damaged by the beast's attack. There were hundreds of buttons, many of which were broken. The largest and reddest by far would have been covered by a glass dome, were the dome not now in shattered pieces. At its base, embossed in metal, were the words: *'Ringmaster ONLY'.*

"Do you mean this—"

"Get on with it!"

Ned pushed it, he pulled it, he even tried punching it, but the button was completely stuck and would not budge. "It's broken!" he yelled, but the Ringmaster and his sidekick were too busy trying to hold the still-bristling beast to help. Ned flicked his eyes upwards to see the Boeing approaching at considerable speed. "Think," he muttered to himself, "what would Dad do?" It was just a button; what mattered was beneath it. He looked at its base and saw a brass ring that fastened the red plastic to the console. He tried turning it clockwise, nothing. He tried again anti-clockwise and… it unscrewed in his hand. A second later the ring was off and he'd yanked the faulty button out of its hole, revealing a metal strip beneath it.

"I think I've found the contact strip!"

"WELL PUSH THE BLASTED THING THEN!" roared Benissimo.

Ned did as he was told. He pushed the strip.

Then, as every single one of the Circus of Marvels' airships dropped out of the sky simultaneously, and the ground rushed up to meet them, Ned suddenly found himself pinned to the roof of the flight deck, along with Mystero, Benissimo and the wolf-thing.

"Is this supposed to happen?" he shouted.

"No, there are secondary inflation devices that should have kicked in, something's gone wrong!" shouted back the Ringmaster. 'Miz, can you do anything?"

Ned didn't wait for a response, instead he did what any thirteen-year-old boy, especially one with a profound fear of heights, would do – and screamed.

***

Pilot John Rickerson was going to enjoy his retirement. He was making his final long-haul trip from Rome to New York and couldn't wait to get home. The 747 was on autopilot, the weather was fine and he had little to do other than daydream about his wife's blueberry pie. It came as a slight shock then when the onboard radar starting flashing uncontrollably and an elephant flew by his window.

"Holy cow!" he cried, spitting coffee across the dashboard.

The elephant was strange but not nearly as strange as the pink bus hurtling past his port side, and he could have sworn he caught a glimpse of an old lady on board sipping tea. He slammed on the air brakes, narrowly missing a merry-go-round and then, just as quickly as it had arrived, it had gone again, leaving nothing but a clear night sky in its wake and the slightest notion of mist. His long-standing co-pilot Hank burst in through the cabin door.

"What the heck's going on, John? I was in the toilet!"

The sudden application of air brakes had caused him to wee down the front of his trousers and he was not happy. John, on the other hand, was in a world of his own.

"I just saw… the circus."

"John? John, are you OK?"

CHAPTER 10

Mystero the Magnificent

When Ned woke again he was still on the flight deck, and felt hugely relieved to be awake at all. The *Marilyn's* secondary inflation devices had kicked in just in the nick of time, saving them from a crash landing, but not saving Ned's face from making a very sudden and painful acquaintance with the floor. While he was out, someone had obviously taken pity on him and moved him into one of the flight deck's chairs. Now he lay still, listening to the conversation that was taking place around him.

"I had a bad feeling about this from the start," said Mystero, trying to keep his voice down.

"You've a bad feeling about everything, Miz. It's part of your glum-faced charm," responded Benissimo dismissively.

"Well, I was right. We could have lost the whole

convoy. Someone helped the beast out of its cage and it had clearly been given his scent."

"The weir was snouting for the boy's blood-key, not his actual blood."

"What about the Boeing? The altered flight path? If they prove anything it's that they'll kill all of us to get at him."

"Look, this isn't what we planned and I don't like it any more than you do, but he's all we've got." Benissimo paused. "Having said that, did you see how resourceful he was with the console? It would suggest a modicum of… *something* about him…"

Ned started to feel bad about eavesdropping and decided it might be time to let them know he was awake.

"Oww…" he said, rubbing his head.

"Sleeping Beauty awakens," said Benissimo, quickly motioning to Mystero that their conversation had come to an end.

But Ned had heard it all. Yes, his life was in danger – this much he knew already – but at least he had earned a scrap of Benissimo's respect.

As he sat up, the bruise on his head started to throb.

"So what happened to 'as safe as a ruby in a crown'?" said Ned with a small smile.

"Well, we're all still here, aren't we? No thanks to you. If you'd done as you were told and stayed in your bunk, George would have dealt with the beast before my *Marilyn* got damaged," said Benissimo sternly, straightening his top hat.

"Well, if you'd told me there was a giant dog-thing walking the corridors I would have quite happily peed in my bed!"

"That's quite enough, you two," said Mystero kindly. "Ned did a great job on the release button, you said it yourself, Bene. If his fingers hadn't been quite as nimble, well, this little adventure would already be over. You did just fine, Ned."

Mystero had a slightly clammy, though now solid face and was still wearing the dinner jacket and bow tie from his last performance in Grittlesby. Though well worn, every crease and button was in perfect order and the outfit suited his serious, sincere demeanour.

"Shall we?" said Mystero, clearly communicating something to Benissimo.

The Ringmaster nodded, and began to speak.

"Ned, Mystero is a Mystral, an elemental force – capable of taking two forms. Part human and part air, hot air if you ask me, but a necessary sufferance. He's saved our collective skin more times than I have toes and I trust no one more deeply with the safety of my troupe. He's also the closest thing I'll allow to a friend."

"What, you mean he actually likes you?" asked Ned.

Benissimo raised an eyebrow, and the corner of his mouth curled up ever so slightly. It wasn't quite a smile, but something in its proximity.

"I'm also an old friend of your father's, Ned," said Mystero.

Ned winced, yet another part of his dad's life that he knew nothing about.

"I expect you know him a lot better than I do," said Ned flatly.

"Terrence is a good man, Ned, and as brave and selfless as any I know. I promised with Bene here to watch out for you, but I'm afraid we have ourselves a definite problem."

The mention of his dad being brave made Ned feel even more of a stranger. It was clearly something he was going to have to get used to.

But now was not the time for hurt feelings; Mystero was trying to warn him about more serious matters.

"Definite problem?"

"The clowns that came to your house used to be ours; a bad decision on my part, I'm afraid. It would appear that the same people who want your father now want you. How they know about your blood-key is anyone's guess, but the weir's attack most assuredly proves it. They won't stop, Ned, and there are plenty of worse things out there than last night's weir."

Ned remembered the monster's smell and shuddered.

"That creature, the weir... it was a werewolf, wasn't it?"

"They've been given many names. The Vikings called them vargulfs or vargs and the Saxons warwoolfs. They are one of three types of shapeshifter. The wolf-pack, the bear-clan and the herd - the last of the great stags. At one time, they were powerful allies, till they lost control over their gifts and their condition forced us to put them in exile. Now they manage the wildlands beyond the Veil for us, in Siberia, and our other Darkling reserves."

"That thing was on your side?"

"Darklings and especially Demons cannot cross the Veil into your world without help, but they can roam behind it. The weirs monitor the Darklings' behaviour and alert us to their movements. In some ways they're like wardens in a jail, only quite often as dangerous as the inmates they're trying to control."

"Siberia's in Russia. What was this one doing in France?"

"It won't talk. Weirs are two parts magic, one part rage, almost impossible to frighten. Yet the forces that put this one in our path have scared it out of its mind. What we do know is, our best attempts to keep you a secret have already failed, which makes my job that much harder. By now the troupe will have guessed you're not a regular runaway. When we get to Shalazaar, you and Benissimo will go into the city alone and in disguise. I'll be going in with one of the younger Tortellini boys and some others to try and take them off your scent. He doesn't look much like you, but I'm banking on the clowns not having had a proper look at your face."

Ned was horrified. Until this precise moment, he'd thought there was still just the slimmest chance he'd gone mad. That this new world of monsters and blood-keys wasn't really *real*. But he hadn't gone mad. His father really was mixed up in this and, Engineer or not, how could his dear old telly-addict dad protect himself? He might well have been brave in his past life, but he didn't have a Mystero or whip-wielding Ringmaster onside. The dad he knew could barely walk to the shops without breaking into a sweat. As Ned's stomach knotted with worry, the intercom crackled.

"*Eagle Eye* to *Marilyn* over?"

"This is *Marilyn*, *Eagle Eye*," responded Benissimo.

"Approaching Veil aerospace, boss. We're home."

At the word 'home' the Ringmaster visibly changed. His rough exterior became softer and his eyes a little more bright.

As he slowed *Marilyn*'s engines for arrival, Benissimo motioned for Ned to come and sit by him.

"Now, pup, you get to see what all the fuss is about; what it is that I'm trying to protect. You never forget your first crossing. Here, pass your eye through my spyglass."

Ned peered through the spyglass. The entire view was a blanket of thick billowing grey.

"But it's just fog, lots and lots of fog."

"Is it?"

Slightly lower than the rest of the convoy and far up ahead, was a much smaller airship. Thick plumes of what looked like steam were billowing out from underneath it. Ned twisted the spyglass by his eye and focused it on the airship's lower cabin. Through the porthole he saw the two Guffstavson brothers, who had lit light bulbs in their mouths back in Grittlesby. They were both red-faced and angry. Sparks of electricity flew between them and were gathered up by brass rods that were in turn linked to a generator. The angrier they became, the larger the sparks of electricity, and in turn the more fog that their ship produced.

"That is nuts," said a stunned Ned.

"No, boy, that is the foginator. *This* is nuts," he turned to the intercom. "Bene to engine rooms – all stop."

The foginator let out a final puff and its propellers stopped spinning. As the sky cleared, Ned's nostrils filled with the smell of strawberry ice cream and burnt caramel. The sounds from the *Marilyn*'s slowing engine began to stretch and blur. Above the convoy, he saw a flock of birds. The birds were flying backwards.

"Those birds… they shouldn't be able to do that."

"No, they shouldn't. But we're at the border, one of many. When magic and non-magic meet, reality bends. I've seen kettles make jugs of ice and rivers flow backwards. It's never the same thing twice," explained Benissimo proudly. "What might look like a lonely wood, or a calm sea, eventually gives way to… what lies behind the Veil."

As Benissimo said it, Ned had a strong sense of… something. They'd 'crossed'. He looked down but all he could see was miles and miles of golden sand. Then shapes started to bend up from the flat expanse, till they became clearer, more solid – walls, buildings, towers. The forming mirage of light and shadow gradually grew into a city. Ned knew from his talk with George what this must be – the desert city of Shalazaar, the city behind the Veil. In its middle lay the Shar's palace. It was ivory white and bore a huge flag carrying his insignia: a set of measuring scales with a two-headed cobra wrapped around its centre.

Ned stared in wonder at the city beneath him, which was unlike any he had seen before. Gothic church spires stood beside ancient mosques and Greek temples. Every surface bulged with giant statues of forgotten gods and unknown kings. Some parts of the city were industrial, huge constructs of iron and steel that spilled out over the old, wrapping themselves around crumbling buildings and broken walls, too ancient to fend for themselves. European architecture fused with Chinese, Japanese with Arabic, as though someone had taken mankind's best efforts and melted them into one. Flying machines whirred over its rooftops, steam-powered vehicles puffed along its streets and Ned even spotted a man on the back of an ostrich. Strangest of all was the sight of people riding other people. Small men in top hats on the backs of great hulking brutes, and, in contrast, huge women laid out on stretchers, being carried by up to a dozen tiny men.

"Over the centuries, as our ancestors crossed into the hidden lands, they brought their gods and customs with them. We descendants like to have our history in plain sight, gives us a sense of place in the world."

To the east, from the foot of a mountain, came a high-pitched whistle, as an enormous steam engine charged out of its tunnel. Instead of a regular engine and chimney, the great metal beast was in the shape of an iron horse locked in mid gallop, smoke pouring from its mouth and nostrils.

"The Indo-China runner," yelled Benissimo over the din of its whistle. "Took old Zaheed fifty years to dig out the track for that little wonder."

Benissimo was explaining who Zaheed was when Ned noticed the statue. It was at least two times the height of the city's tallest building. A rough and weather-beaten image of a giant sitting by the tunnel's mouth. Great tusks the size of streets curled down below its cheeks, and on its back a small forest of pine trees had grown. A village of ramshackle houses had been set up on top of its head, and as they got closer Ned saw its inhabitants desperately clinging to the nearest surface. The ground they were standing on seemed to be shaking. Then, very slowly, the mouth of the statue opened.

"Arooooooooraaa!" It made a sound not dissimilar to that of a whale, only deeper.

"What the..." said Ned in shock.

"Shalazaar, quite a sight, isn't she?" said Benissimo with a proud twirl of his moustache.

"Not the city, that thing!" said Ned, now pointing.

"Ah, you mean Bernie."

"Bernie?" He was still unsure of what he was looking at. "I thought it was a statue. Is it a... giant?"

"Bernaghast is a Colossus, and one of our many wonders. He's a good deal larger than any giant, or anything else for that matter. Colossi are famously slow of foot. He turned up unannounced forty-odd years ago and hasn't budged since. He's waiting for an old friend of his, hasn't seen him since 1732."

Ned looked at Benissimo, smiling happily at the sight of his home. Right here and now, his guard was lowered and for the first time Ned saw him as a man and not a Ringmaster.

"You really love it, don't you? The Veil and all it hides, I mean," asked Ned.

"Every brick and every eyeball, to the bottom of my worn old boots."

Ned could see why. He'd been behind the Veil for

approximately twelve minutes. And despite everything else that had happened to him recently, they were the strangest, most wonderful twelve minutes of his thirteen-year life.

Benissimo handed him a brass-buttoned waistcoat, with a cream shirt and a pair of old-fashioned knickerbockers.

"Err, what's this for?"

"It's your disguise. Misery guts did the picking of it himself."

"Knickerbockers! Who wears knickerbockers any more?"

"Servants to wealthy merchants, young pup. You will be the lowest of the low and I your wealthy and most benevolent master."

There were some lengths that Ned was simply not prepared to go to, lost dad or not, no matter how important the asking, or who did it.

"I'm not wearing them, I'll do the shirt and the waistcoat but not the knickerbockers. I'll look ridiculous!"

Benissimo's moustache started to twitch and his face soured. The Ringmaster had returned.

"Ned Waddlesworth, I'm going to do some speaking and you're going to do some opening of the ears and closing of the mouth. Your father is halfway round the world by now, doing his very best to keep our enemies off your scent… it has not worked. Whether you like it or not, you are now the linchpin of my plans – and the only thing that can save the fair-folk and the rest of humanity on either side of the Veil – for which I need to keep you alive. Those streets you see below are filled with some of the most villainous men, women and beasts the world has ever known. If our spies are as real as Miz claims, then the darkest and most odious of Shalazaar's inhabitants will have been told of your arrival. *WHICH IS NOT A GOOD THING.* When you put those on, you may well look quite astonishingly cretinous, but it is far, far better, than looking dead."

Ned's twelve minutes of starry-eyed wonder had come to an end.

CHAPTER 11

Behind the Veil

The Circus of Marvels set up camp by a shanty town of tents, outside the city walls. Ned was almost trampled underfoot as the troupe unloaded their Darkling cages, and any of his offers to help were ignored. Inexperienced runaways – and especially jossers – were clearly considered a hindrance, though Ned wondered if their mistrustful looks had more to do with the weir's attack. George had told him that tonight there would be a 'Night of the Twelve', so named whenever there was a meeting of the governing council, that ran the Veil's circuses. The council was made up of twelve of the most senior circus members. According to George, rumour had it that they'd asked Benissimo to join several times, but he'd always refused.

One half of the encampment was made up of gypsies

and nomads, the other was circus folk: 'Longhorn's Rodeo' from America, 'the Jade Dragons' from China, 'Putin's Cossacks' just in from Moscow and at least a dozen more, all transporting their captured Darklings for relocation.

The colours, sounds and smells – not to mention the desert heat – were dizzying, and everywhere Ned looked the gathered troupe members were locked in excitable banter. He'd never seen a group of souls so happy to be on familiar soil.

Frocks had been bought, stories exchanged and the food trucks were cooking up some exotic treats. The troupe were readying themselves for a party, all except Mystero and Benissimo. Their minds were clearly focused on the forthcoming mission and the retrieval of Ned's deposit box.

As the sun started to lower, Ned found George sitting by Rocky's wife. Beside them, Rocky was locked in a violent wrestling match with another even larger creature Ned didn't recognise. A crowd of rival circuses had gathered and bets had been placed.

"Hello, Ned," grinned George. It was the first time Ned had seen him, out and about with the rest of the troupe. "You all set?" he added in a rumbling whisper.

"Yup, think so," lied back Ned. The knickerbockers

were as uncomfortable as they looked.

"Abi – this is what last night's fuss was about, my new roomie, Ned."

"Well, of course he is. Ello Master Widdlewoops." At this she winked to let him know she was one of the few in on his secret, along with Rocky, no doubt. "You've caused quite the stir already. Why don't you come rest your bones next to me," said Abigail in a thick West Country accent.

She was the prettiest, smiliest, fat bearded lady that Ned had ever seen and he was just beginning to wonder whether her beardedness was the extent of her specialness, when her beard started to ripple excitedly.

"That's Yuri," she explained pointing over at the fight, "Rocky's cousin. He's a troll like my 'usband – a bridge-troll – and nearly as dumb. Those two have been at it since they could fart. Neither of 'em ever wins, mind, an' every year they meet up 'ere an' give each other another good thrashin'. Big ugly lumps, the pair of 'em," she said with a chuckle.

Crack! Crack! Crack! came a flurry of Rocky's stoney thumps.

"That's it, lover, you teach that big Cossack who's boss!" shouted Abi, cheering on her man.

Benissimo arrived sporting a less crooked hat, a well-groomed beard and what looked like a bit of padding around the belly beneath his shirt. He was not in a playful mood.

"Come along, children, we've grown-up business to be taking care of."

Rocky and Yuri got up off the ground, but not before giving each other a final thump.

"And what of my Kit-Kat?" Benissimo asked, turning his attention to Abigail.

"Gave her a cup o' cocoa an hour ago. She's all lights out an' snuggled up in bed."

"Good, good. And our perimeter?"

"Luigi an' Marco are on the roof an' the other Tortellinis are scattered about all over. I'll be on the bottom floor of Kitty's bus havin' a cuppa till you get back, boss. No one's getting past the Beard tonight."

As if to make her point, Abigail's beard rippled again, like a bicep on a boxer's arm, which was both impressive and deeply unsettling. Ned tried not to stare.

"Be sure that they don't; we've no rudder without her. Miz, if you wouldn't mind?"

Mystero – in his more solid form – followed Abigail inside to make a last minute check on Kitty, reappearing a moment later to give the all clear. Then he headed into the city with his decoy group, while Benissimo handed Ned the rest of his costume. It was a large sack of 'goods' they would pretend to trade.

"You must be kidding; this weighs a tonne!" moaned Ned.

"Well you have to look the part, boy. Now, try not to mess this up, the less chit-chat the better, rich people like me don't talk to their skivvies."

The Ringmaster had now fully returned to his old less-than-charming self.

"You know you were almost nice when we came in to land?"

"A mistake I'll no doubt forgive myself for… in time."

***

Shalazaar's streets and alleys were crammed with stalls, selling all things imaginable, and some that weren't. Ned had to remind himself not to gawp. Behind the Veil, most of the creatures had no need for glamours and the fair-folk were out in force.

Snake-skinned women in pretty lace dresses laughed as a street conjuror pulled wild and rather irritable pixies from his hat. Slightly away from the crowd, a Chinese Kirin was being stroked for good luck by a group of excitable children. The kindly animal – which Ned recognised from a book of mythological creatures, but had no idea actually existed – had a tiger's body, though covered in scales, and a face much like a dragon's with a set of beautiful deer's antlers at the top of its head. What Ned guessed might be an elf seemed to glide by it, all flowing dress and whiter-than-white skin. Outside a food stall, he was watching a group of tiny, leaf-skinned creatures arguing over a sack of plant feed when something sparkled its way between his legs, on the back of a goose.

"Fairy. Avoid at all costs," warned Benissimo.

The more human inhabitants wore everything from Japanese kimonos, to outfits that would have looked more at home in the streets of old Paris. Some carried masks on sticks, others wore white powdered make-up. It was a living, breathing melting pot of mismatched places and mismatched times.

"Everyone looks so… different," said Ned.

"You can trace when their ancestors crossed over, and where from, by looking at their clothes. The last good-sized migration was in the Victorian era. To be honest, some of them are a little snobby about it – especially the ones in togas. Now, button it, underling, or you'll draw attention."

Besides being busy, it was also noisy, as the din of a hundred sales competed with Irish fiddles, banging drums and the calls of jugglers trying to catch the eye of passing trade. The market streets of Shalazaar never closed. The Shar insisted on the selling of goods at all times of the day.

"Veil's on the tumble! Darkling crossings on the up!" yelled a gaggle of 'ink-hawkers', trying to sell the local paper to anyone with eyes. "The end of the world is nigh – and only *The Rag* has it in colour!"

As if to prove a point, a group of 'unveiled' sat cross-legged next to the hawkers. This, Benissimo explained, was the name given to the homeless folk who'd had to move on when their part of the protective Veil began faltering. It had only gone completely in small sections so far, but it was worrying nonetheless. The unveiled were mostly ignored though, and their begging bowls left empty. In Shalazaar, the end of the world was not nearly as important as making a little coin.

"Three bars and an ingot? You must be mad! I ain't payin' nuffin' over 'alf a scroll and two coppertops for that frog's breath," shouted a loudmouthed woman in tatty clothes, who smelt to Ned like she already had all the bad breath she would ever need.

"Aroooooooraaa!" came Bernie's lament over the noise.

"Bloomin' Colossus! Tha's all we need. As if the 'eat weren't enough! All day, all night, 'Arooo' this an' 'Arooo' that. Can't the Shar do nothing about it?" complained a grumpy market trader to one of her colleagues.

"Love charms, gypsy dreams, hag's tears! Fresh in today, three for two, five for three!" barked a rough, three-horned trader, with pale green skin. "You, laddie, you look like you're game, care for a wee sample? The tears really are rather good."

"No tears today, Borrin. As the gods of misfortune would have it, the boy is with me," said Benissimo, putting a firm hand on Ned's shoulder.

"Be- Be- Benissimo, my lord, yes, of course." The trader lowered his head and started to back away.

"We were never 'ere, Borrin, not now, not ever. Understood?"

"Yes, yes of course, your Ringliness… I mean, no sir, whoever you are, Borrin sees nothing."

"Gods of misfortune!" seethed Ned to himself.

Past the spice markets and charm sellers, and down a side road, they came to a smart quarter with beautiful shop fronts and pretty cobbled streets. Smartly dressed lantern-wards were firing up their lamps as the night traders arrived for their evening shift.

For the most part, these shops sold an assortment of antiquated weapons and magic, with names like

'LITTLE WHISPERS: HOME OF THE SHADOWED ARTS'

whose shop window was filled with a moving cloud of inky smoke, making it almost impossible to see inside, and

'THE LIGHTBOX: WHITE MAGIC SINCE THE FIRST SPARK'.

Some of the magic was apparently so powerful it had to be guarded round the clock by the Shar's stone golems, who Ned assumed, like the Colossus, were probably not just statues.

The most impressive shop of all though needed no introduction –

'FIDGIT AND SONS: PURVEYOR OF FINE MEKANIKS SINCE 1066'.

Fidgit's shop front was covered in a thick, gold-leaf lacquer, and delicate Victorian ironwork wrapped around the columns that stood either side of its entrance, giving it a look of grandeur and importance. Peering into the shop, Ned could see its vertically-challenged staff were all clearly minutians like the Tinker, with matching white lab coats. The shop's polished glass windows were alive with clockwork tickers, like Whiskers – eagles, monkeys, mice, all as yet un-furred and un-feathered to show the intricacy of their inner workings. Everything Ned had ever built paled in comparison. The shop in front of him was a thing of wonder, all wrapped up in shiny metal and perfect moving parts.

"There's nowhere quite like Fidgit's," said Benissimo, noting the look of wonder on the boy's face. "Your father's favourite haunt, or at least it was."

Another reminder of his dad's secret life, though this time Ned felt comforted. This was the Terry Waddlesworth he knew and loved.

"I'm not surprised… he would have been in heaven here."

The most impressive piece was outside by the shop's entrance. An un-furred tiger sitting completely still, its polished chrome metalwork glinting in the last rays of the sun. Pistons, dials and gears whirred away quietly, under a patchwork of curved outer casing so detailed and complex it could be described as art.

"So they definitely do sell more than screws then," said Ned with a smile, as he reached out to touch the surface of the intricate metalwork.

"That's not a good idea," warned Benissimo.

But Ned's hands were already on its casing. Deep inside the tiger's chest, a gyroscopic heart started to spin and the beast came to life, its jaws opening to emit a low metallic snarl. Ned jumped back in terror, but the tiger softened, rubbed up against him like a cat and purred.

"Wow! It's amazing!" laughed Ned.

"You wouldn't be nearly as chirpy if it had removed your arm. That's a display unit; the real thing isn't as friendly. Now, are you ready? Is your head screwed on tight, your heart beating steady?"

Ned was still staring at the chrome-plated tiger.

"Not really," said Ned, coming back to reality with a sigh.

"Once I open that box, all this becomes real. I liked Dad and me and the world the way it was. I didn't know how much until now…"

Ned found himself regretting his honesty, and waited for the usual condescending insult to follow. Instead, Benissimo took his arm and looked him straight in the eye.

"We'll get him back, Ned, if you've the heart for it. As for the world, well… it's still out there. You just have to help us save it."

Which was exactly what Ned was afraid of. But before he could have time for second thoughts, Benissimo had spun about and pushed open the shop door.

CHAPTER 12

Inside the Box

The inside of Fidgit and Sons was larger than it should have been, at least five times larger. Everything moved. Escalators, elevators, pulleys and gears all running down to a large circular vault and all to the ceaseless clatter of tiny moving parts.

"This little beauty's just in from Japan," said an attendant, demonstrating the features of a mechanical puppy to an interested buyer. "One of our more popular new models." The puppy proceeded to cock its leg and pee on the man's foot.

"Ahem, completely odourless, of course, and there is the added benefit of the puppy staying a puppy, till you opt for an upgrade."

On the lower-ground floor, they passed through Fidgit's security department, of self-defending doors and thief-battering alarm systems before carrying on down to the basement, where they kept their safety deposit boxes, manned by a single, bored-looking attendant.

"Yes?"

"Box room, please," said Benissimo, passing him Ned's key.

"A blood-key?" said the now interested attendant. "Haven't seen one of these in a while. We discontinued them when people started using other people's blood to get in here. We had one feller turn up with another man's finger once. The lengths the criminal mind will go to…" he said, shaking his head.

He reached into his drawer and pulled out a menacingly long needle. Before Ned could complain, his finger had been grabbed and stabbed and the key transformed. To his surprise, he hadn't felt a thing. The attendant then ushered them through a small door and left them in a windowless marble room the colour of snow. As soon as the attendant shut the door, the marble turned as black as night and all they could make out was a gold-trimmed keyhole, waiting for Ned's key.

With a trembling hand, Ned pushed the key into the lock. When he turned it, there was an almighty thundering of gears as the walls slid apart to reveal a vast warehouse. Black and white marble boxes went on as far as the eye could see, all smooth-sided and completely unmarked. Each was held by a golden arm, and they spun, slid and flipped past each other like a giant mechanical puzzle. From far at the back, one of the white boxes came flying towards Ned, weaving smoothly in and out of the other containers, before stopping abruptly by his hand.

"Now what?" he asked.

"Put your hand to it; it knows who you are."

Ned took a deep breath. People were ready to kill for the contents of this box. Somehow, in some way, those very same contents might be used to save his father.

He touched the box gently with his fingertip, and the cool marble lid flipped open.

Ned and Benissimo peered cautiously into the box. Inside was a letter, and a small metal ring. Ned picked up the letter. It was addressed to him, but the writing was not his dad's, as he'd been expecting. Then he picked up the ring. It looked just like his father's wedding band. In all his years, Ned had never seen it off his dad's finger.

Benissimo sighed with what sounded like relief.

"So the blood-key's 'O' wasn't an O after all," said Ned, "just a symbol for the ring. All this, for a wedding ring? I don't understand. I thought this was going to help us find the girl?"

"It's not really a ring, Ned. Not exactly. And in the right hands it could wield unspeakable power."

"Why is it here then? Why was it left for *me*?"

Benissimo didn't answer.

"Well maybe the letter will tell us," said Ned, and was about to open it when Benissimo stopped him.

"Not yet, pup. Madame Oublier and her council would like to meet you first."

"Who is Madame Oublier?" said Ned, annoyed at being asked to wait.

"It's who the Tinker messaged when we were in France, and they're already waiting for us."

Ned vaguely recalled her name being mentioned, but did not see what she or anyone else had to do with his letter.

"You're kidding, right? In the last three days I've discovered a secret world, been told my dad is some sort of mystical 'Engineer', shared a room with a talking gorilla, been attacked by a werewolf and dropped out of the sky in a flying tent… and you want me to wait to find out *why*? This letter was left for *me*, not some council."

"Wait, boy, you'll thank me for it," said Benissimo, his

tone now more an order than a request.

Ned didn't understand. Why would he thank him and how did Benissimo even know the contents of the letter? Dad had told him on Grittlesby green before they parted that only two people knew about the blood-key. Was the second Benissimo? Was the handwriting on the letter his? Something about the look in the Ringmaster's eye kept him silent, apprehensive even. Were there more things about his father that he didn't know? Things that he wouldn't like? And if so, why wasn't Benissimo telling him?

Once they were back outside the entrance to Fidgit and Sons, the Ringmaster took Ned's items for safe-keeping – without asking – and pulled something from his jacket. It was long and silver, like the tool Ned had seen the pinstripes use on the tourist in France.

"I need to remind our hosts that we were never here. Don't talk to anyone, do not wander off, and try—"

"Not to breathe?" interrupted Ned.

"Not to mess things up," said Benissimo. Then he went back inside the shop and locked the door behind him, flipped the closed sign over and rolled down the blinds.

Ned picked himself a spot under the stars and waited. Whatever Benissimo was doing inside was taking some time and it was starting to get cold. He was weighing up what was worse, being away from his dad or being stuck with Benissimo, when he heard padded footsteps nearby.

"Ooh, lookie nicey boy," came a sinister little voice from the shadows.

"Don' lookie like mooch up close, do he?" said another.

Ned turned around and his blood ran cold.

Walking towards him were three grinning clowns.

The clowns approached Ned with a strange unsettling stagger, their eyes fixed hungrily on him. Ned recognised one of them immediately as the clown he'd seen at his sitting room window. The second one was enormously fat – perhaps the one who had been driving the purple van, he thought – and the third extremely short, even shorter than the Tinker. Each of their outfits was dirtier and more outlandish than the next and when they got closer, Ned could smell a foul mix of bad breath and a distinct lack of soap.

"You lostis? You no heerie froom?" squeaked the shortest of the three.

Ned looked at the one from his house, and a flash of anger boiled up inside him.

"I don't speak clown, but I know who you are. What have you done with my dad?"

"No Cloon spikky, hmmmmm," said the fattest, eyeing up Ned as if he were a plate of food.

"You cooms vid cloons noo, then ve foond Dadda," said the tallest.

The three clowns were now standing between Ned and Fidgit's, so he couldn't bang on the window, and with the shutters closed, there was no chance of Benissimo seeing out on to the street.

"Not scarums boy, facie bad bad," said the smallest, as he inched his way closer.

"Nicey boy, vid cloons noo," added the fat one, licking his lips as he got ready to grab Ned.

Ned did not want to be eaten by a fat clown, or go anywhere with any of them, and as the clown moved in, Ned raised his leg high and stamped down hard on his foot, before bolting.

"Argghhh, boy smush! Flik flak!" hissed the clown. "Getty getty noo!"

Ned had no idea which way to go, only that he needed to run. Benissimo would never find him in the maze of streets, but if he could get away, he was sure to find his way back to the city wall and the camp where the troupe was waiting.

Getting away, however, would be harder than he

thought. Every turn he took seemed to lead him further from the city wall and deeper into the warren of twisting, darkening streets. At one point he took a fork to the left and the fattest of his three pursuers took the other. How were they keeping up? Their baggy trousers and rubbery shoes seemingly did nothing to slow the clowns' progress, and Ned wheezed and panted as he tried desperately to escape them. Hurtling round a corner, his face dropped at the sight of a dead end. His two pursuers had him trapped.

Ned's head was pounding and his chest was on fire. The two clowns hadn't even broken a sweat. Who were these monsters and how could they keep up with a young boy in less ridiculous shoes?

"Gotchi, gotchi, nicey boy," grinned the shortest, as they lumbered menacingly towards him.

Ned had to think fast. In the corner of the alleyway, he spotted a pile of empty apple crates piled against the wall, and made a run for it. Three paces, a high jump and a face full of sandstone later, he found himself at the top of the wall. Usually anything higher than a two-step ladder would make his head swim. But there were some things even worse than heights and these clowns were definitely on the list.

"Grrrrrr," snarled the shortest, grabbing a bicycle horn at his waist.

Honk! Honk!

Ned dropped down on the other side and dusted himself off. His eyes were blurry with sweat and he felt sure he was about to have a heart attack. But he'd made it, he'd got away. Now all he had to do was find his way back to—

HONK! came the deep bass of another horn.

"Oh, come on!" yelled Ned in disbelief.

Standing just a few feet away and not even remotely out of breath was the fat clown. How had he got there so quickly? Ned's spirit was broken; there simply wasn't anything left of him to try and escape again. In no time the others had climbed over the wall and he found himself pacing backwards down a narrow, covered passageway.

"Nicey boy frightie?" grinned the tall one.

"Mo snacka makey," said the fattest, revealing a wide set of perfectly black teeth.

Were these foul lunatics really planning on eating him?

"Eanie, Meanie, heel! Mo, stop that!" boomed the voice of a stranger from somewhere behind Ned.

Ned felt a momentary wave of relief. That was, of course, until he saw the look on the stranger's face.

CHAPTER 13

Face-off

The passageway had led to a small square, where two unsavoury-looking characters were sat around a table outside an otherwise empty café, sharing a pot of evening tea. One of them was the tallest person Ned had ever seen, a thin-lipped cowboy with a checked shirt and grubby yellow scarf. Opposite him was a short barrel of a man, who was almost as wide as he was tall. He had skin like sandpaper and wore a tight leather crash helmet, barely held together with a patchwork of stitching. He was trying to pour a cup of tea with visibly shaking hands, and had the expression of a man who was always angry. Under the table and amongst their feet, a cat was busying itself with a saucer of milk.

"I'm so sorry my boys here startled you; they have the most shameful manners," said the third stranger, smiling again.

Ned had never seen a smile like it. It managed to look kind and cruel at the same time. The rest of him was no less unsettling. He was a large stocky man, with tattooed forearms as thick as Ned's legs. He had a broad face and a wiry, black-red beard. On his head was a bowler hat with two black feathers in its rim and hanging from his belt was a heavy, square meat cleaver, brown with rust. He plucked it from his belt and began cutting an apple, in careful, measured strokes. Each of his fat fingers had a gold sovereign for a ring and his neck was strewn with chains. To Ned he looked like a pirate king, or a butcher, or both.

"The truth is, Ned, we were just a little worried that you might be lost," he continued. "The boys here are so good at finding… *things*."

Ned had been chased by deranged clowns, and come face to face with a werewolf, but nothing had thrown him more off balance than the smiling, apple-eating man in front of him. He had a forced politeness to the way he spoke that didn't seem to fit, like a bulldog trying to eat with a knife and fork.

"Who are you and how do you know my name?" asked Ned, trying his best to look calm.

"Oh, but of course, how rude of me. We haven't

been properly introduced. My name is Barbarossa, and I know your name because I make it my business to know. Nothing happens behind the Veil without Barba finding out."

Whoever Barbarossa was or wasn't made little difference. The clowns were his and Ned wanted to leave as soon as possible.

"Well, it's, err, nice to meet you, Mr Barbarossa. But if you don't mind I think I need to find Benissimo, the Ringmaster, he'll be looking for me and—"

"Oh, but I *do* mind, my lad. I couldn't possibly let you leave. These streets can be so very dangerous at night, especially for a josser on his own. Besides, you and I have so much to discuss. There's your little birthday present, for one thing, and we can't really chat about that without bringing up *daddy*, now, can we?"

Ned felt the strength being sucked out of his belly.

"Do you have him? Please tell me. I just want to know if he's OK."

Barbarossa stopped cutting his apple and laid down his cleaver.

"No, Ned, I do not. Nor will I need him, now that I have you."

Suddenly only two things mattered: firstly, that his

dad was free, and secondly, that Ned needed to find him. Before he could do that, however, he had to get out of here, and Ned suspected that for this he was going to need a miracle. He was trapped again, with these vile men and their terrifying clowns. Something inside him sparked once more, a flare of defiance and fury.

"You don't *have* me, and whatever it is you think I'll help you with, you're wrong. I'm not going anywhere with you. It's a free country and I'm going back to the Circus of Marvels RIGHT NOW."

"That is quite incorrect, lad. This is not a free country. This is my country, and you are coming with me. Cannonball, would you mind persuading our new friend? He doesn't seem to get the gist of what's happening here."

The barrel-shaped man launched from his stool like a rocket and was by Ned's side in an instant. The sheer speed of his movement made Ned jump in terror, he was even worse than the clowns. But as he reached for Ned, there was the loud crack of a whip as Benissimo raced into the square. Ned's heart leapt as the Ringmaster's whip cut through the air, slashing Cannonball across his hand. Barbarossa grabbed his cleaver and he and the cowboy jumped to their feet, knocking over their table with a clatter of falling china and a hissing of frightened cat.

"Welcome, *fratello*," smiled the butcher, clearly trying to remain composed, "it's been a while."

Benissimo's whip coiled and he clenched his fists.

"And yet, never long enough," he replied. Though outnumbered, you'd never have known it from the Ringmaster's glare, a glare, Ned realised, that was also being aimed at *him*. Benissimo's look of blame was both wildly unfair and completely in character.

"All the same, it's good of you to join us, Bene. Now we can take the boy *and* the ring. You did get the ring, didn't you?"

Barbarossa and his men had formed two half circles around Benissimo and Ned. Clowns at the back, Barbarossa and the others at the front.

"Boy and ring are under my watch. You and your… associates will have to go through me to lay a finger on either, and I'm in no mood for letting you have them."

"Surely there's no need for all that? The Shar would be most displeased to have a brawl on his streets, and you really have no hope of winning. However if we must tussle, old Bessy here…" said Barbarossa, looking down at his cleaver lovingly, "…is fair thirsty."

"I'd have a thing or two to say about dat," came a familiar voice.

It was Rocky and Monsieur Couteau. Before anyone could move, the Russian had got both Meanie and Mo in headlocks, while the French swordsman held Eanie at bay with the tip of his sword.

"You remember George, da?" said Rocky, as if announcing checkmate in a game of chess.

George stepped out from the alley, with slow lumbering steps. The mild-mannered giant ape that had been so kind the night before, was nowhere in sight. In his place, the Mighty George stood – feral, simmering with anger, shifting agitatedly where he stood and ready to pounce. Even though George was there to save him, seeing him like that was so terrifying, Ned was glad not to be on the other end of his fixed, dark gaze.

"Let the boy go, Barba," said Benissimo.

Barbarossa fell silent for a moment while weighing up his odds.

"As you wish. But this is not over, *fratello*, not until I get what I want." He tipped his hat courteously at Ned, motioning that he was free to leave.

"It never is," sighed the Ringmaster.

***

They walked a long while in silence before Benissimo turned on Ned.

"I thought I told you to stay put?"

"And I would have done, if it weren't for the three homicidal maniacs threatening to eat me!"

Ned could feel angry frustration bubbling under his skin. Being terrified was one thing, but being repeatedly blamed for things that were quite obviously out of his control was quite another. Why did the Ringmaster dislike everything about him so much?

"I say, boss, I do think you're being a little unfair," snorted George.

But Benissimo didn't respond. It was only when Ned and his protectors had made their way back to the city wall that they understood why Barbarossa had so willingly let them go without a fight.

Squar! came a call above their heads.

The two-headed hawk has many gifts, but its greatest is sight. Aark could see clearly across an entire continent, even on the darkest of nights. Just a second after she raised the alarm, after something in the distance brought out her cry, a frantic Mystero materialised before them.

"I was on my way back… we played right into his hands. The camp, Bene, it's under attack!"

Benissimo's face turned to thunder.

"Devil and damnation… Kit-Kat! Go to her, Miz, like the wind, GO!"

The able number two corkscrewed back into mist, before launching himself forward in a rush towards their beloved Farseer.

"George, Rocky, do not leave the boy's side," continued Benissimo. "Monsieur Couteau, with me. Quickly now! And Ned, this time… *stay out of trouble.*"

CHAPTER 14

Darklings

The night market was in full swing now and they were having trouble making progress. George scooped Ned up with one powerful arm and swung him on to his shoulder, leaving Rocky to lead the way. A strange phenomenon in the mountain variant of the troll species, George explained to Ned, is that their flesh becomes denser and more 'rocky' as their anger rises. The now menacing troll carved a route through the crowds like a living freight train.

"Mek way, circus business!" he bellowed.

"What's going on, George? Who were those people?" asked Ned as he clung to the gorilla's tree-trunk of a neck. It was a strange way to travel – but no stranger than flying in an inflatable tent.

"If those filthy clowns had hurt you, I'd have…"

began the ape crossly.

In truth, Ned was amazed. He had only just met Benissimo and his troupe, and yet they had hurried as one to his aid, even though the Ringmaster now had the contents of his dad's deposit box. Hearing the tone in George's voice something else struck him that he had not been expecting. He had made himself a friend. Albeit a genuinely frightening one. Despite the ape's continued eloquence, 'gentlemanly George' was still nowhere to be seen. Animal anger boiled beneath his skin and he dropped to a gallop on all fours, moving Ned on to his back as he did so, and puffing out his chest like a bull, with nostrils flared from snorting.

"They must want the ring pretty badly. But why, what can it—"

George snarled angrily, not even letting him finish as he punched the ground with a loud *boom*.

"Those people are bounders and scoundrels of the very worst kind. If you ever see them again you find me, Ned, you find me, or you run."

"The big one, Barbarossa, he seemed to know you, and he called Benissimo *'fratello'*. What does that mean?"

"Brother."

"Brother! You mean he's Benissimo's actual brother?"

"Brother and nemesis, with a soul as black as coal. Poor Bene has dedicated his life to undoing the beast's wrongs, for as long as anyone can remember."

"What sort of wrongs?"

"Atrocities of the very worst kind. Some people are born beyond reasoning. Barbarossa is beyond *everything*. As for his accomplices, Slim, the cowboy, when un-glamoured, is a long-elf, different to their shorter cousins, and prone to acts of cruelty. They weren't always so heartless, though thankfully they're now uncommon. The little one is a dwarven berserker, which keeps him both enraged and unbreakable."

"I could brekk him," chimed in Rocky from the front, before barging his way through a group of disgruntled potion makers in the midst of selling their wares.

In his current mood, Ned had no doubt he was right.

At last they made it back to the shanty town of tents, where the visitors continued with their festivities, unaware of the danger that the Circus of Marvels was in.

The Night of the Twelve was by now in full swing. African drums and gypsy wailing filled the sky, accompanied by an endless shimmer of beyond-the-Veil-made fireworks. A procession of beautifully painted bull elephants marched round the camp while dark-skinned nymphs with cymbals on their fingers floated and chimed between them.

Just near their camp, the Longhorns and the Cossacks were arguing over who had captured the most dangerous Darklings, the Russians settling the dispute by displaying a heavily-chained chymera; a petrifying beast, with the heads of both a lion and goat, and the tail of a thick-fanged snake. If Ned hadn't been chaperoned by his two hulking bodyguards, he was pretty sure the sight of it would have frightened the skin off his back.

High above them, a large rocket exploded, briefly turning the night to an eerie semblance of day.

When the first scream came, it was piercingly loud. The second was enough to silence the drums. What followed, was a tidal wave of terror and sobering rage. Half the valley ran, the other stood murmuring in disbelief before leaping to arms.

Darklings. A stampede of oil-skinned assassins came tearing through the night. Iron-tinged hellhounds the size of rhinos on four legs; poisonous, razor-clawed nightmongers on two; and above them, a flying escort of dark-fanged imps, like bats, but with arms and legs and long spine-covered tails. They were all coming from the Circus of Marvels' encampment. As the beasts spread through the valley, they sought out their own kind and cage after cage was flung open. Somewhere in the distance a wyvern roared before launching a plume of its noxious, flammable spit.

"Good lord. You'll pay for this, Barba," grunted George.

"Boy, hold on tight," growled the troll.

As they charged forward an imp swooped down low, narrowly missing their heads, before cutting through the Russian chymera's chains. In a heartbeat, the monster had ended three Cossack lives. Ned was horrified. This was what the world would look like without the Veil – running, screaming, and the gleeful delight of Darklings doing what they do best: killing.

When they reached Kitty's bus, the troupe were out in full force and all carrying torches. At their centre stood Benissimo and Mystero, two links in an iron chain holding everyone together.

"High toppers to the roofs, magic casters use your visions. Turn every shadow, scour every plain. We must find her!"

The Circus of Marvels cages had been opened, and Kitty was missing.

No longer a rag-tag group of misfits, the troupe split

into squads, each with their own well-practised role. Couteau and his sword-wielding unit marched through the corridors of trailers and tents, like a cohort of Roman soldiers quickly dispatching any Darkling that moved. Even Daisy prowled the shadows. Above them, the Tortellini boys called out threats and where necessary launched a flurry of daggers with lethal precision. At the centre of the camp, a ring of heavies, impervious to fire and more exotic projectiles, shielded the magic casters as they used their skills to search for the Farseer. At one point the Guffstavson brothers managed to power every bulb and fairy light in the valley, but their current became too strong and they were all plunged into darkness again. Of everyone, Ned thought, the image of George leaping from rooftop to rooftop, beating his chest with rage and sorrow was the strongest. There was no remnant of the gentleman within, only raw animal instinct as he launched himself on the Darklings fool enough to find themselves within his long-armed reach.

Suddenly Rocky barged past Benissimo and his number two towards Kitty's bus, in search of his wife.

"Rocky, wait! Don't go in there…" pleaded the Mystral.

But the troll was not in a listening mood. Moments later, his sobs drowned out the sound of shouting and fireworks, drowned out the sound of everything.

"Noooooooo! Niet! Niet! Babooshka! My Babooshka!"

Ned followed Benissimo and Mystero on to the bus where they found Abigail's seemingly lifeless body in Rocky's arms. Her beard hung limply to one side and a brown tea stain ran down her front, the pot and saucer smashed beside her.

"There's a pulse, but it's weak, and she is non-responsive," said Mystero. "It's like she's in a strange sort of coma. I've never seen anything like it." He paused a moment before continuing. "Now we're here, I have to tell you something else, Bene. It's not good. The spirit-knot, the one Kitty made for Ned. It's gone."

Benissimo's face turned to the colour of ash.

"Ned, Miz will take you to your bunk. Do not leave there till sun-up. No matter what your ears tell you... *do not open the door.*"

"But... but can't I help? Can't I help with the search?"

"Surely you must get it by now, pup?" Benissimo looked at him with exasperated eyes, before shaking his head hopelessly. "Either way, they've taken your spirit-knot as well as my Kit-Kat..." Benissimo's eyes dropped. "Just stay in your bunk. Please."

Ned did not get it. What he saw quite clearly though,

were Rocky's tears and a circus that had lost its rudder. This world wasn't his. And yet somehow, in some way, he knew that he had to help. But following the Ringmaster's orders would have to do for now.

Miz escorted him over to George's container and Ned had to duck as an angry fireball flew past them after missing its intended Darkling. The Shar had sent his stone golems to help restore order but all around them bedlam still raged, the smell of brimstone and magic heavy in the air.

"Will they find her, Miz?" yelled Ned over the chaos.

Mystero pushed open Ned's door. "If Kitty's our eyes, Ned, then Finn's our nose and ears. If anyone can find her, it's the Irishman and his beasts."

"My spirit-knot, the one they stole – why is it so important?"

Mystero paused, as though picking his words carefully.

"There's only one thing that would stop your father from saving the Veil, the very same thing that has kept him hidden for more than thirteen years."

"What? What thing?"

"You. Whoever controls the spirit-knot can control you, Ned, and in turn your father. He will do *anything* to see you safe."

Beads of moisture were streaming down the Mystral's face.

"Are you OK?"

"Sure, just a little thinned out. Now get in there and keep that door locked. I'll send George to keep watch."

The Mystral smiled softly and walked out, locking the door behind him. Ned changed out of the knickerbockers into his ordinary clothes and sat on his bunk. He looked at his powerless phone and his empty picture frame.

"What am I doing here, Dad? Why didn't you tell me about any of this?"

But the phone stayed silent and the frame remained empty. What he really wanted, more than anything in the world, was to hear his dad's overprotective voice say that it would all be OK.

But it was not OK. At last he understood why Terry Waddlesworth was the way he was. The world really was a scary place, things did indeed hide in its shadows, and as it turned out, those things wanted Ned.

Just then the lights in the container sputtered and went out. Ned thought it was probably either the Guffstavsons causing another power cut or the Darklings attacking the generators. He thought that until he heard the lock on his door click. Until he heard the door open. Until he felt the air move – without footsteps, without breathing – then a hand, just a hand, hard and strong, clasp itself over his mouth. Then there was the incantation of a spell, before George's container, with its books, beds, phone and picture frame, became small and out of focus, and the kidnapper's magic carried him silently out into the night.

CHAPTER 15

Something in the Smoke

Ned felt heat, the kind of heat that dried your tongue and soaked your hair. The shouting from the troupe's desperate search became muffled, till there was no sound at all. He found himself in a bank of thick, dark, grey. It was more like acrid smoke than the foggy dreams he'd had of Alice. Billowing plumes of hot ash and embers streamed past him and he could barely open his eyes. The hands that had taken him had gone and Ned was alone.

Through the smoke he saw shapes beginning to form. They looked like they'd been painted, from ash and oil. A house... He was outside his home at Number 222, except he wasn't.

The black billowing version of 222 was unfinished and strange. Giant black Lego-like bricks floated above a half-formed roof and the street continued on forever, though there were no other houses.

"What is this place?" he asked aloud.

"Not what, Ned, but where. You are in the Shades," came a deep booming voice.

Ned jumped. The voice came from inside his head and all around him.

"Who… who's there?"

"A friend," said the voice.

"If you're a friend then why can't I see you?" asked Ned, looking everywhere for some sign of the speaker.

"I'm too far away, Ned, you're going to have to come to me."

"Well that's a great idea, voice, only I don't know where you are."

"Just follow my words."

Ned walked forward and Number 222 melted away. He saw pieces of his school classroom come together, he saw his bedroom and the empty picture frame.

"That's it, Ned, you're doing just fine."

The voice was calming him somehow. It was strong, powerful even, and it made him feel safe.

"Is it much further?"

"No, Ned, you're nearly there . . ."

Parts of his dad's toolbox floated in front of him. A spanner, then a ratchet, then hundreds and hundreds of tiny black screws. He thought of his father and the smoke thickened, till it became like treacle, holding him back and heavy to the touch. He found himself having to push his way forward.

"I have to find…"

"Yes, Ned, that's it, fight it, harder!" came the voice, spurring him on.

"Kitty, she's missing, I…"

As he mentioned her name, something changed. In front of him, the last fragments of his father's tools dissolved, making way for something more human. It was lighter, brighter, a beacon amidst the blackness. It was a cloudy, billowing version of Kitty.

The old lady was on her knees and her face was contorted, as though she were screaming at him, or concentrating with all of her will, or both. From her lips, he heard syllables, soft and faraway.

"F…I…N…? Finn? Yes, he's looking for you. No, wait, I see… FIND… FIND ME. She needs my help! She wants me to find her."

And as he spoke, the image of Kitty began to break apart.

"*My voice, boy*, follow my voice," boomed his friend again.

Her face was the last thing to dissolve. There was a flicker of a smile, and she was gone. Blackened, boiling smoke rose up from where she'd knelt. It clawed and climbed around Ned's limbs, over his chest and up his neck. It started to feed into his mouth. His lungs burned with oil and ash and his world returned to darkness.

"Get up!" commanded the voice.

But Ned was tired and his limbs would no longer do as they were told. His eyelids drooped heavily, blinking in and out of black.

"Open your eyes," came the voice again. Though its pitch was different somehow, more real.

It took Ned almost a minute to open his eyes and another to make them focus. There was no smoke or burning embers. He was, in fact, in a sumptuous, four-poster bed.

"Young Master, I trust you slept comfortably? I am Mr Sar-adin, your servant. You will look to me for your needs while staying with us. I have brought sustenance. It is what young Masters enjoy, is it not? Pancakes, and sweetnesses." Very slowly, Ned registered the figure of a butler standing at his bedside.

He wore a black turban, with a black button-down jacket and looked to be of Arab descent. His eyes were dark and hollow.

Ned felt groggy, as if his thoughts couldn't quite connect.

"I think I was dreaming, but… I can't remember anything. It's… it's gone," he murmured.

"The dream is still there, young Master, it merely waits for your return," answered the servant, while pouring Ned's tea.

Ned looked about – he was in the height of luxury. Vaguely military, black marble covered everything and on the far wall was an elaborate carving of a coat of arms. It was a set of scales with a two-headed cobra. He'd been rescued, though why the Shar's golems had brought him to the palace was anyone's guess. If Ned was safe, maybe Kitty was too?

"Kitty? Is she OK? Is she here?" he asked, rubbing his eyes.

"Yes, young Master, the Farseer is in very good hands."

Ned sighed with relief. There had been something else, something urgent. He couldn't quite put his finger on it, but was sure it had something to do with a letter. It made his head hurt and he shifted his attention to the stack of pancakes in front of him. Their smell was intoxicating and he took a bite. It was perfect. Light fluffy butter mixed with hot sweet syrup. It had just the right amount of cinnamon. And something else. Something he'd never tasted before but already wanted again.

"Delicious," he mumbled, more to himself than anyone else.

"That is most pleasing. I shall tell the kitchens to prepare more."

"Oh yes… thank you," whispered back Ned. He found himself staring at a forkful of pancake for a long time. How long he couldn't tell. It glistened as the sun rose and Ned felt as though he might watch it all day.

"Is something troubling you, young Master?"

"On no, just feel a little sleepy that's all…" replied Ned dreamily.

"Indeed. You should rest your eyes, for this evening you dine with His Greatness and there is so much for you to discuss."

Ned could barely stay awake. All he could think of was syrup, syrup and pancakes with a nice dollop of jam. As his eyelids gave way, he did wonder whether there would be enough to go round.

"Will Benissimmm be joininnnng ush…?"

"That would be next to impossible. You see, he has no idea where you are, besides which he would be most unwelcome here."

"Oh goood, I nevver reallly liked himm muchhh."

Ned was oblivious to Mr Sar-adin's answer as his head was already on the pillow and the forkful of pancake had tumbled to the floor. Through the sweet aroma of syrup, he sensed another, strangely familiar smell. It was smoke, thick black smoke, and was followed by a powerful voice, a voice he knew, and though he didn't remember where he knew it from, it was a voice that made him feel safe.

"There you are," said the voice.

CHAPTER 16

A Prisoner

Ned dreamt for hour after hour. His head and sheets were soaked with sweat. Memories of his past were swept away till he was left with a single guiding voice and a grey billowing nothingness. He was woken, from somewhere outside the dream. By someone or something, trying to burrow its way in.

"OWWW!" he yelled, jumping out of bed.

Out of his window the sky was pitch black, except for the stars and a smattering of cloud. His room was also hot, very hot. Fumbling in the dark, he tripped over a chair and landed on the ground with a thud. The pain had woken him so rudely that it made his eyes water, but it wasn't till he checked his trouser leg pocket that he found the culprit.

"Whiskers, you're back!"

The Debussy Mark 12 had returned to his old self, without any sign of a cog or gear anywhere.

"I've had such a weird time of it, boy. It's good to see you again."

Whiskers looked up at him and nodded in tiny mouse agreement. In the past Ned had often spoken to his pet, never truly expecting an answer. Nodding was not something the mouse had done before.

"Err, Whiskers, did you just… agree?"

The little mouse nodded again.

"Whoa!" yelped Ned. "Do you understand what I'm saying?"

The Debussy Mark 12 bobbed its head one last time, before looking up to the ceiling, seemingly with a 'now he gets it' expression on his face. Ned was over the moon.

"That's amazing. I bet you've been able to do that all along, haven't you, boy?" Whiskers shrugged. "How did you get here?" went on Ned, as his sleepiness started to lift.

Whiskers flashed his eyes again, then pulled at his fur as though looking for loose change in an imaginary pocket.

"Ahh, in my pocket. Good thinking. Have you seen the others yet? Kitty or Benissimo?"

The mouse shook his head so vigorously it looked like it might come off.

"What's got into you? Are you having a malfunction? Whiskers? Whiskers…"

Ned's voice trailed off when he spotted the fallen fork by his bed. Mr Sar-adin must have missed it when he'd tidied away the plates. The ticker's antics suddenly seemed less important compared to another taste of the Shar's syrupy pancakes. His eyes softened and he reached over to pick it up.

"Oww!" he yelled, as the Mark 12 sank its teeth into his thumb. "What was that for?"

He went for the pancake again, this time Whiskers bit him so hard that he drew blood.

"You don't even eat food! This is not mouse-like behaviour! Any more trouble and I'll ask my butler for a screwdriver!"

Whiskers answered by pricking his ears up over his head, in the shape of two tiny horns. Ned stared blankly till the mouse started shaking his head, tapping one foot on the floor and hopping about all over the place. Finally he snatched up what was left of the pancake and ran out of the room by scurrying under the door.

"Oi, come back here!"

Ned was surprised to discover that the door was locked, apparently from the other side. He yanked at it, banged on its frame and was about to yell when he heard approaching footsteps and what sounded like chanting. It was the same phrase, low and deep, over and over again. The lock clicked and in walked Mr Sar-adin.

"Young Master," bowed the butler. "I had thought to find you asleep. Is something causing you discomfort?"

"Well, um, no not really, it's just that there was… a mouse in here and, well, he's gone now." Something told Ned not to mention that the mouse was actually his. The combination of Whiskers' odd behaviour and the locked door had unsettled him.

"A mouse, you say? Oh dear oh dear, that will not do at all. We take a dim view of mice here." Mr Sar-adin paused, eyes peering about the floor suspiciously.

For a moment, they seemed to flicker with a light of their own.

"Mr Sar-adin, why was the door locked?"

"To keep you safe. It was deemed better to have such an esteemed guest kept away from the ship's corridors. Especially on a ship such as this."

The hot marble walls of Ned's room felt as if they were closing in around him.

"Ship?" he said, frowning. "Mr Sar-adin… where are we?"

"Young Master, you are aboard the *Daedalus*. The first dreadnought-class airship of its kind."

"A dreadnought? Why would the Shar want a warship?"

"The Shar merely paid for the vessel to be built, as a show of support. The *Daedalus* belongs to His Greatness, Barbarossa."

"Oh good," Ned said. "I can't wait to see him."

Somewhere, in the back of his mind, he knew it was the wrong thing to say, even as he said it. He wrestled with trying to find the right thing, but his mind went blank, leaving only the strange cloudy sensation of feeling safe.

He was led through a maze of hot metal corridors, the ship's crew going about their business in ordered silence. Near the engine room the heat was almost unbearable, though you would never have known it by looking at Mr Sar-adin's dry sweatless face. Up on the top deck, Ned saw that they were floating far above sea, with no coastline in sight. The ship cut an angular, intimidating silhouette, a great gouge of sharp iron against a star-spattered sky. It was large, much more so than the *Marilyn* and her entire convoy put together. It had the shape of an axe blade, tapering to a sharp point at the bow. Everything about its design was menacing, from the myriad protruding cannons to the steel cages of its wyvern escort, their un-muzzled mouths smouldering with intent. It differed entirely from the other Veil-made circus ships that Ned had seen. The *Daedalus* didn't convert to a series of obscure-looking vehicles. It wasn't built to be hidden, it was built for war.

It took Ned some time to notice but the ship was different for another, even more alarming reason. There was nothing keeping it up. No balloons or propellers – nothing. Where the balloons should have been, were six enormous chimneys, belching out a constant stream of oily black smoke. Its crew of cutthroats and pirates looked to Ned like they'd been scraped from the lowest dregs of the Hidden's criminal underworld and seemed to him like morgue attendants, working some vast angular machine that had been built for the bringing of death.

On their way to the captain's quarters, he caught the unmistakable stench of clown hanging in the air.

"Enter," a deep, familiar voice rolled out of the cabin's open door.

Inside Barbarossa sat facing them. Here in his element and aboard his ship he looked like a pirate-king at court. Two plates had been set. Crystal glasses, silk napkins and dozens of gold-domed dishes had been carefully laid out for their dinner. The rest of the room, like Ned's, was a grand gesture of black marble. There were two cabinets full of antique weapons and the air smelt vaguely of polish and cigars. It was a room where serious men planned serious deeds. What had no place in a room like this was the scene being played out between Barbarossa and the ship's cat. The same cat, he vaguely recalled, that he'd seen under the table in Shalazaar.

"Poor Fang, poor little creature. You only scratch when you need to, but nobody understands, do they?" The huge man was crooning over the animal as if it were barely a kitten.

The cat purred in his arms contentedly.

"What you need is a little feeding up. Mr Sar-adin, I don't think he looks well. Have the kitchen send up a saucer of warm milk, would you?"

"I will see to it right away, your Greatness."

"And make sure it's fresh, my personal store."

Barbarossa put Fang down carefully, before turning to Ned with a smile.

"Thank you for joining me. I trust you're well rested?"

By now Ned knew he was a prisoner, taken by force, and there was no doubt that the "good hands"

Mr Sar-adin had told him Kitty was in were Barbarossa's. But for some reason, he found himself happy to see him. He was everything his brother wasn't – warm, courteous even, and the smile that had looked so cruel in Shalazaar made him feel safe here, safe and at peace.

"Now, Ned, I know we got off to a wrong start, but I really don't want you to feel like a prisoner here. I merely want to talk to you, after which you are most welcome to leave, if you wish to do so," Barbarossa continued.

Despite his soothing tones, despite the strangeness in Ned's head, some small part of him managed to remember where he was and who he was with.

"If I'm not a prisoner then… why was the door of my room locked?"

"I don't know what prisons are like on the outside world, but in the Hidden lands they do not come with silken sheets and a butler. This is a warship, Ned. Warships carry weapons and explosives which do not, I'm told, mix well with thirteen-year-old boys."

It made good sense and when he tried to look for a reason why it didn't, the cloudiness in his mind returned. It left him with the feeling that he was talking to a reasonable man.

"I… I suppose you're right," whispered Ned.

Barbarossa switched from amiable host to attentive waiter and began lifting the golden domes from their dishes.

"I hope you don't mind, I took the liberty of ordering us some supper."

In front of Ned was a banquet of sugared treats. Candied apples, chocolate cake, giant éclairs, meringues, toffees, every possible flavour of jam, and of course pancakes, mounds and mounds of hot syrupy pancakes. Ned's jaw went slack and he found himself licking his lips.

"I trust this is to your liking?"

Ned hardly heard him speak, lost as he was in a world of sugar.

"I'll take that as a 'yes' then. You know your mum always had a soft spot for sweets. It must run in the family."

Ned came out of his daydream with a hard thump.

"You… *You* knew my mother?"

"Indeed, and your father. In a way, that's where I need to begin. With the truth, Ned. The truth no one is doing the courtesy of telling you. The truth about *everything*."

CHAPTER 17

Secrets and Lies

The word truth had taken on an abstract meaning since Ned's birthday and yet the man in front of him – Benissimo's nemesis and brother – was offering it freely. A sugary treat reached Ned's lips and he listened quietly, like a child with a bedtime story.

"My sources tell me you have yet to read the contents of your letter, is this true?"

"Bene wouldn't let me."

"My brother," said Barbarossa with a sigh. "Always so controlling, when sometimes all you really need is *honesty*. You see, Ned, the fact that you were born the other side of the Veil and raised as a josser does not change who you are. Your father is an Engineer, that much you already know. What no one has been kind enough to tell you is that you too, Ned, are not in the slightest bit average."

He was enjoying the story so far, though he thought the last bit was a little far-fetched. Barbarossa opened a drawer from beneath the table and pulled out a roll of paper.

"The truth," he announced.

It was an old circus poster, faded and brown with age. Across the top in beautiful hand lettering it read, *'Benissimo's Circus of Marvels presents: Mentor the Magnificent'*. And beneath the letters stood a handsome young man with a flowing cape. His eyes were shut in concentration and levitating in front of him was a half-constructed model of the Eiffel tower in miniature, perfect in every tiny detail. To his right stood a beautiful assistant, dressed in a costume that made her look half woman and half bird.

Ned squinted. There was something about the young man, something familiar. A few less wrinkles, a slightly thinner face and a little more hair. It was like a younger version of his…

"Daad?" he slurred, as chunks of cake fell out of his open mouth and on to the image of his father.

"And next to him, your mother."

For a second Ned couldn't focus his eyes. He blinked frantically through warm tears at the one thing he'd always wanted more than anything.

"My mu- mum?"

Right in front of him was a picture of his mother. A lifetime of painful longing and here she was.

"She… she was beautiful."

"The prettiest headliner a circus ever had. Though no doubt she'll have changed a bit when you next see her."

Ned almost swallowed his tongue.

"That's not funny."

Barbarossa pushed a plate of meringues across the table.

"It wasn't supposed to be. I know this is hard for you, but I'm going to help you, Ned. I'm going to help you with everything. I'm afraid you've been a pawn in a very drawn out game." Barbarossa's brow crumpled in sympathy. "I'm only sorry it had to be me to tell you… your mother, she's alive."

Ned could feel his heartbeat soaring, as a jumble of emotions raced through him.

"That's not true, she died in a car crash, I was still a baby."

"And who told you that?"

"My dad."

"And he's always told you the truth, has he?"

The question hurt. Terry Waddlesworth or Terrence Armstrong, depending on what side of the Veil you inhabited, had led a double life. Ned was still coming to terms with that. But to lie about his mum, to let him go on thinking she was dead when she wasn't? His dad would never do that… would he?

"Yes, I mean no… I- I don't know."

"Then let me tell you what I know. Your parents were two of the finest operatives the Circus of Marvels ever had. There was no car or accident, but they did have to make a choice. Two children were in need of protection, Ned, you and the girl. Like your father, your mother, Olivia, has been deep undercover. A false name and a false existence. You're not going to like this, I can't think of anyone that would, but the truth is, she could have given the task to someone else, but your mother chose to be with the girl and… not with you."

Something within Ned screamed, *YOU'RE A LIAR, YOU'RE ALL LIARS! LEAVE MY FAMILY ALONE!* But all he could muster from the noise and raging hurt was silence.

"I believe their plan was hatched shortly after you were born. You see, at the moment, you and the girl are the last of your line."

"I don't understand. What line?"

"Your family have always been Engineers, Ned, and Lucy's Medics. Lucy, for now at least, is the last Medic and you and your father – you are, as it stands, the last Engineers. That's why both you and the girl are so important."

Ned was still reeling from the revelation about his mum. Could his dad really have kept this from him too?

"But I can't be. I'm just… me."

"It takes a special kind of parent to put the mission before their own son. The genius of their plan was in not telling you. Here you are, a genuine key to saving the Veil, and you didn't even know it."

It dawned on Ned that his dad was not the only one to have lied.

"So Bene, Kitty, George, Miz, even Rocky and Abigail… they all knew about me being an Engineer?"

"It's hereditary, and you're your father's son, Ned, of course they knew."

Ned was feeling both joy and sickening rage. Here was a picture of his mum, and she was alive, but she'd chosen to be some stranger's guardian… chosen someone else. Terry Waddlesworth was a liar, and Ned was some pawn in an elaborate game of chess. Had his dad only been worried for his safety in order to protect the Veil? Surely there was more to it than that? Surely he loved him? Maybe not though. His mother had abandoned him, after all; left him for Lucy. Did she care? Did either of his parents really care? Till now the thought of Lucy Beaumont had given him comfort – maybe they could have helped each other? Not any more. This girl had taken half his childhood, the half that was his mum, and Olivia Armstrong had helped her do it.

Tears now rolled freely down his cheeks. He took another bite of cake. With each mouthful the pain in his chest subsided. Something in the sugar seemed to help.

"The ring you retrieved in Shalazaar is one of a pair, your father wears the other. Both the rings and the skills necessary to wield them are passed down every generation. Its technical term is an Amplification-Engine. Like your father and his mother before him, your brain is perfectly wired to control and work with it. To explain it simply, it gives your bloodline the power to create things, nearly anything, using only their mind."

"Bene tol' me... i's like magic..." slurred Ned, as his hand drifted to a plate of éclairs.

"Science, magic, nature, even the arts... they're all related. The Amplification-Engine is limited only by what an Engineer is capable of seeing in his mind's eye and how clearly, how completely he can put together and hold the picture. Skilled Engineers spend lifetimes perfecting their craft, but it's the strength of their imagination that determines their level of power."

"So… what can the Medic do?" It pained him to ask but he had to know.

"Lucy Beaumont is a healer. Her skills are not dissimilar to that of an Engineer, though they focus on the living. She can control the structure of cells, reverse damage, restitch what's broken. It is the combination of these two skills, yours and hers, that we believe will fix the Veil's source of power."

Ned was finding it hard to grasp what he was being told, his thoughts were getting increasingly confused with every bite of his food. What he did understand – quite clearly – was that for the first time in his life he was being given the truth.

"Why are you telling me all this? The truth, I mean… aren't you…"

He looked down at his plate.

"The bad guy? Wicked? Working with Darklings and Demons?"

Ned didn't answer. His eyelids had started to droop once more.

"I'm sure my brother and his cronies have told you all manner of nonsense. All the dark ones really want is freedom, freedom which the rest of the world takes for granted. That's what they fight for, Ned, despite what you've been led to believe. They simply want to come out of the shadows, to walk free. What if I told you that Mr Sar-adin is an Ifrit, otherwise known as a djinn, or genie. A high ranking one at that. Ifrit means 'fire-demon', Ned. Yet here he works for me, changing your sheets and bringing you breakfast. Hardly end of the world stuff, is it? Now, your father has been leading my men on quite the merry dance, I think he hoped I wouldn't find out about you, that you could go and mend the Veil while we chased him through half of Europe. But I have you, Ned, and they *will* catch him soon enough. Rest assured, their orders are not to harm him, that's not what I want for either of you. Stay here with me, let Lucy remain unfound, and the Veil will tumble of its own accord. Then and only then, the world will see the truth. Think of it, Ned, no more secrets, no more lies, and all because of you. Join me and we could build glorious things together… you and me in our brave new world."

His smile was so broad and his words made so much sense, yet somewhere deep inside of Ned a little voice still whispered. He wanted to ask Barba something, something about a cat, a Kitty-cat. But the voice was little and his host's, so deep and strong… and soothing.

Ned's eyes closed and the room spun. Maybe he'd eaten enough? Maybe he could just have a rest, get back to his food later…

"You look tired, Ned, why don't you sleep a while? Let me look after your troubled head."

Barbarossa clapped his hands and a fireplace appeared at Ned's side, flushed orange with heat. From the hottest part of its burning coals came the sound of footsteps.

"Yesss, your Greatness?"

As the room faded, it occurred to him that Barbarossa had let him eat all of the food, without touching a thing. What a generous host, he thought, so much nicer than his brother.

CHAPTER 18

Awakenings

Ned drifted in and out of a feverish slumber. The hours in his cabin seemed to blend into each other. Thoughts about his life before the *Daedalus* were strangely distant, as though somehow out of his reach. He didn't feel too bothered about being lied to any more. He didn't really feel anything, except that something wasn't right. He was trapped, trapped with a pain somewhere deep inside his gut.

Time stood still.

"Time," he murmured, lost in a wash of smoke and shadows.

There was something about time, something urgent, something at stake.

"No time."

What was it? He was angry about something, or

jealous, or both. Was it a girl? A father? A mother? Somewhere inside of him, the boy that was before the Veil, before sugared treats and lies about lies, started to fight. Things were coming back into focus, things he'd put away, or hidden behind syrup and jam. He found himself thinking of his dad, the one he knew, not the one people kept telling him about. Lies, he thought, and the pain in his belly broke free.

"Blearchhhhh."

Pancakes, waffles, doughnuts and cake came flying out of his mouth, landing with a sickly splat on the floor. He lay groaning on his bed, the combination of stomach cramps and heat keeping him awake. And then it came to him. A flood of bright memories: building Lego sets, then Meccano, for hour after hour; sitting with his father and studying the pieces, of anything, of everything. His dad might not have told him why, but he'd been looking out for him all along… training him. Terry Waddlesworth was an Engineer and unbelievably, completely unthinkably… so was Ned. As he remembered, everything in his thirteen-year-old head and heart shifted.

"The letter! What's inside it? My mum… she's alive! I have to find my dad and mum and… Kitty! Kitty's here, she's here on the ship…"

Whoever had or hadn't lied was no longer the issue, at least not now in his marble-clad cell. Kitty was in danger and he had to try and help her. He thought of all the cakes and sweets he'd devoured in the last twenty-four hours and his stomach churned. *That's how he got to me,* thought Ned. Something about the pirate-butcher's food had turned his mind.

It was then that a small, fast moving rodent scampered over to Ned's bed and climbed up on to his pillows. The Debussy Mark 12 ticker had a deep scratch in his side, revealing some of his shiny inner workings.

"Whiskers, you don't look too good. Was it the cat?"

The metallic mouse stared at him as if to say, "Well, it's about time you woke up!" Then did some violent "yes" head bobbing.

"You knew about the food?"

The Debussy Mark 12 responded in the most extraordinary way. It carefully lowered its head so that it was flat to the pillow and opened its mouth.

Bzzt, ching, bzzt, ching ching.

Through its lips streamed a flow of perfectly typed ticker-tape. A Hidden-made version of a telegram. It was from Benissimo.

ned stop eat nothing stop find kitty stop
get off ship stop TERRIBLE DANGER stop

All sound advice, if a little late. And getting off the ship was a good idea in theory, but the last time he'd looked they were floating over a barren sea. Ned was going to need more than advice.

"Right, well I think we need to send old tash-face a reply. How does this tape thingy work, Whiskers?"

Bzzt, ching, whrrr, bzzt ching, went Whiskers.

PS stop, recordo-gram works only one
way stop

Ned's heart sank. Whiskers bit off the end of the tape and went back to normal.

"Right, thank you, Whiskers, that was brilliant and um… extremely weird."

His mouse nodded.

"So it looks like we're on our own. What we need is a plan. Dad always loved a plan, or at least a set of instructions. Have you seen Kitty? Do you know where she is?"

Whiskers scanned the room, looking about as lost

in thought as a clockwork mouse can, till he found the answer directly behind him. A portrait of Barbarossa hung by Ned's bed. It was the first time Ned had noticed it. For a moment, he thought he might be sick again.

"She's with Barbarossa?"

The mouse shook his head vigorously.

"She's near him? No… she's in his quarters?"

Bingo.

Ned found himself thinking increasingly clearly and angrily. More so than ever before.

"Whiskers," Ned said at last, "I need you to do something for me. I need you to go out there and find me a key for that door."

Whiskers tilted his head to one side, as though mulling over what he'd said. Then he did a slightly robotic salute, before reaching up a front paw and… unscrewing the end of his nose.

From the new opening, two small metal rods came into view, one with an L-shaped bend at its end, the other curving up into a small hook. Ned gawped.

"A torsion wrench and a hook pick?"

His key-faced mouse nodded.

"Whiskers, I know you're just a bundle of pistons and cogs, but you're brilliant."

Effortlessly the Debussy Mark 12 had supplied him with the next best thing to keys – a basic set of lock picks. When Ned was little one of his dad's favourite games had been 'Free Up the Pudding'. After supper he'd lock the kitchen door, giving Ned a set of picks with which to open it up again and retrieve his prize. It had taken him six months to master the skill; to be able to visualise the inner workings of the lock and tinker it open each time. In later years he'd thought of it as a typically eccentric Waddlesworth pastime. He was just beginning to understand how much of his childhood had been about preparing him for the eventuality of… now.

"Thanks, Dad," he whispered, as he gingerly worked his pet mouse's tools. It didn't take long for the lock to click loose.

Unfortunately, it took Sar-adin even less time to raise the alarm after they'd broken out of Ned's room, and within minutes of their escape the ship's corridors tremored with the pounding of feet.

"Search every inch!" yelled one of the crew captains ahead.

He was thick-skinned, swarthy and part ogre from the look of his bulky stomach and green mottled skin. He was also blocking the way to Barbarossa's quarters.

"Whiskers, now what?" hissed Ned.

But his ever-resourceful rodent had the problem in hand and was already pointing nose-first at a small hatch in the ship corridor's wall to Ned's left. Ned managed to prise it open with a few hard pulls. He crawled through the gap after his mouse and closed the hatch behind him carefully. Inside the ship's labyrinthine network of ventilation shafts the pipework was searing to the touch and what little air they had was almost too hot to breathe. But at least here the sound of the search parties was muffled and distant.

They crawled inch by sweat-pouring inch and Ned had to clamber up and down almost vertical chutes till he was bruised and battered. With Whiskers leading, however, they finally made it to the ship's map room. It was directly next to the captain's quarters.

"Gather the crew and unleash the Darklings. Get EVERYONE! I, WANT, THAT, BOY!" Barbarossa screamed.

Then there was a screech followed by the sickening crunch of bone and muscle. In his rage, Barbarossa had kicked the ship's cat out of the room and into the corridor. Ned watched through a grate in horror as Fang skidded to a halt, then lay motionless.

"No crossy Ba-ba, slippty boy findee," whined a fearful Eanie.

Ned hated clown speak, almost as much as clown smell.

"Oh Ba-ba is very crossy, Eanie. As is Bessy." The pirate-butcher stroked the meat-cleaver at his belt ominously. "The damned boy was nearly mine. With his help, I could have had an Engineer and a Medic. Now, find him, or I'll have Sar-adin peel off your skin! AND TAKE A DAMNED BATH!"

Ned used the butcher's rage and the cowering clown talk to crawl by unheard. Finally at the vent for Barbarossa's quarters, he peered into the room beyond and saw Kitty. It was only when he slipped through the grate and closed it behind him that he let himself breathe once more. The captain's quarters were dimly lit, but Kitty's pale skin and grey-white hair shone in the darkness. Her eyes were closed, her hands tied, and her body lay still. Ned's chest tightened. Was he too late? Had she died at the hands of her captor?

"Kitty, it's me – Ned," he whispered, standing over her. "Are you all right? Say something, Kitty…"

"Well, of course it's you, silly, I'm blind not demented!" beamed back the old woman as she sat up and smiled.

"I've been so stupid. Thank goodness you're OK, you looked so…"

"Pretty? Oh Ned, really, I'm far too old for you! Tell me the truth, you're after another reading, aren't you? I would so love to slap your face…"

She was frail, but she was still Kitty.

"I've come to get you out of here, I just need to figure out these handcuffs and then I'll… erm…"

"What's the weather like outside, dear? Will I need my umbrella?"

Though cheery, the Farseer seemed unusually demented, and unlikely to help with Ned's escape plan, which was a problem, because Ned didn't have one. Just then, out in the corridor, he heard footsteps approaching the door, most probably Barbarossa and his Demon-butler. Ned looked about frantically for somewhere to hide, then he heard the welcome squeak of Whiskers over by a cupboard.

He picked him up quietly and popped him into his pocket. The cupboard was bare except for a few hanging clothes and a belt. The belt held a holster, which in turn held a Hidden-made musket. Ned patted Kitty on the arm, scrambled desperately into the cupboard and closed the door behind him. Squinting through its keyhole, he saw the cabin doors burst open as two of Barbarossa's men approached and took positions on either side of the Farseer. As big as they were, they still looked as if they were worried the old lady might spring up from her seat and fly out the door. Ned found it all a bit ridiculous. Were they really that frightened of an old woman? A moment later, Barbarossa entered and began pacing the room, closely followed by Mr Sar-adin, who took his place behind her, before starting to talk.

"*Dear old Kitty*. How long will this foolishness go on? Your loyalty to him is endearing, but I will find a way in. I always find a way… in."

"*Foul, stinking Demon*. How long are you going to prattle on for?" teased back Kitty. "What you need is a hug and a better role model."

The Demon-butler scowled.

"We do not have time for this, witch! If you will not give us the assistance that we seek, then I will meld with your mind and make you."

"Oh, please! You Demons are all the same, all big demands and no manners!" cackled Kitty.

The Demon shot a glance at his Master, who nodded.

"Very well."

Mr Sar-adin unlocked Kitty's cuffs then lit a dark blue

candle. Next, he took something from a silk bag and burnt it over the flame. It smelt vaguely of incense mixed with cloves. Holding his hands by her temples he began to chant, much to Kitty's apparent amusement.

"*Am, ra, tra-va. Am, ra, tra-va,*" repeated the Demon, over and over.

"*Tra-la, Da-di-da,*" mocked the old lady in return.

The candle seemed to suck the light from the room, while the smell of burning grew stronger. Ned covered his nose. Both Kitty's and the Demon-butler's eyes closed for a moment and Mr Sar-adin fell silent. When they opened again, the whites of both sets of eyes had turned to an oily black.

"There, Kitty. I have found you."

The old lady remained silent.

"I can feel it all, yes… yes. Open the door, witch, open the door…"

Without warning, Kitty smiled, and Mr Sar-adin howled. Ned felt the temperature in the room soar and the two of them broke free from their trance.

"Arrgh!" screamed the Demon, falling to the floor in violent, pained spasms. "Get out of my heaaaaaaad!"

"Enough!" roared Barbarossa. "Take him downstairs and plug him back into the heat-generators. If he can't break an old woman, at least he can power the ship!"

Mr Sar-adin was still babbling incoherently when one of the men dragged him out of the room.

"So little Kitty-Kat still has claws?" boomed Barbarossa, pulling up a stool.

The Farseer did not answer back. Instead she played with her Hello Kitty hair band, as though an innocent schoolgirl, idly passing the time.

"There are plenty of ways to skin a cat, Kitty. And you know I know all of them."

"Really? Well it seems to me that the great Barbarossa can't even turn a boy, not with a Demon's magic or his sugared treats, not even with a spirit-knot!" said the old witch, now very present and in the moment.

Barbarossa fumed. "The girl *must die*. The boy will lead me to her, and you, old woman, will help him do it!"

"I've already told you – you'll never break him, Barba. With or without the ring – or me – he won't tell. I've seen inside his heart. He's his parents' son through and through."

Ned realised with a shock that they were talking about him, though he didn't really understand how he was supposed to lead anyone to the Medic. He didn't even know what she looked like, never mind where she was.

"You're wrong – I never fail. I'll get my hands on one of those rings just as easily as I did the boy. As for you, you are not the only Farseer behind the Veil. If you won't help me, I shall find another…"

The remaining henchman produced a set of sharp, polished instruments. Barbarossa picked out a spike and studied it carefully. *The truth*, thought Ned. How could he have been so stupid? Ned had been wrong about him in Shalazaar. Barbarossa wasn't a rough pirate, or a butcher. He was a surgeon, a precise and clinical mastermind who would do and say anything to get what he wanted.

"Now, why don't we try again?"

He raised the tip of the spike to Kitty's face and Ned reached for the musket beside him. He didn't know how to fire a gun. But even thirteen-year-old boys can kick open a cupboard door, no matter how scared they are of it actually opening.

"Let… her… go," he stammered, pointing the weapon directly at Barbarossa.

His target lowered the spike and turned around slowly. He looked unnervingly calm for a man with a musket pointed at his head.

"Now, what did I say about wandering around on your own? You could get yourself hurt, my lad."

Though Ned's thoughts had become his own once more, he found himself weakening again, under the full weight of Barbarossa's gaze.

"You, you let her go, or… I'll shoot."

The remaining lackey began inching his way towards Ned, till Barbarossa motioned for him to stop.

"You talk as if you have a choice," said the surgeon, reaching into his pocket and pulling out Ned's ribbony bundle of hair. "I'm impressed you resisted for so long. Even in your sleep you managed to stop yourself from turning completely. But I have great plans for you, Ned, far beyond the finding of silly little girls. Now, turning the mind is what I do. I enjoy it. So… point the gun at Kitty's head. If she doesn't say what I want to hear, you will pull the trigger."

Ned felt his arm move, like a puppet on a string. As much as he willed it to stop, the musket was now pointing directly at Kitty.

"For the last time, old woman, will you help me find her?"

"No," smiled the Farseer, before turning to Ned. "It's all right, dear, don't be frightened. This will all be over in a second."

"As you wish. Ned, kill her."

Tears welled up in Ned's eyes as he fought his own finger pressing down on the musket's trigger. Barbarossa's eyes grew wide.

"By all that's Dark, how are you doing this? You're just a boy. No one is strong enough to resist me, Ned, no one!" His face seethed and twisted with renewed effort.

And he was right.

"I... I can't stop it! I'm sorry, Kitty, I'm really sorry..."

BOOM.

CHAPTER 19

The Truth

Time slowed. To Ned's right, the wall flashed with light, before exploding inwards. Through a mess of fire and tearing metal came first a cannonball, then George. Barbarossa's face flickered, from surprise to anger as the metal projectile hit him and he was flung to the other side of his cabin. His remaining henchman was still standing; he lifted his dagger and thrust it towards the giant ape's chest. But it might as well have been a sewing needle for all the good it did him. George roared, a roar so deafening, so loud, so utterly enraged that the henchman dropped his weapon and curled to a whimpering ball on the floor.

The great ape sniffed at the air. A second later his powerful hands had scooped up both Kitty and Ned before retrieving the boy's spirit-knot from their dazed but still breathing captor's hand. How Barbarossa had survived a direct hit to the chest, or how Kitty had known the ape was coming, was unimportant; Ned's nightmare was over.

Holding them both tight, George leapt back through the hole in the *Daedalus*'s side. Two of the elder Tortellinis were waiting outside, hovering in the air, the engine of their small scout-ship revved and ready. George landed on its deck with a wood-splintering thud. The open-topped vessel had no cabin or hold and the ape used his two great arms to shield his precious cargo from the wind while they made their hasty exit.

"I told you, my dear chap," George rumbled, "if you ever saw that man again to either find me or run. Well, you wouldn't come to me, so here I am."

With the cover of night and a little Veil-born magic, their fast moving scout-ship was in and out before the *Daedalus*'s crew knew what had hit them. By then it seemed Kitty's extraordinary mind had already reimagined their ordeal as some sort of pleasure cruise.

"George, dear, we've had the most marvellous adventure! Benissimo's brother has a magnificent ship, you know, delicious food, and the rooms, such attention to detail…"

It started to spit with rain.

"Oh, fiddlesticks," she said. "I knew it. I really should have brought my brolly. I do so hate to travel with wet hair."

Ned let her gabble on, and stayed quiet himself – he had a lot to think about.

***

The convoy had set up camp outside the Veil, in a remote part of the Italian countryside. As they came in to land, the first beams of sunrise were creeping over the horizon.

When he set foot on solid ground, Ned's eardrums were nearly blown apart by a blast of Alice's trunk.

"Oh, I am sorry, Mr Waddlewats, but she's been beside herself with worry. Poor luv ain't eaten in days and she's even started sheddin' her feathers. 'Alice, old girl,' I says. 'Not a squeak out of you, you let the poor lad come 'ome in peace,' I says. And here she's sat. Ain't so much as twitched an eyelid waitin' for you to come back," explained Norman in a rush.

"Hello, Alice." Ned smiled slightly, while fighting off her affectionate trunk.

"Grooooar!" replied the elephant.

"Yes, I'm fine, Alice, it's nice to see you too."

Despite his ringing ears and Alice's continuous attempts to lick him, he was almost happy to see her. As far as he knew, winged elephants did not tell lies.

"Welcome back, Widdler," said one of the kitchen hands as he crossed the field.

"Well done, kid," said another.

"Bless you, Ned, welcome home!" called the Glimmerman in passing.

Till now, most of the troupe had largely ignored him, or treated him as a josser. Today was different. Even Finn gave him a nod, with an unintelligible grunt, and George had already told him that Finn never spoke to anyone except his hawk or lions. But the friendlier they were, the more he boiled inside. Why bother with the pretence of Waddlewats or Widdler? Surely they knew he was an Armstrong by now? Knew who and what he was and how much danger he was in? Their journey to Shalazaar had not been about saving his father, but about retrieving the Amplification-Engine, and Benissimo had known all along that it would then probably fall to Ned to find Lucy and mend the Veil. Why else would his dad have given him the blood-key? Whatever Barbarossa was, he had at least told Ned about being an Engineer. More importantly, he'd told him the truth about his mum.

By the door to George's container stood Benissimo, brows furrowed and whip coiling. Ned strode towards him.

"Ned Waddlesworth, thank the heavens you're safe."

It was the first time the Ringmaster had called him anything other than josser, pup or boy, and it infuriated Ned even more than those hated nicknames – because his name was yet another lie.

"Don't touch me – you're a liar, you're all liars!" he seethed, brushing away Benissimo's hand, storming into the container and slamming the door shut behind him.

"I'm guessing my brother told you then?" asked the Ringmaster, but the door did not answer.

Benissimo was not known for his apologies, but he did send his able number two to try and break Ned's silence, armed rather foolishly with a plate of Scraggs's pancakes. Mystero managed to 'mistify' himself in time and did not take it personally that the tray, plate and breakfast had been hurled directly at his head.

Ned did not want a pancake or anything else remotely sweet, ever again. A short while later, however, George's giant hand braved the doorway, waving a white handkerchief... and the letter that Ned had found waiting for him at Fidgit and Sons.

"Ned, dear chap. I come in peace. Can I enter?"

By now, Ned was in such a fury that even his beloved Whiskers didn't dare look him in the eye. But the giant gorilla had risked his life to rescue him, and besides, it was really George's trailer.

"Come in," said Ned eventually.

"If I come in, do you promise not to throw anything at my head?"

"No."

George approached him carefully and handed him a letter.

The letter was from his mother.

He looked at it a moment, then opened the envelope, and read what was inside.

My darling boy,

As I write this, I am on the run, hounded by Barba's men wherever I turn, and you, my darling child, have just turned one. If you are reading this, then your father is now on the run too — or worse — and only you are free to save us all. My only hope is that you have grown big enough and strong enough to understand the choices we have made.

Lucy Beaumont's parents were murdered two weeks ago and I

was delivering her to safety – one last mission for our friends behind the Veil. But our contact on the other side has been turned, and I have been forced into hiding. Everyone I go to for help loses their life and I fear for all of our safeties.

I cry for you and your father every day, for the lies that must be told, for the secrets that must be kept. If I leave my ward, she will perish, and perhaps the world with her. If I come home, I bring this nightmare to your doorstep, and to you. You may never forgive us for lying to you but I hope and pray you will see it for what it is: the only way to keep you, and the world as we know it, safe.

This ring holds power and danger in equal measure. Only you can decide whether you will wear it. When the time comes, if it comes, I know you will find the courage you need inside of yourself. We have a lifetime of love to catch up on, but only the slimmest chance to live it.

I love you, my dearest, to the stars and back again.

Your Mother,

Olivia Armstrong.

Ned could hardly breathe – there were so many emotions rushing through his heart and mind. It was not as the butcher had suggested, his mum hadn't chosen anyone over him. The truth was that she'd had no choice at all.

"So… so what happened?" Ned asked.

The great ape removed his spectacles.

"I'm still trying to put all the pieces together, old bean, but so far this is what I've managed to garner. Years ago, when Terrence went under the name of 'Mentor', rumours began to circulate that the Veil might be weakening. Barbarossa became obsessed with letting it fall. He insisted it would usher in a brave new age and asked your father and Lucy's mother – the Medic at the time – to let it happen. Obviously they refused, aware of the disastrous repercussions that would follow, and went into hiding shortly after. The place from where the Veil's power springs – the Source, as it is known – has been kept secret for centuries. Its location, even its form, is to this day a mystery, as far as we know. Their plan was to somehow locate and mend the Source, after Barbarossa had stopped hounding them. But he didn't.

"Two years later, he finally caught up with the Beaumonts. And, well, you know now how badly that ended." Ned nodded. "Lucy and your good self were barely past your first birthdays. Now, Barbarossa did not know about you, dear chap, but it was quite clear that he would do anything to get what he wanted. For your safety and any hope of the Veil's, your parents chose to separate themselves, and you and Lucy. They've lived in total secrecy ever since. It was no doubt a bitter sacrifice. They must have believed it to be the only way. But when the Veil did truly begin to fail, Barbarossa upped his search, your dad realised this and, well, here we all are…"

"I don't get it, though. Why bother kidnapping me? Surely it would have been easier to just have me killed?"

"That's what we can't figure out, old chap. Whatever the reason, he most definitely needs you for some purpose and I should venture, given his new warship, it's utterly foul."

"He did mention something about 'great plans' when I was on the *Daedalus*…"

"As for all the secrecy, your dad held out on you for the same reason as Benissimo did. The less you knew, the more safe your cover. As you've seen first hand, Barbarossa will use unspeakable means to get what he wants, Ned… unspeakable."

Ned felt the last of the numbness thaw and the wound in his heart reopen. "Nothing I know is real…"

"Your parents, Ned, they're real," grunted George kindly.

"Are they? You probably knew my mum. I expect half the troupe knew both my parents and the girl… Lucy, she'll be like a daughter to her by now. But I don't, George. I don't know them, or this world they come from, or even what I am, not really… not any more."

George sighed.

"That makes two of us, old chap, at least it did. I never knew my parents at all. And I've read every tome on every species on both sides of the Veil and I'm the only 'me' I know of."

Ned looked up to see what might have been tears forming in the giant ape's black eyes.

"But if this circus of oddities has taught me anything, dear boy, it's that your family is who you say it is and that your home is where your heart beats loudest."

Ned thought of his dad and how he'd lived on the run to keep him safe, missing his wife and pretending to be something he wasn't. He thought of the old poster he'd seen of his mum, how pretty she'd looked, how alive. And then how different she'd sounded in the letter; how alone and how afraid.

"We don't know what kind of dastardly pact Barba's made with the Demons, Ned," George continued, "but if the Veil falls and they fight for him, there will be no stopping them. Unless…"

The great ape looked over at Ned's bunk.

"That picture frame over there. It was meant for a picture of your mother, wasn't it?"

Ned nodded.

"And you mean to tell me, that now you know she's alive, and with Lucy Beaumont, you're going to lock yourself in this room and mope?"

Ned said nothing, feeling a rush of emotion as it all finally clicked into place. Barbarossa had crushed his parents' bravery and stolen his childhood. And no matter what he'd claimed on his ship, the Darklings Ned had seen weren't fighting for freedom. They fought because they liked to kill.

Whatever Barba's plan, his parents, the world on both sides of the Veil, needed him to be so much more than average, more than Grittlesby and jam sandwiches. Now was his chance… why wasn't he leaping on it?

"Waddlesworth or Armstrong, it makes no difference. Turning people is what that brute does best. There isn't a man or monster that's lasted even half as long as you did. You're special. And you're the next Engineer. Now, old boy, you get out there and prove it!"

CHAPTER 20

The Amplification-Engine

Ned burst into Benissimo's trailer, jabbering wildly.

"When you told me the blood-key was a way for us to unearth Lucy, you knew the ring was waiting for me, didn't you?"

"I hoped—"

"Well, I don't know about you," Ned rushed on, "but where I'm from people earn each other's trust by being truthful. You've been lying to me all along, about everything, and if I'm going to do this, then I need to trust you, so you're going to not do that any more, right?"

For the first time since they'd met, Benissimo – fearless Ringmaster of the Circus of Marvels – was at a loss for words.

"And while I'm at it, every time you give me an order, like 'stay in your bunk' or 'wait outside the shop' or 'go to your trailer', someone tries to hurt or kidnap me. So from now on you're going to stop treating me like a baby, right? Because... because I'm an *Engineer*. And I know you don't think I'm up to it, but right now I'm the only one you've got!"

"Being an Engineer is much harder than just saying so, pup. You have to have what it takes."

"Do you know what..." fumed Ned, feeling all the injustice of the last few days, of his life, rise up inside him, "your brother might well be the end of the world on legs, but at least he's *polite*!" Ned was on a roll now, furious anger pouring out of him like molten lava. "And at least he doesn't look like he's got a rat strapped to his top lip!"

Benissimo raised his eyebrow. There was a long pause. Ned held his breath and wondered if he'd gone too far, until Benissimo broke into the first actual smile Ned had seen since the two of them had met.

"Why are you smiling?" Ned suddenly found himself annoyingly disarmed.

"Because that fire inside of you now, the one burning so brightly in your belly, is what I've been waiting to see since you joined us."

"Oh... right."

But Benissimo's smile faded as quickly as it had

appeared, and he furrowed his great brows. Ned had already worked out that it was the kind of furrow he liked to use when he was about to give a warning.

The Ringmaster got up and began pacing his trailer. "I know you think I've been harsh on you, Ned, but I've been around a very long time, and I've seen a lot of people I care about die, and the truth is… I've lost the stomach for it, and sending you in to do your father's job just doesn't feel right or fair. You weren't even born our side of the Veil – whereas most of your predecessors have been, for many decades now. Your lack of size, age and training, it all counts against you… but there it is. Your father isn't here, and time is pressing. Barba obviously knows about you now, making your father's distraction attempts futile. So we've sent out word, but what we don't know is whether the message will get to him in time, or even if it will find him at all. Maybe he'll make it back to us, but maybe he won't. But if he doesn't… it's all up to you."

Ned sighed. "No pressure then."

"The fact that your gift passes down the bloodline doesn't guarantee success. The Engineers in your family don't always 'connect' right with the ring. Even those older, more learned in the ways of Amplification. Sometimes it has to go to the nearest relative, a sister, brother, uncle or aunt, to pick up the reins. If things go wrong... you could wind up with even more loose screws than Kit-Kat, or six feet under in a pine box. Once bound to the wearer, the Engine cannot be removed, not until their final breath. Your forefathers have tried and failed."

"Failed?"

"Died."

"Right. And what about the ones that bonded OK?"

"Honestly?"

"Honestly."

"Some became corrupt, ruined by their greed for power. Many died in the thrusts and parries of battle against the Darklings. Some led more ordinary lives, in quiet times, others did not. They say one simply vanished off the face of the earth. A whole Engineer, just up and evaporated. You may have noticed, Ned, but you don't have any other relatives. Your bloodline just doesn't seem to last."

"So not the best odds for survival?"

"Not the best, no, but despite my concerns, it seems there is something about you, something that Kitty saw in you when you first came to us, the very same thing that made you work that red button aboard my *Marilyn*, and stand up to Barbarossa where countless others have failed. Your dad also thought that you could do this…"

And Ned realised he was right. His dad *had* believed in him, even if Benissimo was still unsure.

"There's one more thing," continued the Ringmaster.

Ned wondered how there could possibly be anything else.

"If my brother manages to find and kill Lucy, the Veil cannot be saved. The same could be said for you and your dad, but for some reason my brother wants you alive, and is getting information about you from a source which I can only assume is within our circle. Miz and I have turned over every bunk and trailer a hundred times looking for the culprit, but we can't find them, or work out how the messages are getting out. If you succeed in bonding with your ring, Ned, his spies will send their whispers, and when they do, he'll come after you again, but this time with everything he's got. The question is, are you up to it? Are you man enough to face whatever he sends us? To do what needs to be done?"

Just the thought of Barbarossa made Ned shudder. But the Waddlesworths or Armstrongs or whatever they were had done more than enough running. He might not be man enough, or even really boy enough, but he was certainly going to try.

"Let's make a start tonight."

The Ringmaster half-smiled. "Welcome to the circus, my boy."

***

When Ned and Whiskers got to the infirmary, Kitty was sat at her desk in a particularly bright pink outfit, writing swiftly on pieces of parchment, one after the other. She was not alone. At her feet were the strangest assortment of creatures Ned had ever seen. They were green, very small and partly transparent blobs but with bright glowing eyes, warm, smiling faces and short stubby limbs. One had little wings that beat away furiously, another was short and stout with at least eight eyes, another had a mouth as wide as its waist. Like Kitty, they were writing on pieces of parchment, matching the speed and movement of her hands perfectly, as if joined by invisible thread. When they heard Ned enter, they squealed, changing colour from green, to yellow, to bright orange, before running behind the Farseer's legs. Whiskers squeaked at them distrustfully from his perch on Ned's shoulder, his fur on end, as though he'd been plugged into a wall socket.

"What... are... those?"

"Good evening to you too, dearie. These are my familiars, and be nice, please, you're scaring them."

"But what are familiars?" asked Ned, bending down for a better look.

"Good spirits are the closest thing that might make any sense, dearie, though they're not human in origin. Familiars are, to the witching kind, friends, butlers, protectors and mischief-makers. Though I'd call this little lot of lemon-drops my family. You can come out now, boys, Ned's one of us."

One by one, the little creatures crept out from their cover.

"That's better. Now Ned, this is Frimshaw, Hookscarp, Orazal and Groir."

Each one bowed in turn, their colours changing to placid blues and washes of green. At the back of the infirmary, what Ned had thought was a shadow, started to move.

"Oh, and that's Gorrn, don't mind him," whispered Kitty, "he's a little shy on account of being so large and… colourless."

Ned's mouse still hadn't moved a single hair, and his tail was sticking out as straight as a pin.

"All right, Whiskers, you can stand down now," said

Ned, and the little mouse scurried from his shoulder, down his leg and on to his foot, keeping his eyes firmly on the familiars as he went. "Were they with you on the *Daedalus*?"

"Oh no, my little lamb. I was taken in my sleep. Familiars only cross over to our realm when we're awake. They can appear wherever we are, but only if they know where that is. Poor mites couldn't find me."

Whilst they worked, Whiskers sat with Ned and eyed the little creatures suspiciously. They helped Kitty prepare the last of her parchments before burning them and sprinkling the ashes around a chair at the centre of the infirmary.

Next, Frimshaw and Hookscarp poured rice wine vinegar around the room's perimeter, before the others scattered M&M chocolates. Apparently M&M's could befuddle an intruder's mind, especially the red ones.

"What's all that for?"

"A little insurance."

"Insurance against what?" asked Ned, who was already dreading the answer.

"During the bonding process, part of you will be in the Shades. It's the place we go to between asleep and awake," explained Kitty.

"Is that how Barbarossa talked to me in my dreams? When we were on the *Daedalus*."

"Exactly. Unfortunately for us, not everyone the butcher employs is from the outer world or the Veiled. Some inhabit the Shades. A bargeist is what happens when you mix a dead Darkling with the blood of a Demon. Sar-adin owns one. Like my boys here, bargeists can cross over from the Shades if they have your scent, and I'm fairly sure that after our stay on the *Daedalus*, his beast would have both of ours. Best to just keep your eyes closed. You can only see them when you're scared, and if you do see one, you will be. Not very nice, let me tell you. But quite containable, if you know the way of it."

"So you think once I put this ring on you might be able to help me find Lucy?"

"Most certainly, dear. I saw a link between the two of you when I first read your mind. Every generation of Engineer and Medic have a connection, which is magnified even further when they both come to bear their rings. Your father could work with Lucy – but it's you two who are meant to be as one. After tonight, and a little time spent with your Engine, we shall have our first real chance at finding her."

There was a knock at the door.

"Enter," said Kitty.

They were joined by the Ringmaster and the Tinker, along with what looked like roughly half of his lab. Ned caught a glimpse of George pacing anxiously outside on all fours, muscles rippling beneath black fur, before the door closed behind them. Benissimo motioned for Ned to sit in the central chair, and handed over his ring.

"Well, my boy, if you think you're ready, here it is. The moment of truth."

Ned perched Whiskers back up on his shoulder. If he really was going to carry the weight of the world up there, then he would do so with his mouse at his side.

The Tinker got out a magnifying glass and held it up to the ring for Ned to see.

"Beautiful, isn't it?" he whispered.

And it was. Under the lens, Ned could see that what had appeared to be solid metal was in fact made from thousands of tiny strands. More astonishingly, they looked like they were moving, some together, others in different directions, forming shapes and patterns that constantly evolved from one thing to another. It was like looking at a kaleidoscope of moving metal.

"It looks like it's… alive," said Ned, admiring the patterns and the workmanship.

"Indeed," replied the Tinker. "The folk that made it are no longer with us. So although we think the Source may use similar technology, the truth is, no one really knows, sir. We don't even know what it's made of; not exactly."

"Kit-Kat, some privacy if you will?" said Benissimo, who was now impatiently twisting the end of his moustache.

Kitty mumbled something unintelligible, took a small black pebble from her pocket, and swallowed it. A mushroom of darkness blew up over their heads, so that they appeared to be under a perfectly black dome. The outer world, for all intents and purposes, had gone.

"Well, dear," she asked, "are you ready?"

Ned took a deep breath, and put on the ring.

At first nothing happened. Then, ever so faintly, he felt an itching sensation on his finger, just where it touched the metal. The itching grew stronger and was followed by a little heat. He closed his eyes. Somewhere on a microscopic level, the ring was trying to connect with him. He could feel it. Its thousands of little live wires were literally burrowing into the pores of his skin. In no time at all, the faint itching became a burning.

Whiskers squeaked in mouse alarm and Ned opened his eyes and looked down at the ring. Hundreds upon hundreds of tiny metal wires were growing out of it. They moved like snakes – up his hand, his arm – becoming longer and longer till they reached his forearm.

"Err, g- guys, are you sure this is supposed to happen?" he stammered.

"Oh don't worry, Ned, apparently your dad asked exactly the same thing!" grinned Kitty, who seemed to be enjoying the spectacle enormously.

"Twenty-eight percent connectivity and rising," read the Tinker from his dials.

The wires started to twist their way up his arm. They were making a kind of pattern, like a giant loom stitching together cloth, only they were stitching themselves into Ned's skin. The heat intensified and he had to hold back the urge to yell.

"Stay steady, pup, you're doing just fine," said Benissimo sternly.

But Ned did not feel fine, or steady. It was then that he had the feeling that someone else had entered the room. Ned heard a kind of growling, and the chattering of teeth, followed by paws padding across the floor behind him. He looked around, but could see nothing, so said nothing.

"Forty-six percent," announced the Tinker.

"Guys, this is getting pretty weird," said Ned.

"We'll deal with the weird. Just focus on the ring,"

barked back Benissimo.

But Ned still felt like something was horribly wrong. He heard a pained howl, and looked down and saw pawprints in the ash. Clearly they had an uninvited guest – Kitty's first line of defence had slowed the bargeist, but not stopped it. He was about to say something when there was a sudden stabbing pain in his arm as the wires tightened their grip.

"Ow!" he spat through gritted teeth.

"The ring wants your undivided attention, dearie," trilled Kitty.

"Sixty-two percent."

His arm HURT. He closed his eyes and tried to concentrate on the ring. But the bargeist had tiptoed over the vinegar and was now on the M&M's. He could hear its horrid grunts as it gorged on the chocolates. It then occurred to him that Kitty hadn't told him what would happen if it made it past her defences.

"Seventy-three percent, and… ahem, vital signs are… oh, that is strange…" said the Tinker nervously.

The ring's wires crept further and further up his arm, under his T-shirt and around his neck.

"I don't know if I'm enjoying this very much," Ned hissed anxiously.

"Eighty-eight percent."

"Don't open your eyes, dearie, it can't hurt you if you can't see it," chimed the witch cheerfully.

When he was a much younger boy, that logic might have worked with Ned. But not today, and certainly not now. There were angry snarls as the bargeist tried to break through the ash ring.

Whiskers squeaked furiously as the wires at Ned's throat snapped tight, and burned. He tried to yell, but he had no voice.

"Ninety-five percent. Readings are not good, Bene. He can't take much more of this!" yelled the Tinker.

The snarling suddenly stopped, and he felt the little footsteps of his mouse running down his back and heading for cover. Ned hoped for a moment that the thing had gone too till there was a horrid breathing noise and what sounded like the licking of lips. Ned snapped open his eyes and saw two long fangs floating in the air beside him. The more scared he became, the more of the bargeist he could see – teeth, lips pulled back, and then a blackened lolling tongue. The wires burned and tightened and the world started to spin into darkness.

"QUICKLY, KITTY!" ordered Benissimo.

"Gorrn, Groir… Now, please, my loves, be done with it."

And with that, two of her familiars sprang out from

hiding and lunged at the unsuspecting beast.

"Ninety-nine percent… his vitals, Kitty!"

Ned felt himself fall without moving, his friends, family, mission simply ceasing to be important. Overwhelming pain, unlike any other, shot through his arm, and from somewhere deep in the vast folds of the Shades, he felt a great, empty Darkness, longing to be free.

It watched without eyes and spoke without lips.

"Ned."

"NED."

"*NEDNEDNEDNED…*"

A hungry cacophony of hisses, mumbles and whispers, all calling his name, exploded in his mind.

"Ned?" called out Benissimo. "Can you hear us?"

"Something's wrong… we're losing him!" shrieked the Tinker.

"DO SOMETHING!" roared Benissimo, grabbing on to Ned's shoulders and shaking him.

From somewhere beyond them all, somebody did indeed do something. In the midst of the blackness, Ned saw a pinprick of light, and felt an echo of a thought, a glimmer of a notion… that was not his own. He saw the girl's hands first, and in them he saw a flower.

The Darkness did not like the flower.

CHAPTER 21

French Steel

Everything seemed to move slowly and all to the pounding beat of his heart. That was, until his heart stopped. He did not notice George tearing Kitty's door from its hinges, after she'd lowered the black-domed barrier. He was not aware of how close the Darkness had come to taking him, nor did he know how hard the Farseer had fought to stop it. The only thing he remembered clearly was the notion of a girl holding a flower, that and a room raw with shouting before George's great arms carried him back to his bunk.

Much later, when Ned woke, the thought of the terrible voice and the girl who had reached out to him were still fresh in his mind. The voice had been ancient and frightening. Different again to the one aboard Barbarossa's ship. But if not Barbarossa then who or what was it? He decided to say nothing about it, at least until he had a better understanding of what it meant. As for the girl, it must have been Lucy Beaumont. Kitty had been right – as soon as he'd bonded with the ring, their connection had come alive. He switched on his sidelight and studied his hand. The band of metal looked quite normal. From the outside you couldn't tell that it was connected to him through the pores of his skin, as much a part of his nervous system now as the hand that carried it. He'd survived the bonding. Ned had become an Engineer, just like his father before him. It was at this precise moment that he felt something he had never felt before. Ned felt special.

"Well this is weird, Whiskers," he whispered, but his Debussy Mark 12 was pretending to be asleep. "Oh and yeah, I'm fine, thanks pal," he added, which was when his mouse turned over and started to snore.

Ned left Whiskers 'recharging'. He was met outside by Monsieur Couteau who was waiting in full fencing gear, rapier in hand, with his customary expression of French severity.

"Monsieur Neede, follow me."

"It's actually Ned, Mister Couteau."

"Swish! swish!" said Couteau, as the tip of his blade did just that in front of Ned's nose.

"*Monsieur* Couteau, if you please, Neede."

Ned had had little to do with the man since their run in with Barbarossa in Shalazaar, but had heard from the others that he took his job and the Ringmaster's orders *extremely* seriously.

"Er, yes *Monsieur* Couteau," replied Ned now, eyes fixed on the rapier's tip, only inches from his nose.

With Ned's new status as an Engineer, Benissimo had evidently given the French Master at Arms instructions to begin his battle training immediately. Having Ned taken again, by whatever means, was not an option. He needed to be ready for anything.

Couteau led them over to the big top, where Finn was wrestling with a level two tiptoe – a slim, grey-skinned, oily-looking creature that reminded Ned of something between a snake and a frog. He'd caught it giving nightmares to young children throughout the Italian countryside. The tracker was about to demonstrate how best to deal with the nuisance when Couteau dismissed the gathering for his one-on-one session with Ned.

One of the younger Tortellini boys smiled at Ned on his way out. "Good luck," he said, as Ned realised that the smile had actually been more of a knowing smirk.

"Under this great canvas," began the Frenchman, "you

will learn the secrets of ze blade. You will learn to be ze blade. Work hard and you will become an artist who paints in steel."

Ned was starting to wish he was still in bed.

"Choose your blade, Monsieur Neede."

Ned went to the armoury and picked out one of the lighter-looking foils. As he turned around, he came nose to tip with the end of Couteau's blade. This time it made contact with his skin. It was razor sharp and it hurt.

"Never turn your back on your enemy," said Couteau icily.

"But we're not enemies, we're just training," grimaced Ned, though he was beginning to wonder.

"Monsieur Neede, *en garde*!"

Startled, Ned tried to raise his foil, but it was only halfway up when Couteau struck with such speed and force that it went flying from his hand. The Frenchman was not playing games.

"Again. Faster, please," ordered Couteau.

Ned tried again. This time Couteau let him raise his foil, but no sooner had he done so than the Master at Arms attacked with a flurry of such ferocious blows, he thought his foil might actually shatter. There were three more attempts, each one ending with Ned's blade lying in the sawdust. The Frenchman was irritatingly calm, as though he'd been casually swatting a fly throughout. Ned, meanwhile, was already dripping with sweat.

"Faster, Neede, faster! Take me down!"

"I can't!"

"Why can't you?" challenged Couteau.

"Because I'm just a boy and you're the finest blade in Europe!" Ned quipped.

"Non, Monsieur Neede," said Couteau, still duelling. "We are nothing, there is only steel on steel. Ze blades do not care who holds them, only who wins. Forget me, forget you, strike faster, win!"

"But—"

Ned was about to try to lighten the mood once more, but Couteau's face turned ice cold with intent. His eyes narrowed and he lunged forward, hacking at the air so fast, that Ned couldn't see which blade was which. Had the Master at Arms gone mad? All Ned could do was stagger backwards, trying desperately to fend off Couteau's attacks, till he tripped and fell to the floor. Couteau disarmed him with a flick of his blade and cut Ned across the cheek. The cut was so fine and Couteau's blade so sharp, that there was no blood, just a hot sting of pain.

"All right, that's enough!" yelled Ned indignantly,

grabbing at his cheek.

"Non, Monsieur Neede, it is not. Do you think ze butcher will stop when he comes back for you? What will you say? 'That's enough'? Will he listen? Will he show you remorse if you will not do as he demands? Ze boy that would save ze Veil? Non, Monsieur Neede, he will not."

Couteau's point had sunk in. Ned stood up, readied himself, and they went again. Properly this time.

The Frenchman finally let him go after two disheartening hours and sent him on for the next stage of his training, which would be with Kitty. As Ned wandered to the infirmary, he felt pretty sure his tutor hadn't been as hard on the rest of the troupe, and he had no doubt that Benissimo was behind his 'special treatment'. On top of that, despite his best efforts, he didn't feel like he had improved at all.

On his way to Kitty's infirmary he passed by three white-skinned elves, a large family of bearded gnomes and what looked like a Minotaur, all of which were being offered shelter. Ned hadn't noticed the day before, he'd been too angry to see it, but the unveiled were arriving, and in increasing numbers.

Aboard Kitty's bus, things were no better. As Ned entered, he saw Rocky attempting to trim Abigail's beard.

He was doing so rather hopelessly, and with a pair of garden shears.

"Don't worry, Babooshka, Rocky mek you pretty again."

But 'Babooshka' did not answer, nor had she since the night her Farseer was taken. Her skin was as white as a sail and her mouth open in a permanent and silent scream. Despite Kitty's best efforts, they had yet to find a cure for the strange coma that had so cruelly taken her.

Rocky nodded to him. "Dey upstairs, boy."

Ned nodded back and continued up the stairs. Though his session with Couteau had made its point, it had done little to encourage him. Could he really help? Would he really be enough to make any kind of difference, and if he was, what was he actually going to do?

When he reached the top deck, the Tinker and Kitty were both waiting with his answer.

CHAPTER 22

A Single Grain of Sand

"**S**and? The world's falling apart out there and you want me to use my Amplification-Engine – one of the rarest devices on the planet – to make sand?"

"It's just the one grain of sand, dearie, though it is a lot harder than it sounds." Kitty twirled her Hello Kitty bracelet merrily.

"What about finding the Source… and Lucy? I don't know how, but last night I'm sure I sensed her, Kitty. She's got to be more important than… sand?"

"Oh, my little gum-drop, don't be such a fusspot. Trust me when I tell you that everything is in hand. I am a Farseer, after all, and I'm quite sure that the Source's location will reveal itself to me momentarily. As for Lucy, the power of your connection with the girl is quite unprecedented, and will only grow as you master the Engine-ring. When it's strong enough, we'll use it to find her, dearie, together. First things first, though – a grain of sand."

"Well, if you think it will do any good?"

"Think? Oh no, my little apricot, there's no room for thinking. You have to *know*."

The Tinker tried to explain in a bit more depth.

"The Amplification-Engine works at an atomic level, using your thought as fuel. Whatever you hold in your head, it uses as a template, literally reforming the atoms you focus on, till they become something else. It takes pure mental focus to create enough energy. In other words, you need to do more than just *think* about it – you need to become one with the vision in your mind's eye in order for the ring to make it so. There can be no doubt."

"So if I want to make water, I need to *feel* wet?"

"See, Tinker? I told you he'd pick it up quickly," beamed Kitty.

The minutian presented him with a small leather-bound book, no bigger than a man's wallet.

"*The Engineer's Manual*, Master Waddlington, passed down through your family for generations. Your father gave it to us for safe-keeping when he left the Veil."

For the first time, Ned felt a sense of ownership towards the Armstrong name mixed with the fear that he was not strong enough to carry it. But he didn't bother to correct the Tinker – he knew what he meant. On the book's cover embossed in gold was a small ring, and beneath it a row of unintelligible symbols. It had a clasp along one edge, which Ned unclipped carefully.

WHOOSH!

There was a loud yawn of stretching leather as the Manual sprang to life, leaping out of his hands.

"OW!" shouted Ned, as he received a violent and leathery slap to the face from the Manual's rapidly expanding cover. The tiny pocket book was now a large and heavy tome, hundreds if not thousands of pages long.

"You knew that was going to happen, didn't you?" Ned grinned, marvelling at the pure magic of it, despite his stinging cheek.

"Course we did, dumpling, but it wouldn't have been nearly as much fun if we'd told you."

In front of him, were the combined notes and experiments of the world's Engineers. Its first entries were in symbols he'd never seen and some were in languages that were no longer spoken. There were countless blueprints and diagrams, notes and sketches – many focused on how to work the ring. It was like looking through a family album that went back thousands of years. Suddenly Ned's little family was something else, something vast and connected. It was a good feeling, like being home again.

The Tinker cleared his throat and continued his explanation. "The methods of Amplification, they're all in there, sir. The single grain is the building block with which all Engineers begin their journey. Air to fire would be simpler, a matter of speeding up the atoms till the air ignites, but compressing them down to make sand means changing the mass as well as the form, so it's a good place to start your learning. Metal will turn to stone, all right, but you'd probably need all the air in this room to make a ball of lead from scratch; not advisable if you want to breathe. If you can grasp the principles, though, then you can make just about anything."

The last entry, and easiest to read, explained the importance of holding a clear picture in your mind's eye, and how practising with any number of construction sets and building blocks might help a young mind become more attuned to the art of Amplification. It was easy to read because it was in his dad's handwriting. At the bottom of the page was a simple message:

Look before you leap.

It made Ned's stomach knot. It was clearly a message intended for him. Even in his absence, his dad was trying to watch over him.

"He used to say that a lot."

"It's the Engineer's way, lamb-chop. It's called Seeing and it's what we're going to start with. Now, empty your noodle and relax. You need to think of the air first, then see it form into a grain of sand. If you can, try and feel it changing. Hold the end vision in your mind, as if it were under one of the Tinker's lenses. See every microscopic detail. The more clearly you see it, the better the transformation."

Kitty's words became soft and Ned's thoughts drifted. 'Seeing' air felt next to impossible to him, but in his mind's eye he imagined it as best he could. He held it there, a nothingness that shimmered with form. Soon it thickened in wisps of undulating motion till he blew it up in his thoughts so much so that he could almost visualise its tiny molecules being drawn together. This was the hard part, the change in mass – from gas, to liquid, to solid and all at once. Harder and harder he pushed his brain till beads of sweat started to trickle down the side of his face. Finally something solid started to form before his mind's eye in hues of orange and brown. In his head he saw its tiny ridges, every miniscule imperfection. He thought of it like the blueprints and instructions he had followed over the years – the pleasing way that parts felt in his hands; how the details all fitted together; how they made sense of each other…

"That's it, oh crumbs, *that's it*…" whispered Kitty.

And all of a sudden the machine on his finger came alive, its microscopic parts moving as one. A tickling sensation flowed from his finger up his arm and ran right into his mind. A strange power seemed to flow between Ned and his ring in a high-pitched, humming loop. The air around him buzzed with static, making the hairs on his neck stiffen, till he heard a crackle of energy.

A ripple formed between Ned and the world. Light folded in on itself, bending the image in front of him with the faint sound of air being drawn together.

"Wow…" breathed the Tinker.

Ned opened his eyes. There, inches from his nose, was a perfectly formed grain of sand, just as he'd seen it.

"Wow indeed, dearies, wow indeed. What did I tell you, Tinker?" said Kitty, beaming. "Just as clever as his daddy. Now, my little bag of sweets, you're going to turn it for me."

"Turn it?"

"Imagine it spinning, Neddles, atom by atom, and it will spin. Just try not to force it, or you'll take out your eye."

Ned did as she asked. It was like trying to juggle a ping-pong ball with a hairdryer. Ned quickly found he couldn't really move the grain itself, just suggest where it went to in his mind. He felt the turning all the way to his belly, so much so that it made him queasy. Again, the ring at his finger hummed with life, and to his utter and complete amazement, the little granule turned in the air.

"A vital part of Amplification, sir, essentially telekinesis. Your sort call it Telling," said the Tinker.

Ned reached up and plucked his grain of sand from the air. A grain of sand which, until he'd thought of it, had not existed. Since his thirteenth birthday, Ned had experienced one impossibility after another. Walking, breathing fairy tales, and monsters straight from nightmares, all of them real. Magic was real, flying tents were real, even wind-up robots the size of a mouse… they were all real. Nothing, however, was more incredible, more life-changing or strange, than the minuscule grain of sand on the tip of his finger. Average boys like Ned Waddlesworth did not make things with their minds. But he was Ned Armstrong, and he was no longer an average boy.

For a moment Ned's mind raced with possibilities. "Can I make anything?"

"Not quite, Master Ned. It does have limits – gold, silver and precious gems. They're all off the menu, so to speak," explained the Tinker.

Ned's dreams of limitless wealth evaporated before they'd even formed.

"Well, that's a bit disappointing."

"Steady your paws, little leopard," urged Kitty. "Precious knick-knack's are nothing to what you and your ring will be making eventually. Seeing and Telling a single grain is only the first step. You'll need to learn much more to mend the Source of the Veil's power. Normally we wouldn't try this quite so quickly, but with time being what it is, we'll need to start you off on multiples."

"Multiples?"

"Making and moving more than one thing at a time; bringing together complex parts. Tricky. We'll try two grains of sand first. Now be careful, we don't want you spraining your head, not when it's so nice the way it is."

He shut his eyes and slowed his breathing. His mind took him back to the shimmering air as it jostled into position. There was the high-pitched hum again, between Ned and the ring, followed by another crackle of energy, till finally, miraculously, he saw two grains of sand forming in front of him.

"Turn them both, dearie. In opposite directions. Gently now my pear-tree, and for as long as you can."

The first started to spin, just as it had before, but as soon as he focused on the second, they both started to wobble and disintegrate. He panicked, trying to compensate with one and then the other, till they slipped from his invisible hold and tumbled to the floor, evaporating back to air as they did so. A part of him felt as though he were tumbling with them, and he reached out to steady himself.

"That was *really* hard."

"Actually, dear, it's only ever as hard as you make it," answered Kitty.

The room was still swaying. "But the granules... I couldn't stay focused on more than one at a time."

"The only limit is what your mind is trained to believe is possible or not. If I'd asked you to Amplify a whole bag of sand it would be just as easy, dear, but only if you let yourself think it. When your daddy went on stage he could turn a knife into a metal spider's web, a pane of glass into a pool of water. To reach that level, you need willpower, and your resistance to Barba shows you have it in spades. You also need belief, in yourself, your own imagination, and what you're trying to create. This is not beyond you, Neddles, it's within. Believe me when I tell you this – no one shone brighter than your parents, in or out of the circus ring," said Kitty warmly. "Mark my words, little Armstrong, in time you'll do the same."

It was the first time the elderly witch had used his real surname. It hurt because he wanted so desperately to believe that this was who he was. To be like they had been, to be the same.

"If you say so," he mumbled.

"No, dearie, if *you* say so," said the Farseer, this time without a smile.

Just then, a grim-faced Benissimo came pounding up the stairs, his whip writhing like a snake on fire, his top hat askew.

"Murder and mayhem, mud and mischief! You had best all follow me."

"What is it, boss? What's the matter?" asked the Tinker.

"Madame Oublier has sent news – and it is not good!"

CHAPTER 23

Oublier and Co

Madame Oublier was Prime of the Twelve, the governing council that watched over all of the Veil's circuses. Their word – and by definition, hers – was law amongst the travelling kind. She was also, like Kitty, a Farseer – a woman with the gift of sight. She had sent as envoys two agents from her pinstripe brigade bearing a letter. To not entrust the news to an air-modulator, largely accepted as the Veil's safest form of communication, could only mean two things. The news was both highly sensitive and extremely dire.

Mystero and George were already waiting in the Ringmaster's trailer to hear what the pinstripes had to say. It was Ned's second visit there, though he'd been too frantic to take it in the first time. Benissimo's quarters looked as if they had been lived in by a hundred Ringmasters before him and were strewn with the costumes, wigs and weaponry of his trade. His standing mirror was so covered in photos of troupes gone by, that there was little mirror left to actually see into. Looking about the trailer, Ned realised that the Circus of Marvels was more than a troupe that required a Ringmaster – to Benissimo, it was his family and home.

The oversized ape and head of security were sitting far apart and George looked upset, not animal-rage upset, more gentleman-seriously-miffed upset.

"You OK, George?" asked Ned.

The ape's fur bristled.

"Apparently that is for our clammy-handed head of security to decide."

"George, no one is suggesting that you're the actual spy," said a stern-faced Mystero. He was in his solid form, and his suit looked as tired as he did. The constant checks on the troupe's security were clearly taking their toll.

"But you want to search my container?"

It was Benissimo who answered.

"George! This is not the time for hurt feelings. Ned was taken from your quarters, and Miz merely needs to inspect it for tickers."

If an ape's face could go red with anger, then George's

would have been scarlet. Instead he busied himself with the angry elimination of a banana.

Ned gave George a sympathetic smile, then took his seat with the Tinker and Kitty.

"Now, if we're all ready to be civil…?" said Benissimo, pausing to peer at George before he began reading Madame Oublier's letter.

"*Bene, I am forced to send envoys as the news they bring is grave. Secrecy is of the utmost importance, for I suspect more than one rotten apple in my basket and suggest you look to your own over the coming days.*

"*The Veil is indeed failing, old friend. For now, our circuses and operatives on the outside are containing things as best they can. The human press may not have joined the dots, but those in power are beginning to. They don't know what they have yet, but they know they have something. We are not dealing with a foolish incursion by that idiot Bigfoot, or Nessy showing off in Scotland, nor is it a few isolated sightings of fair-folk forgetting their glamours. As the Veil continues to falter, piece by alarming piece, we can only wonder at what will be revealed next. I leave it to the pinstripes to explain further, as I do not trust even the ink or paper that this letter is scribed upon. If the child's sighting of the Shar's insignia aboard your brother's ship is true, then I fear a cabal of enemies has already formed.*

"Keep your eyes open on the road ahead, I see a perilous ride for us all…"

Benissimo finished reading, and looked to the two men with matching slicked-back hair and pinstripe suits standing quietly by his side. The same two men that Ned had seen with Finn in France. They bowed politely to Benissimo, then Kitty, before the stockier of the two cleared his throat and began.

"Masters… over the past twelve months, myself and Mr Cook, along with the other pinstripes have been monitoring activity in every nook and cranny of our borders. I have to report that the amount of high-level Darklings crossing over has increased at an alarming rate."

The other pinstripe laid out a collection of magazines and newspapers, from the josser side of the Veil. Most of them were local, small-scale papers with tiny readerships, but all had one thing in common: their leading stories revolved around unexplainable phenomena.

'FLAME-BREATHING
REPTILE IN PARIS SEWERS!'

'HALF-EATEN HUMAN REMAINS
FOUND IN MOSCOW SUBURB!'

'WHAT CREATURE MADE
THESE CLAW MARKS?'

'ELDERLY LADY ATTACKED IN SLEEP
NEAR BATTERSEA POWER STATION!'

From England to India, America to Australia, the Veil was faltering and at an alarming rate.

"With all these rumours circulating, we're seeing widespread panic on our side of the Veil. The more defenceless of our folk are understandably terrified and would be far more so if they knew the extent of the problem. More troubling still is our timeframe. That is to say, what is indicated by the lengthening duration for which the Veil falters each time. The science guilds and the elder librarians of Aatol have cross-referenced the dates and lengths of incident with their geographical positioning and I'm afraid the Astronomicus has given us its date, Masters – we have just thirteen days. The level thirty-sixes – the Demons – are less than two weeks away from breaking through."

Mr Small's words lay over the room like a great dark blanket. For the first time since Ned had met the man,

Benissimo hung his head, and both George and the Tinker looked like they'd forgotten how to breathe. Only Kitty remained unshaken. To Ned's complete amazement, she was happily thumbing the pages of a Hello Kitty sticker book.

"Ooh, snap, two matching lollies!" she squealed, though she had no way of seeing that they were no such thing.

"Really, Kit-Kat! You could at least take this seriously," scolded Benissimo fiercely.

"Oh, but I am, dearies! Has the room forgotten our young Engineer? The brave wee boy who will save the Veil?" said Kitty, though without her usual mischievous grin.

All eyes turned to Ned, who gulped and looked at his lap sheepishly.

"Kitty, the prophecies are all good and well," said Benissimo, clearly trying to watch his words, "and we are all no doubt grateful to the boy for agreeing to help in his father's absence. But we are clearly running out of time. Can we really put our futures in the hands of, of… a child?"

Kitty gave the faintest of smiles.

"I did. On your brother's ship. I knew the boy would

resist the butcher's magic and that he would find me, just as I knew he'd bond with the ring, and with the girl. Is the Beaumont girl herself not a child? Is she not as much a gamble?"

"He's had no training."

Ned felt another pang of jealousy. It was true, he was horribly ill prepared, whereas Lucy had no doubt always known about her gift. Had his mother trained her, made her better than Ned?

"Now is not the time for sowing doubt, Bene, not when we are asking so much."

"Fine. You're right," said Benissimo, now looking at Ned. "Tell me, how goes his tutoring?"

Ned had to force himself not to walk out of the room. The Ringmaster was back to talking about him as though he wasn't even in the room.

Kitty suddenly looked less defiant.

"Tip-top, though it's only his first day and—"

"And how long did it take his father to come into the fullness of his gifts?" interrupted the Ringmaster.

"Well, I wasn't involved in his training so I can't be sure," said Kitty, suddenly wearing a distinctly faraway expression on her face.

Even Ned could see that she was putting on an act.

"Kitty, please! I may not be able to read minds, but I can tell you know very well the answer."

"Well, but the boy is a natural if ever there was one, took to Seeing right away, so there really is no comparing them."

"HOW LONG, KITTY?" barked the Ringmaster.

The witch stopped smiling and looked up at the ceiling sulkily.

Of all the people in the room, no one was more impatient for her answer than Ned.

Eventually, Kitty looked at Benissimo.

"Eight months."

CHAPTER 24

So Jump!

The meeting had come to an abrupt ending. Only Kitty remained behind with the two pinstripes, who had a private message from Madame Oublier to pass on. Ned left feeling that everything was against them, but nothing more so than their – or rather his – lack of time. Ned's initial wonder at creating his first grain of sand was long forgotten in the face of the enormous task he now faced in getting his skills up to scratch in time for them to find Lucy and reach the Source before – quite literally – all Hell broke loose.

And so Ned's training continued, each circus member taking it in turn to test his skills and pass on what wisdom they had.

"What are the three main staples of Amplification?" tested George a couple of days later as they sat in his container having their lunch. George was peering at Ned's Manual over his specs, one huge finger pressed delicately to the page.

"Seeing, Telling and Feeling," recited Ned.

"Nicely done, old bean. And now, what is Feeling?"

"How about some definitions? 'Telling' or Telekinesis; a skilled Engineer can make an object move. The more complex the thing the harder it is to control. Then... 'Feeling' is when, by adding one's own anger or calm to a creation, an Engineer may imbue it with an intent. The results are often unpredictable and highly explosive – not to be undertaken lightly. Learning these forms till they are second nature is the key to advancement. Shall we look at subsections now? The creation of weapons or—"

"Ned, we have been over every translatable entry a hundred and one times. If you keep going at this rate, your brain is going to combust."

"It's either my brain or the world. You heard what the pinstripe said, George – I have DAYS to figure this out. The newspaper reports are getting worse and—"

"And how many hours' sleep have you had since that meeting?"

"Plenty," said Ned dismissively, finishing off his sandwich.

Whiskers looked over at George from where he was sitting on Ned's bed and shook his head emphatically.

"Fibber," rumbled the ape.

Ned's ring hummed into life as he brought something into his mind. He was learning fast. Fast enough to See the orange on George's desk turn into a rock and fast enough to Tell it to fly at the ape's head.

"Good lord! That, old chap, is an unpardonable way to treat my second favourite fruit."

"I've got a grasp on the beginnings, but I can't manage multiples, George, and Kitty says that until I do, I won't have enough control to find Lucy or the Source, never mind fix it. Besides, just look at this Manual, I've still got so much to learn. Benissimo's been right about me all along. I'm going to let *everyone* down... and the chances of seeing my dad again... or finding my mum are—"

"Stop that!" said the great ape, lumbering to his feet. "Don't be so hard on yourself! I hate to see you rattled like this. What you need is a break from all this confounded studying."

But it was no use. The harder Ned tried to be the boy they needed, the more he seemed to fail. When he wasn't training with Kitty or studying with George, Benissimo had him train with Monsieur Couteau and Grandpa

Tortellini, hoping to get his fight and flight skills up to speed. And every day, he would fail at those too. Over and over again, he found himself humiliated by Couteau's sword, or burnt by Grandpa Tortellini's rope as his fear of heights got the better of him and he slid back down before ever getting anywhere near the top.

"Come on, Whatiwhat!" said Grandpa Tortellini. "How am I gonna teach you to fly, if you don't climb-a da rope?"

And although Ned had been hopeful that his skills with the blade would improve, even that turned out to be a disaster. In his second session, Monsieur Couteau cruelly paired him with Daisy, the innocent-looking seven-year-old he'd seen on his first day, aka Daisy 'the Dagger', who was in fact a military grade assassin.

Ned didn't mind being humiliated, or having the troupe know he was scared of heights. He wasn't proud. What he did mind was wasting time. All of the Veil's combined circuses were working round the clock to manage the border crossings and prepare their weapons for the inevitable struggle. What was the point? If he was unable to master multiples, let alone connect with Lucy, it would all be over in a handful of days.

Ned was waiting glumly for Grandpa Tortellini in

the big top one day when his trainer bounded in with a particularly sparkly smile on his face.

"Whatiwhat, what's-a da matter?"

Grandpa Tortellini was a half-satyr. He had the horns of his father, but not the mountain goat legs. Even so there was something about his walk today that was unusually springy, as though he had a secret that he was dying to tell.

"I gonna cheer you up and today we gonna try something a little little, OK?" smiled Tortellini encouragingly, as he led him over to the other side of the big top.

There in front of Ned was indeed something "a little little". A thin high-wire had been tightly strung across two short poles, no more than a foot off the ground.

"You no like-a da heights, so I get rid-a da heights!" explained Grandpa Tortellini proudly.

Ned smiled at him – it was hard not to – and stepped up unsteadily on to the wire, Whiskers perched as usual on his shoulder. To Ned's surprise, he found himself laughing. So close to the ground, walking the wire was a completely different proposition. It felt solid and strong. With every step Whiskers gave an encouraging squeak.

"I's-a good, no?"

"Yeah, it is actually."

Without the threat of plummeting to his doom, he managed to focus on the task at hand. Walking on a wire at any height was hard, but Ned discovered to his complete amazement, that he was actually quite good at it.

"BRAVO! BRAVO!" yelled the half-satyr almost bleating with excitement. "Trust yourself, Whatiwhat. See how good you can be when you do!"

He spent an hour with Tortellini enjoying his new talent. By the end of their session he was walking backwards and had even tried it blindfolded.

"Good boy, Whatiwhat! Feel your foot on da rope before it lands, feel it in-a your mind."

Ned did as the old man asked and his foot followed.

"How you feelin', Whatiwhat?"

"Great! I'm not bad at this!"

"Why, Whatiwhat, *why*?"

Ned stopped on the wire and balanced effortlessly. What had changed? The poles had shortened, but that wasn't it. Maybe it was at first – the ground was close, so he wasn't scared. But now it didn't matter how high or low it was. It was just a wire, and he knew how to do it now. It was Ned who had changed. Something inside.

"Because… I believe I can do it?"

"Finally! The Whatiwhat, he's-a fix his block of a brain!

Take off da blindfold, Mr Whatiwhat!"

His aged trainer was red in the face with excitement.

"Kitty-Katty, if you don't-a mind?"

Kitty walked sideways out of the shadows. She had been there the entire time. She looked at Ned and chanted under her breath. Ned felt his legs wobble. The big top's stalls, sawdust and floor suddenly dropped away, as though falling through the air. Just as suddenly, they stopped. Ned twisted around to see that the two-foot-high poles at either end of his wire were now at least thirty feet in length. Grandpa Tortellini and Kitty were far below him, looking up delightedly.

"Just a little illusion, my newly feathered bird. We thought it might help with your fear of heights," squeaked Kitty.

Ned had been up there all along. His head hurt trying to work out the magic, but it didn't matter. He was high up at the top of the big top and he was… OK.

"I's-a little sneaky, no?" bleated Tortellini. "But you feel-a good, no?"

"I… do!" agreed Ned shakily. "I feel great!"

"And if you fall, nothing gonna happen, right?"

Ned looked down at the safety net beneath him.

"Nothing!" he shouted.

"SO JUMP!" roared the satyr.

Ned was dizzy with excitement. His rodent companion was shaking its head in a vigorous "no", but Ned felt so happy and free, so completely removed from his problems, that he did just as the old man asked. He took his mouse in his hand and leapt off the wire, and as he did so, four words came with him: *look before you leap*.

Ned tumbled through the air, wearing the biggest grin of his life. The way he felt now, he could move a hundred grains of sand, hell, he could move a whole truckload if Kitty asked him to. He was an Engineer, the newest recruit of a warrior circus... and he and his wind-up mouse were flying!

In the blink of an eye he had landed on the safety net, his indignant Debussy Mark 12 beside him. As the bounces slowed, he lay back, eyes closed, and let the power surge through him. Suddenly the air around him began to crackle. His whole body hummed as hot energy flowed between Ned and his ring, coursing up and down his arm. He was dimly aware of Kitty and Grandpa Tortellini, and the small crowd of gathering onlookers who had come to see what the commotion was, but he pushed them from his mind as he focused, and the light folded in on itself.

Then with a loud whooshing of air, grains of sand

began to fall from the big top's canopy, not ten or twenty, but thousands, tens of thousands. He pushed at them gently with his mind. Not one or two but all of them at once, as though they were one connected body, a universe of yellow stars now gracefully pivoting in different directions. He held them all still a moment, suspended motionless in the air, then let them fall, like rain, landing in his eyes, mouth and even up his nose. It was the most beautiful thing he'd ever seen. As his mouse squeaked in approval, Ned whooped and the circus clapped and hugged each other excitedly.

"Two grains, Kitty," laughed Ned. "Here's your two grains!"

***

Word spread like wildfire and those not scouting the perimeter were given the rest of the day off training for a morale boosting celebration. In the morning, he and Kitty would attempt to link with Lucy Beaumont, and the Farseer was quite certain that this time it would work. Until then Ned was under strict instructions to leave his Manual alone, enjoy the party and get a good night's rest. He agreed reluctantly.

By the time Ned left the big top, the entire troupe had gathered outside.

"Well done, Widdlewack!" the Guffstavson brothers chorused.

"You did it, Whatters!"

"Way to go, Ned!"

But it was the Ringmaster's words that meant the most, minimal as they were.

"Not bad, pup. Not bad," he said with a tiny smile and a tip of his hat, before striding off again.

Scraggs outdid himself by enchanting their food. Great roasts of beef and pork floated out of the ovens. Huge plates of crackling and magically crisped potatoes were stacked sky high on all the tables, and all you had to do was hold a cup and say the word and it miraculously filled with whatever you wanted. When the last plateful had been devoured, they lit fires, and sat round them singing and laughing. Ned's hair was ruffled, his cheeks pinched and Alice could not be deterred from licking his face, however hard he tried.

For the first time, Ned felt like he actually belonged in the circus. He had earnt his place amongst them, not by name, but because of what he could do.

"All right, all right, you drivelling buffoons. Let the

poor fellow breathe," said George eventually, lying flat on his back beside Ned having eaten an embarrassing amount of bananas. Ned leaned into him happily, and thought to himself it was like leaning against a large hairy cliff, and surprisingly comfy.

By the end of the night everyone had partaken of some of the feast at least – bar four people. Benissimo, who never celebrated, Rocky who would not leave his wife's side, and Mystero, whose ever-vigilant eyes decided instead to take the opportunity to check the troupe's quarters again while they were empty.

It wasn't long before Ned felt his eyelids droop and decided to make his way to bed. Back at his bunk, he stared at the empty picture frame and the powerless phone by his bed, and thought of his parents, and for the first time since he'd joined the circus, he felt hope.

He forced himself not to look at his Manual and decided to imagine himself a treat of his own. It was going to be harder than a single grain of sand, more complex in form, but at least this time it was just the one. He meticulously envisaged air being drawn into chocolate, its sugar-coated casing, its soft brown insides, how they came together as one. And there it was, the familiar humming. In a ripple of light, the molecules in the air in front of him were drawn together noisily and reformed into a perfect, crunchy, hard-shelled chocolate drop. He plucked it from the air and popped it in his mouth.

"Bleuch!"

Next to him Whiskers squeaked, in what sounded uncannily like mechanical laughter. Ned had never actually tasted slime, but he guessed this came close. He'd created a perfectly brown ball of disgusting goo. He was clearly going to have to work on his flavours, he thought happily and seconds later he drifted off to sleep.

***

Chocolate drops, loving mothers and Engineer fathers were not, however, what he dreamt of.

It started as it always did. A wall of dull, grey fog that turned ever so slowly to smoke. Deep in its oily, acrid shadows, something sinister lurked, waiting.

CHAPTER 25

Something in the Mirror

The Glimmerman loved a good party. He'd eaten an extraordinary amount of crackling and was more than ready for the comfort of his bunk, but Ignatius P Littleton III never went to bed without first checking his beloved mirrors. An ordinary Hall of Mirrors bent your shape, to make you look wide or thin, skewed or straight. The Glimmerman's mirrors took things a little further. When you looked at them, the image in the mirror stayed exactly the same – what changed was the actual person looking. From one mirror to the next, you'd grow a huge belly, or shoot up in height. Some made you older and some a child. He had hand-crafted each one to give just the right effect, walk away and the magic would wear off.

But there was one special mirror that had a different

purpose entirely.

Deidre was a gateway, a portal which could be accessed from anywhere in the world. You simply had to step through another mirror, any kind would do, and you would be magically transported to Deidre – the basis of the Glimmerman's circus act. Obviously there had to be security measures. After activating, the path between the two mirrors would close again. How long it remained open was largely down to the quality of the glass. You also needed light, the slightest glimmer would do, but if Deidre was in complete darkness, the path to her would always be closed. Finally, you needed a key. When made, at least one shard of a gateway mirror was always kept aside, to act as that key. Those trying to cross without one wound up with a bloody nose.

There had never been a breach, at least not until now. Deidre's cover was on the ground and a small lantern burned brightly beside her. Ignatius snatched at the light and blew.

***

The Demon could smell his fear. He could smell his hair, his fingernails, his sweat. To his kind, there was no fouler stench than that of a human. He had often asked himself: why?

Maybe it was their endless capacity to love, an emotion that all Ifrits fear and loathe in equal measure. How he longed to be back in the earth, with the fire and the ash. Back with his own kind's dark and cruel ways. But he was bound to Barbarossa, given as a gift by his one true Master, to do his bidding until he set him free. And the fat one would never set him free. He needed him for his ship's great engine and to do the work that the others wouldn't. Or maybe if he succeeded in this one task for him...

Behind the Ifrit, a row of pitch-black eyes blinked open – his army of destruction. Though vaguely human in size and shape, gor-balins had none of those loathsome human emotions Sar-adin so hated. His were raised from ash and lava, fire and darkness, they were – much like himself – bred for murder.

***

The air in Ned's dream stank of sulphur and burned at his lungs, as it had done so many times before. He staggered through the shadows, lost and afraid. There had been no guiding voice, no hope, no anything. Just a perpetual nothingness of ash and grey. His foot struck a kerb. It was hard and familiar. He was back once more, at Oak Tree Lane, though not the one he knew.

His home was on fire and beyond it street after street raged red and orange. London was ablaze. He kicked at the door to Number 222 and it yawned open.

"Dad! Dad! You've got to get out of here!"

There was no answer. From the sitting room he heard the television, blaring over the flames.

"And the answer is… Edelweiss."

Smoke started to fill the hallway and Ned pulled his T-shirt up to his mouth.

"Dad! Da…?"

Instead of his father, he found a girl. Instantly he knew it was Lucy. She was holding a flower, cradling it in her arms, away from the closing flames. She looked proud and brave.

"Help us," she said, without the smallest hint of fear.

But before he could answer, his knees buckled and his lungs filled with smoke. He closed his eyes to the boiling darkness and waited for the end.

"Get up, Ned! Get up!" called a voice.

"Can't move… the girl, she's gone…"

"Get up, NOW!" shouted his Mystral protector.

Ned opened his eyes to hot stinging fumes, no different to in his dream. George's container was full of smoke, his beloved bookshelves already ablaze.

"What's going on, what's happened?"

"Barbarossa's Demon – Sar-adin – he's come for you. We have to get out of here. Get up! MOVE!"

Ned was up in an instant, had grabbed the short sword Monsieur Couteau had insisted he sleep with, and was bolting for the door, Whiskers following at his heels. But Ned had forgotten his keepsakes. When he turned around, he saw the photo frame by his bed crack and splinter, and beside it his black plastic phone turn to a molten puddle.

"Wait!" he cried, but Mystero, in solid form, grabbed him and shoved him hard in the direction of the door. Just as Ned landed on the grass outside, the walls of the container fell inwards, collapsing to a jumble of timber and flames. The pale-faced shapeshifter had saved his life again.

Smoke and fire were eating their way through the campsite and those that weren't fighting the flames were fighting Sar-adin's gor-balins. The creatures were on a mission of sabotage, incinerating every vehicle in the Circus of Marvels' fleet. Half dressed in pyjamas and dressing gowns, the troupe did their best to counter the attack, but Sar-adin's well-armed assassins struck as only the soulless can – without fear or mercy. It was smoking, burning, chaos.

Ned shoved Whiskers in his pocket as Alice thundered past, trumpeting loudly and in the process of a wild charge, the three emperors riding furiously on her back. Monsieur Couteau and the satyr-headed Tortellini boys were doing a valiant job of protecting the youngest and most defenceless, as wave after wave of black-clad assailants jumped out from the shadows. Ned heard bellowing and the ugly crack of bones breaking in George's hands, and outside the food truck the Guffstavson brothers fought back to back, their anger so all-consuming that they were frying both the gor-balins and the occasional ally. Somewhere in the darkness, Ned heard the roar of two lions and the screeching of a hawk. Finn and his friends were fighting the assassins on their own terms.

Of everyone, however, Rocky was the most fierce. He stood outside the infirmary like a solid wall, cracking the heads of anyone fool enough to go near. No one would ever hurt his Abigail again.

"We have to get you to safety," yelled Mystero over the noise. "I'll not have you taken on my watch again!"

"But... but we have to help!"

"You'll help by getting out of here. Half the convoy's already up in flames – if they take you as planned we'll all go to hell!"

Ned knew he was right. But it felt like déjà vu – the last attack, the last time he'd tried to hide, it had not ended well…

"How do we even get out of here?" Ned asked. "They're everywhere!"

"The same way they got in," said Mystero. "Follow me."

Mystero was leading Ned through the chaos towards the Glimmerman's tent when Ned caught sight of Sar-adin, dressed now in full military garb with a broad scimitar clenched in his hand. Benissimo was holding the line against him, flanked on either side by magic casters foolhardy enough to attempt pushing back the Demon's flames. Sar-adin was positioned at the centre of the campsite like a volcano, eyes glowing with heat. With a wave of his right arm, a wall of fire engulfed a trailer; with a wave of his left, another sprang up at Benissimo's feet.

But the Ringmaster barely flinched. He cracked his whip and it turned itself to water, curling around him like a protective shield. What magic he'd used to stay unhurt was beyond Ned, but without help he would surely burn just as fiercely as his tents and wagons. Ned was pulled away from the vision by a yanking on his arm.

"He won't be able to hold the beast for long, Ned, we have to go, NOW!" yelled Mystero again.

"We can't leave him like that."

"They're *his* orders, not mine!"

"I don't care, I'm not going!"

Just then there was a scream from inside the Glimmerman's tent. It was Kitty.

CHAPTER 26

Mr Sar-adin

Gor-balins do not know fear and yet the incantation Kitty had screamed had clearly taught them it.

"Nasty little gobs were waiting for you," said Kitty brightly as Ned and Mystero ran over to find her in the doorway of the Glimmerman's tent wearing a fluffy pink and white Hello Kitty dressing gown.

Three more gor-balins came out of the shadows of the tent towards them. Though roughly the size of an ordinary human, their eyes were lifeless and black. Their ears and noses were sharp and crooked, and their skin a mottled grey, with veins of pitch-black ash and lips the colour of coal. They opened their mouths in unison and bright red embers poured from their lips. Whatever burned in their chests in place of hearts stank of sulphur and soot. Two of them ran at the Farseer, their sword arms poised to strike.

"*Famil-ra-sa*," she whispered.

And from out of her pink sleeves poured Frimshaw, Hookscarp, Orazal and Groir. The demure little creatures Ned had seen at the bonding were gone. Now they glowed a hot scarlet and their faces were twisted with anger. Frimshaw and Hookscarp leapt at one gor-balin, and in an instant had reached into its mouth and pulled out the fire that burned in its chest. In its final smoky breath, the gor-balin opened its lips and hissed like a steam engine, while its lifeless body shrivelled to ash. Orazal and Groir dealt with the other in the same way, which left only the third.

The gor-balin was closing in on Ned at a pace. Mystero – in his half-man, half-mist state – was braced, and Ned held his sword before him, trying for all he was worth to channel everything the French Master at Arms had drilled into him – when the gor-balin suddenly stopped dead. Its shadow, however, did not. The blackness beneath the assassin grew larger and began to pulse as two great arms reared out of its edges and pulled something else up and out of the ground. The gor-balin dropped its sword. Even a creature without a soul knows its end. The shadow was Gorrn. It grew upwards violently, till it had completely engulfed the gor-balin, before closing up around it like the mouth of a whale and swallowing him down into the ground.

"Wow, that was gross," said Ned in disbelief.

"Yes, I think it was a little," agreed Kitty, while looking rather pleased.

From somewhere beneath their feet, Ned could have sworn he heard a belch.

***

Across the grounds, the battle was starting to even. Most of the troupe had now given up their attempts at dousing the flames. With their homes lost, there was little to do but fight. Sar-adin's assassins were being beaten further and further back. All, that was, except for Sar-adin himself.

The Ifrit fumed and raged more fiercely than ever, like an animal being forced back into its cage. Except that Sar-adin was fiercer than any animal.

Benissimo ordered Scraggs to turn one of the firetruck's hoses on him, with no effect, and every bolt or bullet launched in his direction was a spit of ash by the time it struck.

"You've got to talk some sense into Ned," said Mystero

to Kitty. "He's refusing to escape through the mirrors, and the Demon won't stop until he has you both, Kitty, not now the boy's come into his powers."

Kitty looked Ned up and down.

"We're supposed to run away together, you and I, but I think it's about time you got to make your own decisions, dearie."

"I'm tired of running, Kitty. Besides, they need us."

"Oh for goodness' sake," muttered the Mystral.

"And we would be missing all the fun, now, wouldn't we, my little cracker-jack?" agreed the Farseer with a smile. She took Ned's hand and marched him through the raging battle to the centre of the encampment, where Benissimo stood, head to head with the Ifrit.

Maybe the letter was right. Maybe his mum really had put the bravery he needed inside of him. Now facing the Demon, he hoped that he would find it before his legs buckled.

"Why don't you leave my family alone and pick on someone your own size?" shrilled Kitty.

The sight of an old lady scolding a fire-Demon would have been funny, had it not been real. Benissimo spun to face Kitty, then Ned, with a look of absolute fury.

"You two are NOT supposed to be here! And you're

DEFINITELY not supposed to be drawing his attention to you!"

"Oh do stop bleating, you old goat. You can't possibly beat him without us." As she spoke, the witch put a hand on the Ringmaster's shoulder and started to glow. It was gentle at first, but her light quickly grew brighter and brighter till Sar-adin winced with pain. The Ifrit shook for a moment, before steadying himself and launching a fireball directly at the Farseer. She stood her ground as a protective shield of energy bubbled in front of her.

"Your light will not harm me, witch. Give me the boy," roared the Ifrit stubbornly.

"I'll do no such thing," said Kitty, her face still locked in concentration as Benissimo braced to support her. "You know, Ned, a little help would be nice. After all, it's you he wants."

"Help, err, OK, and umm... how exactly would I be doing that?"

Ned was already racking his brains, trying to recall a helpful page from his Manual – something he could create that might vanquish this fiery Demon...

"Well, you can clearly make sand, dearie, so I'm fairly certain you could knock up a little rain. On the count of three..."

It didn't seem very imaginative; what about a defensive wall or even a weapon? But even though the hoses were having no impact on Sar-adin, Ned knew better than to question Kitty, wise, brave and potty as she was.

He shut his eyes tight, blocking out everything around him and cast his mind to the skies. It would be easier than making sand, he thought, as he looked up at the sky. The elements had already done half the work for him.

"*One*."

High up above the campsite, he focused on the clouds. He could use them, use their water vapour to form his rain. He willed their atoms closer together, saw the strands of vapour compressing to his will and the ring hummed at his finger obediently.

"*Two*."

It was enough to See the droplets form – gravity took care of the rest and they plummeted towards the Ifrit.

"*Three*," said Kitty.

In the split second it had taken for Ned's mind to both power and guide his Engine, Kitty had focused all of her strength. She stood, like a white beacon to Sar-adin's darkening fury, and unleashed her attack in a shockwave of pure light. It hit the Ifrit at the precise moment that Ned's first raindrop landed on his head. To Demons who are born in the ground, fresh falling water from the skies is like acid, especially when already weakened by the light of a Farseer.

"Roarghhhhh!"

Ned closed his eyes and concentrated, till every muscle in his face and neck felt like it was going to break. A great deluge of water poured down on the Ifrit, the rain now coming so thick and fast it forced Sar-adin to his knees. As the droplets cut at him, steam poured from each new incision. He arched his back and roared with anger, his disguise breaking away, falling in boiling chunks to the ground. Bit by bit his human form dissolved, till the real monster beneath rose up for a final stand. The horned monstrosity became a crumbling vision of darkness and hate.

"This is not over, witch!" he half-bellowed, half-rasped, any semblance of humanity now gone from his voice.

The Ifrit burst into flames and launched himself at the Farseer in a last act of blazing violence. Still drained from her outburst, Kitty's shield faltered. In the beat of a second, Ned tried to conjure up a barrier of his own making, his ring finger buzzing noisily. The air between the Demon and Farseer crackled with strands of Ned's hastily woven ice. If he'd had more experience, or time, they might have held. But Sar-adin splintered his creation into broken shards and Kitty was flung to the ground. When the smoke cleared, only Kitty lay there, alone in the mud. Sar-adin and his embers were nowhere to be seen.

CHAPTER 27

Edelweiss

"**O**h, do stop fussing, you big baboon..."

Even at her weakest, Kitty was always Kitty. Though Ned's shield had not held up to Sar-adin's strike, it seemed it had blocked the Demon's blow enough to keep Kitty from any fatal harm. But under her bluff exterior Ned could tell, as George's long arms carried her off to the infirmary, that she was badly wounded.

The troupe worked on until sunrise, dousing the last of the flames and salvaging what little they could. After daybreak, Benissimo gathered everyone by the food truck for breakfast, and an open ear.

"Today is a black day. Barba's struck as we knew he would, and though we still have the boy, our Kitty, our compass, lies broken in her bunk. You've all paid a price too – your homes, your possessions – and as always without my asking."

He paced up and down the tables, whip twisting menacingly, looking each of them in the eye.

"You're the best troupe I've ever worked with, but there's a stench amongst you, a dark and ugly growth. One or more of you gave that Demon the mirror-key and told him when best to attack, that much we know. The Tinker's machines can't find you and neither could our Kitty, but by blood and thunder, I'll sniff you out whoever you are and, when I do, you'll know *my* anger and you'll know *your* fear."

Not for the first time, Ned was happy that the enigma that was Benissimo was on his side and not the other.

"You tell 'em boss!"

"For Kitty, for Kitty!" they cheered.

Mugs and plates were banged together and those that could got up and clapped. Only Mystero sat silently, watching for a chink, Ned thought. A chink in the spy's armour that would let him be found. But the spy was cunning and would not be roused.

Benissimo had not wanted a celebration the night before; his number two had convinced him that Ned and the troupe needed it. But anything that took them away from their goal was wasted time to the Ringmaster. With that in mind, he marched an exhausted Ned and Mystero over to Kitty's flame-scorched bus as soon as he was done with his speeches.

"I'll have to check the Tinker's lab now," said an ash-stained Mystero as Ned hurried beside him. "Like it or not, he has our only air-modulator. If messages are getting out, there's every chance that's how they're doing it."

Beinissimo looked doubtful.

"No one is above suspicion, Bene, not after last night."

The Ringmaster's face darkened. "Fine, do what you have to," he said, and Mystero misted away.

The idea that the Tinker was under any kind of suspicion seemed absurd to Ned. Though it was no more outrageous than suspecting George. The way Mystero had been behaving lately, Ned wouldn't have been surprised if he'd turned over his own quarters to try and oust the culprit.

In the infirmary they found the Farseer puffed up on a mountain of Hello Kitty pillows, with George tending to her wounds. His huge fingers were surprisingly dexterous.

"Damn your stubborn kindness, Kit-Kat," said Benissimo, for once betraying a sliver of emotion, in a now much-softened face.

"Yes, yes, you can thank me later," pouted Kitty. "Now where's my little sugar-plum?" she added, peering past the Ringmaster towards Ned.

"Hello, Kitty, how are you feeling?" asked Ned.

"Never better, dearie."

For some reason her brave act was making Ned feel even more responsible.

"I'm so sorry, if we'd just gone when Miz said…"

"…Then everyone else would most probably be dead, dear. You did very well, no apology needed! Besides, I'm fine, though I do have the most ferocious craving for a doughnut."

At that, Ned couldn't help but smile.

"Now, you and I have some unfinished business, my little seedling. Let's find ourselves that girl, shall we?"

"Kitty needs rest, Bene, surely this can wait till she's back on her feet?" said the great ape beside her.

"There'll be time for rest, George, when we fix what needs fixing," insisted Benissimo coldly.

Despite his momentary softening and his almost fatherly way of treating the Farseer, Ned wondered if Benissimo ever put the people he was trying to protect before his mission to save them.

Kitty took Ned's hand in her own and explained what

they were about to do.

"My powers work through empathy, Ned. I can sense a person's emotions, in the past, present or future, but the way my visions form is abstract. I can't pinpoint Lucy or your mother. I can sense them, but not where they are. We've searched both sides of the Veil, so has Barbarossa."

Kitty paused and gave him an encouraging smile. "But you're ready now, dear. Take everything you've learnt, that concentration, that harnessing of pure will and *find her*. If the connection is strong enough, you'll be able to see where she is, not just feel it. Look for any clue, anything at all that might tell us where she is. I'll do what I can to help."

Ned was jealous of the time Lucy had had with his mother, of what she'd always known. But without her he would never see either of his parents again, and the world as he knew it would be lost. There was no choice, only the lingering fear that he might not be up to the task.

Kitty closed her eyes and tightened her grip on his hand.

He felt his thoughts soften and blur into one. But instead of Kitty scanning him, it was like she was opening a doorway into her own thoughts. The hopes and fears, loves and hates of… everyone.

"Whoa…"

As Ned was battered by a barrage of emotions coming from countless creatures and people, he gained a new-found respect for the Circus of Marvels' Farseer. No wonder she was a little unhinged.

"Exactly," said Kitty, though Ned hadn't actually spoken out loud. "Now," she continued, "concentrate, Neddles, find her in amongst this mess and we'll see what we can see."

Ned focused, as hard as he could. But the noise in his head was overwhelming. The chattering of a thousand voices, with a thousand dreams, and a thousand, thousand nightmares. His stomach started to turn.

"Kitty…"

She squeezed his hand hard. Despite her frail condition, she held on to him like a steel trap.

Ned fought, he forced himself deeper into his own thoughts. Somewhere in his mind's eye he saw a light, different from the others, form and enlarge until it filled his vision completely.

"Just a little longer, dearie, and… THERE!" yelled a triumphant Kitty.

Ned was seeing what the old witch was feeling,

and together they were peering into the mind of Lucy Beaumont. He had the extraordinary sensation of looking through somebody else's eyes. Looking out of a window at a beautiful valley. He felt a longing for adventure, a longing for escape. He felt... he felt like a girl.

"Eeuuw, this is horrible!"

His eyes blinked, he had such pretty eyelashes... wait, why did he just think that? He felt a tug of war happening between himself and... himself.

"Kitty? What's happening?"

"By my useless old eyes... she can see you! You're like mirrors. I've never seen a connection this strong... never."

Kitty sounded genuinely surprised, and people who saw the future were *never* genuinely surprised.

"Keep your eyes closed, whatever you do. If she sees back into this room it will probably frighten the life out of her."

A second voice spoke to him, from somewhere far away and from just inside his head. It was Lucy Beaumont.

"Hello? Is it you? What are you doing? Look, this is really weird, you shouldn't be in here, not like this!"

His, or rather her head, started to shake violently.

"Quickly, Ned, find something, find a clue, anything!"

squawked Kitty. "We're going to lose her!"

Ned looked round quickly, there was something on her windowsill that seemed to matter. A moment later he was back on the bus with Kitty and the others.

"Go on boy, spit it out!" ordered Benissimo. "Where is she?"

"I'm not sure, but I saw a… flower…" said Ned, suddenly feeling sheepish. "Does that, err, help?"

There was a long disappointed silence. Whiskers, who'd barely left Ned's pocket since Sar-adin's attack, gave him a comforting nip and George patted him on the back, nearly knocking him over.

"You tried, Ned – that's what counts," he rumbled.

The Ringmaster nodded curtly. "Like I said, pup, who and what you are – or are not – is not your fault. You didn't ask for any of this."

For once, the Ringmaster was not trying to be unkind. His words simply spilled out of him. Ned's disappointment, on the other hand, was all-consuming.

We have a lifetime of love to catch up on, but only the slimmest chance to live it.

Was his mother right? Would he ever get to meet her? Would he ever see his dad again, glued to his screwdriver and his TV…? And that was when it hit Ned. His dream, on his birthday, and again last night, when he'd walked into the house… There'd been a game show on the telly, the answer had been the same both times. It was the name of a flower. And then there was the girl; she'd been carrying something…

"Wait! The flower. It does matter. I saw it last night in a dream. And Lucy had it in her hands when we bonded, and on her windowsill … I think it might be called an… Edelweiss? It means something, it has to…"

George grunted thoughtfully. Somewhere in the great mountain of his skull, a light had been lit.

"Stay right where you are." Suddenly the ape dropped to all fours and pounded away. The caravan had barely stopped shaking from his abrupt departure when he reappeared with two burnt tomes and his favourite spectacles. He slammed the books down on the table in a great cloud of ash and started flipping through their ruined pages.

"Luckily for you lot, I'm something of an expert in several fields, but none more so than the rare and 'unfound'. *The Botanicus Maximus*," he said, thumbing the index. "A fascinating read, what's left of it. Let's hope the page we need has survived…"

The others closed in around him.

"Page three hundred and ninety-seven. The *Leontopodium Alpinum*, or as Ned so rightly put it, the Edelweiss. There she is…"

And there, in pen and ink, was Ned's, or rather Lucy's, flower.

Sensing Benissimo's impatience from the writhing coils of his whip, George quickly read on.

"Now let me see here, blah, blah, blah, prefers rocky, blah, blah, ah yes. The Edelweiss is a protected species… in Switzerland. Switzerland! Of course! Well, that explains it…"

"Explains what?" asked Ned, confused.

"Why Kitty could never locate even Ned's mother…"

"Oh, George, you are so very clever for a monkey," teased Kitty.

"I'm no monkey!" retorted George merrily. "You see, in Switzerland lies one of the few known places across the globe, five in all, I believe, that lie on neither one side of the Veil nor the other, but, as it were, right down the middle. The place in Switzerland I'm thinking of is a long-forgotten convent in the Val Lumnezia, or 'Valley of Light', which, according to this entry," said George, excitedly tapping the page, "was famed for its abundance of Edelweiss! Centuries ago a sect of nuns known as the

Order used St Clotilde's to smuggle the weak and weary across the Veil, one way or the other. At one time, they were powerful, with strong connections to both sides. It was thought they'd been disbanded, under orders from Rome. It would appear that the Order had different ideas. It was a safe house then, and I've no doubt it's a safe house now. I'll wager a bet – the Order have her. They've been hiding her since the beginning. Well done, Ned – you've found your Medic!"

***

The circus's battered campsite was whipped into action as its only two remaining airships untouched by Sar-adin's attack were readied.

"We'll need somewhere to resupply after St Clotilde's. Somewhere nearby and off the radar, *anyone's* radar. Miz?" Benissimo twirled the end of his moustache thoughtfully as he spoke.

"Well, there is one place I can think of, but you won't like it… Theron's Keep."

Benissimo's face darkened.

"Not *the* Theron. Theron Wormroot? A fairy's motives are rarely understood, Miz, even by themselves, and if

I remember it rightly, Theron's in the situation he's in because he's greedy and can't be trusted."

"It's his greed I'm banking on. Nothing is more compliant than a well-paid crook."

"Risky but true. And you're sure there's nowhere else?"

"Not nearby, old friend, and not if we want to stay hidden."

Despite his protests, Mystero was ordered to stay with the rest of the troupe and lead them to Theron's Keep. It would be up to him to whip the Circus of Marvels back into shape, besides which he was the only man, or Mystral, that Benissimo trusted to watch for spies.

The Ringmaster's final instructions were for the Tinker. Firstly, he was to send a message via his air-modulator to Madame Oublier. The message was simple – *Send Jenny*. She would know what it meant, he said. This was followed by some other, quietly mumbled instructions that Ned was not party to, about which the two disagreed for some time, the minutian grumbling that it "couldn't be done" before agreeing to have a go. Whiskers was also left with the Tinker, on some kind of surveillance operation. Neither Ned nor rodent were happy about this, but the Ringmaster was adamant.

After a hurried goodbye to Kitty they assembled outside. Their sortie consisted of the troupe's finest – Benissimo, George, Monsieur Couteau and the Tortellini boys. Even Rocky emerged from his vigil over Abigail to join them. If there was to be any opportunity for payback, the Russian troll wanted in on the action.

Ned turned down Couteau's offer of another sword. Engineers before him had always imagined their own weapons with the help of their rings and, ready or not, Ned had decided he would do the same. Besides, he was useless with a blade and he knew it. As the airship took to the skies, Ned sat alone on deck a while, trying to study his Manual, but he couldn't concentrate. He knew he had barely scraped the surface of what he and his ring could do, and he still had no idea how they were going to locate the all-important Source. Kitty had told him to leave that problem to her for now. But he just couldn't study any more. The dizzyingly complex notes and diagrams in front of him had lost their form. They'd become curves and dashes of meaningless ink, compared to the reality of being about to see his mother. Would she remember him? Would she care? He rubbed at his face, trying to get rid of the night's ash, and attempted to straighten his hair.

"I wouldn't worry about all that, old chap. She's been waiting to see you since before you can remember…" said George, swinging down from the rigging above.

"You… you think she'll be happy to see me?"

"Happy? Good lord, Ned, you're about to get the hug of a lifetime.

CHAPTER 28

St Clotilde's

The convent of St Clotilde had had the good fortune of remaining hidden for most of its many years. The few children who had come across it, from either side of the Veil, shared one thing in common – a need of protection. It was immaculately clean, full of laughter, and a safe cocoon from the outside world.

When Olivia Armstrong had arrived, she'd been carrying a small bundle in her rain-soaked arms. The bundle was Lucy Beaumont, recently orphaned for the sought-after gift that she shared with both her mother and grandfather before her. Olivia would not leave the child unguarded and was granted permission to stay. An unprecedented decision, in view of her background as an operative of the Twelve.

It was here that Lucy Beaumont had spent her life.

Only Sister Clementine was ever allowed out, and she had been 'reassigned' without warning. Lucy missed Sister Clementine's stories of the world beyond her window and longed to see it with her own two eyes; a longing that the Mother Superior had promised would one day be answered.

"I've told you what you are. The world will come knocking, Lucy, you might not be so pleased to see it when it does."

***

From the air, the Val Lumnezia looked to be a picture of tranquillity. Two of the Tortellinis had kept a constant vigil for any sign of a tail and they were quite certain that no one had followed them. The troupe were relieved as the airship descended into a lush meadow, surrounded by flower-peppered hills. Bees buzzed around them noisily and overweight goats grazed happily on the grass.

Ned watched with amusement as a shiny red apple flew off the ground and floated up to the branches of a gnarled apple tree. As Ned had come to learn, things were rarely as they seemed when sitting on the Veil's borders.

The grey stone walls of St Clotilde's were much smaller than Ned had imagined, sitting undisturbed as they did on the hillside, looking down on the rest of the valley.

Walking up the hill towards the convent, they soon realised that the building they'd assumed was St. Clothilde's was in fact only its gatehouse. The rest of its structure lay behind it, which they couldn't see from their approach.

As they passed through the gatehouse and crossed into the Veil, Ned's ears started to hum, with muffled, stretched-out sounds too distorted by the Veil's magic to make out.

"Quiet," hissed Benissimo. Monsieur Couteau drew his sword.

As they came closer, the sounds grew louder and painfully clear. Low, lumbering groans soon rose till their pitch rested on a high, painful scream. It was a woman's, and one of many. The world had indeed come knocking for Lucy, using fists and swords and muskets.

Ned tried to register the horror before him.

In the central courtyard a battle raged between the Sisters of St. Clotilde's and a large group of

Gor-balins. Their young wards were running from the fight, with a wall of the Sisters' rapiers to cover their exit. Pools of blood framed several of the children's valiant protectors who had already fallen to the assailants' onslaught.

But it was not the attacking creatures' violence that made Ned's stomach turn so much as the expressions of joy on their pointed, sallow faces.

"Mud-gobs," muttered one of the Tortellinis.

These variants of Gor-balin were thick-necked and heavy, bred as blunt instruments for the breaking of bones – with skin like tree bark and hair a mess of tattered roots. They did not know what the Medic looked like and Ned could only assume from the multitude of fleeing children that they had been ordered to kill… all of them.

"Mum…" he breathed. His eyes fixed on the fresh corpses strewn across the courtyard's floor.

"Guns 'n daggers," spat Benissimo, his whip already in hand.

There were rules amongst the fighting kind. No matter how bitter the battle, children should never be harmed, and the church, whatever its creed, was sacred ground.

"That fire in your belly, boy, does it still burn?" roared the Ringmaster.

"Yes!" Ned exclaimed.

"Then I suggest you use it! Strike swift 'n' hard boys!"

And with a furious bellow, Benissimo and his men charged. Somewhere, amongst the smoke and the screams, was Ned's mother. His head, hands and heart filled with a rush of furious fire and for the briefest moment, he forgot that he was just a boy.

They hit the unsuspecting marauders hard. Rocky's Abigail was still in a coma and the great mountain became a running juggernaut of stony vengeance. Benissimo turned his whip to a coil of flames, before hurling three stone runes at a cluster of assailants. When the runes' magic was spent, the cluster had turned to a pile of salt. Meanwhile the half-satyr Tortellinis had vaulted over the gor-balins' heads and landed by the nuns' sides, weapons already raised. Monsieur Couteau turned one of the Darkling captains into a walking pin-cushion. From its wounds poured a gurgling mess of tree sap and dirt. George stayed loyally by Ned's side, cracking heads together as he lumbered past.

Not all of the marauders had been taken unawares.

At the centre of the courtyard stood the Darklings' 'heavy weapon' – a thick-skulled swamp ogre. Green, vast and angry, it was covered in slimy, lizard-like skin, with eyes to match, and it had set its sharp-toothed sights on Ned. It was grinning wildly, while stroking the edge of a large scimitar.

Ned thought fast – he was determined to tackle this like a true Engineer. What would take out the beast's weapon most effectively? One of the descriptions in his Manual came to mind. It was a design for one of many listed weapons, but less complicated than the others. Two weighty iron disks on top of one another, with serrated edges, and a single bolt to join them – a 'spindisk'. Perfect for breaking the ogre's blade. The hard part would be Telling them to move, counterclockwise to one another, before launching them at the ogre. As rudimentary a weapon as the manual said it was, it would still be stretching Ned's new skill-set considerably.

The ogre roared and George paced forwards, beating his chest in an attempt to draw attention from Ned.

Ned stilled his mind – blocking out the sounds of both ape and ogre – and focused on the cobblestone paving at his feet. Stone to metal, their density would work, they were a good fit; he just had to will the atoms to move on his command. He saw the surface of the stone in his mind as if it were his own skin. He probed its very substance, willing it to reconfigure, and immediately felt it begin to harden and shimmer with the reflectiveness of metal. His ring fired, its energy shooting through his body, and two cobblestones came loose from the ground, changing before him. He Saw their edges sharpen, and it happened. For the bolt, he chose a shard of brick from one of the convent's shattered walls and altered it in the same way. When he tried to meld the pieces, for a second the vision faltered as he struggled with the details. But his mind knew what to do, after all those years of building sets with his dad, it pushed and pulled the pieces together until finally there was an angry spark of energy, and the spindisk hung in the air before him. His calculations were off, it was smaller than he'd intended, but it would have to do.

Ned had only dabbled with Feeling, but knew that the more emotion you put into the Amplification, the more violent the reaction. As he thought of his mother, the spindisk glowed a fiery red. He channelled his worry and rage into the weapon's moving parts and the spindisk flew angrily at its target.

"Argh!"

Ned was shocked, as much by the ferocity of his projectile as that the creature was still standing. The ogre had lost three teeth and its lips were bleeding badly, but it still managed to grin as it barrelled towards him, scimitar untouched and ready to hurt. His Feeling had been too raw, and the disk had flown wider than Ned intended. But the ogre soon stopped when the black mound of furred muscle that was George came smashing into it. A second later and George the Mighty had it pinned to the ground, with one of his great feet at the creature's throat. As it struggled beneath him, the ape became a frightening blur of strength, suddenly yanking the ogre aloft, swinging it about his head, before launching it into the air. The flailing beast flew over the convent wall and out of sight. Ned had never seen anything like it.

"I know you're on my side, George, but sometimes you *really* scare me."

But before the ape could answer, there was a sudden shriek of loud gunfire from a corridor that opened to their right, followed by screaming. And a pair of unwelcome newcomers.

The absurdly tall American, Slim, walked into view like a spider looking for a fly, and to his side, the stocky ball of muscle that was Cannonball, his teeth chattering with excitement.

"Well ain't it our lucky day?" grinned Cannonball.

Ned braced himself. If Cannonball was half as quick as he'd been in Shalazaar he'd have little time to use his ring.

"Now we get to kill the girl and take the boy. The boss is gonna be reeeal happy," agreed Slim.

But the ever-vigilant Ringmaster had spotted the threat.

"George, get him to his mother, and Lucy, quickly now!" ordered Benissimo.

Monsieur Couteau and Rocky stepped in to aid their escape, cutting off the American and his dwarven sidekick.

"Ready fer a lil dance, Frenchie?" asked Slim.

"*En garde*, theen man."

The long-elf's arms blurred with gunfire as Cannonball made ready to charge. But bullets were just like any number of projectiles the Master at Arms had sparred with in his shows, and he blocked each and every one, with the angry roar of metal on metal.

Beside them, Cannonball tensed before firing himself across the courtyard. The charge downed three of the Tortellinis and several nuns, and he was closing in on a fleeing Ned and George when a large Russian fist swung out to greet him.

"Niet niet, little tank," boomed Rocky.

CRACK!

The fist connected and Rocky's forearm broke. In seconds Ned and George were speeding through the convent's corridors searching for his mum, behind them the fury of ricocheting bullets.

"Don't worry about them, old chap, Couteau and Slim have an old score to settle and a dwarven berserker is no match for a vengeful mountain troll."

But one floor up, Ned looked down at the courtyard to see a broken-armed Rocky and a group of nuns shielding three of their wards, cornered by a muddy wave of gor-balins, and Slim poised to shoot with a freshly loaded revolver. It was pointed at the Ringmaster, who was too lost in his own battle with another gor-balin to notice.

Even as Ned screamed his warning, there was a loud BANG.

He watched in horror as Benissimo fell to the floor.

He lay unmoving. To Ned's amazement, Monsieur Couteau and Rocky fought on as if nothing had happened. Only a moment later, Ned could see why. Though the bullet had made a large hole in his military jacket, right where his heart should be, Benissimo's eyes suddenly opened. He gasped for air, before quickly hopping back to his feet and continuing the fight. Of all the things Ned had imagined the Ringmaster to be, this was the eeriest. He wasn't a monster or one of the fair-folk – he was something else entirely.

"Quickly Ned, we have to find them before the gobs!"

George was up ahead, filling the stone corridors with his fast moving bulk. Ned chased after him, his mind suddenly screaming with worry. If they were too late, his mum or Lucy could already be dead. Up the final flight of stairs, they came to another group of heavily armed nuns.

"You'll not pass us by!" yelled one of the women. "Come along Sisters, send them back to hell!"

And with that, a seemingly meek and bespectacled Sister, in her sensible shoes and perfectly turned-out habit, prepared to lead the charge.

"Wait! Wait, we're not with them. We're looking for

someone. Olivia, Olivia Armstrong? Do you know her? Is she here?" pleaded Ned.

The Sister froze.

"It can't be… oh dear lord, you must be Ned. Be quick child, the Mother Superior needs you."

CHAPTER 29

Mother's Day

Upon the convent's flat roof, they saw a group of huddled children from both sides of the Veil. One was partly elven and taller than the others, another was a full-blown satyr, and two more had the pearlescent skin and fire-red eyes of the duarliis, an uncommon variant of sand-nymph even behind the Veil. The rest were entirely human-looking, but they were all wielding daggers. Rather than seeming afraid, they were steely-faced, guarding the bell tower's entrance and whoever was inside. In front of the children, stood the protective figure of their Mother Superior.

She had raven-black hair, a beautiful face and even managed to make her robes look glamorous. She didn't really seem to fit in her convent surroundings, and she most certainly didn't fit back in Grittlesby. The thought of her at home on the sofa, eating a microwave chicken korma and watching *This One's Easy*, made about as much sense as a bottle of crisps. The Mother Superior – Olivia Armstrong – was definitely above average. Ned felt his nerves stiffen. He could be skewered on the end of a gor-balin sword at any minute but the only thing worrying him now was talking to a nun.

She was in the process of dispatching a gor-balin who had climbed up the convent's walls, when she saw them approaching.

"George?" she asked softly.

"Yes, Livvy, in the flesh."

Seeing his chance, the gnarly-faced-gor-balin lunged at her back. The Mother Superior remained rooted to the spot, her wrist however did not. With the slightest of flicks it twisted behind her and the blade sliced the Darkling's nose. The agonised creature grabbed at the wound before falling back over the edge of the roof screaming. With her assailant taken care of, Ned's mum continued staring. At Ned. Her lower lip started to tremble, and her eyes glistened with the welling of tears. Then she did the most unexpected thing, she started to straighten out her hair.

"I, I wasn't expecting you…"

It turned out that Ned's mother was just as nervous as Ned.

"M-Mum?"

Her sword dropped with a clang. "…Is it really you?"

Ned couldn't speak as his mum pulled him into a long-awaited hug.

For a moment, he was oblivious to the screams coming up from the stairwell. One of the gor-balins had made it past the Sisters' blockade, only to be hammered by George's fist.

"Do you mind? They are trying to have a reunion!" he snarled.

But the gor-balin at his feet was completely unconscious.

"Oh Ned, let me look at you," Olivia said, her face now clammy with tears. "You're everything I hoped you'd be."

She could not have said anything kinder.

"I… I, um…"

"What about your dad – where is he?"

"Well… um."

Behind them, there was a loud clash of ape against steel.

"Ned, dear, I need to protect the children. We'll talk when this is over."

"Um… I…"

Ned had lived without a mother for twelve years. Finally reunited, he'd managed to say "Mum", "I", "well" and "um". It had been the best talk he'd ever had, ever. He watched like a spectator in his own dream as his mum spun away, effortlessly disarming a gor-balin with another flick of her wrist. His new-found mother was beautiful, brave and wonderfully weird. Ned didn't want to be normal any more. Being the Engineer son of Terrence and Olivia Armstrong would do just fine.

But his daydream was cruelly interrupted by an unpleasant stench and a shock of white make-up. The Sisters' blockade below had now completely fallen and Ned and his companions were joined on the rooftop by Eanie, Meanie and Mo with a full squad of murderous mud-gobs.

"Get behind us, old chap, this might get a tad ugly," bellowed George, loping in front of him and the other wards. He beat his great chest with his fists angrily as Ned backed behind him and his mum.

When Mo saw Ned he stared at him like a man who'd spotted a long-lost friend, either that or a favourite dish he hadn't eaten for some time.

"Ooh, Jossy boy yum yum. Mo supa hoppy!"

Looking at the gathering before him, Ned realised

that they were now vastly outnumbered, both above and below. Down in the courtyard, Benissimo and his men were fighting as a wall of steel and snapping whip. But even they would fall to Barbarossa's numbers at this rate – the flow of gor-balins into the convent still seemed unending.

In front of Ned, George and his mum did their best to hold back the clowns' forces, George's fists swinging wildly, the Mother Superior's sword lashing with deadly precision. But clowns rarely take the most dangerous route to their targets, and as Meanie led another push towards the belltower, Mo seized the moment and found a gap that landed him squarely beside Ned.

"Jossy boy smush, bones makie cricka crack."

Ned tried to think of something. But panic does a strange thing to the mind. His brain whirred, his ring crackled and the air around him hissed, but nothing came. All he could do was look on in horror as the clown's club was raised, sack at the ready, to carry him away once he was rendered unconscious. One of the other children yelled a warning.

"Ned!" screamed his mum.

She turned quickly, launching a flurry of blows at the clown's stomach. But it was the wrong tool for the wrong job. Mo's 'gift', though simple, was highly effective. He had an impenetrable belly. And with her back turned, Ned's mother had no way of seeing the threat behind her. Ned had read about Hidden-made gas muskets in one of George's books. Almost completely silent, they were only used by assassins or cowards. Eanie the clown was both. There was a low hiss and Olivia Armstrong arched her back. She looked at Ned, smiled sweetly and fell to the floor. Blood trickled down the side of her mouth and her eyes flickered with pain.

"Ned darling, Lucy… must save Lucy." She raised her hand to stroke his face, before slipping into unconsciousness.

Ned felt all the light and laughter being sucked out of him. Barbarossa's hand had struck too great a blow. Somewhere deep in his soul, something snapped. Something that the clowns and gor-balins at St Clotilde's would regret having broken.

"NOOOOOOOOO!"

His cry was not entirely human, more like that of a wounded animal. Ned's mind raced with rage and with hatred. A hatred so dark and unrelenting that it burned inside his belly. He wanted to smash everything, to break the world in half, to tear every stone from the convent's rooftops and bring them down on the clowns' heads. Darkness enveloped him and the darkness had a voice.

"Yesssssss."

His insides vibrated with Feeling and the Amplification-Engine did as it was told. It started with the little things at first. As the humming at his finger grew, screws in the walls nearby unscrewed, mortar came undone and slate tiles lifted. The Engineer in Ned was trying to unmake the convent and what he'd seen, piece by meticulous piece, till his anger became too strong and a shockwave poured from his head and hand in a great crackling blast of pain. Seeing, Telling… and FEELING.

Concrete turned to liquid, bricks burned, wood froze. With the deafening rumble of shearing and breaking, a wave of moving stone that had once been the convent's roof flew at the clowns and their gor-balin soldiers, turning itself as it did so to bubbling metal and daggers of ice. Below them, windows shattered and concrete tore. Slim's revolvers burned in his hands and the still slumbering Cannonball was covered in a heap of broken flagstones and twisting metal. The very fabric of the convent was becoming undone, a mess of bending, bursting atoms and unrelenting rage. There was no order to the chaos, no blueprint or plan. Ned's anger moved like a living thing, picking out its targets while leaving Ned's allies and the residents of St Clotilde's unharmed.

In minutes, the battle had been won, and all it had taken was a broken-hearted boy to do the winning. He lay in a curled ball on the remains of the convent's rooftop.

"Ned, dear boy, it's me, it's George, are you OK? Ned? Ned!"

But Ned was somewhere else. His hand and heart were alive with pain. His vision was blurred, his ears were ringing and his belly was a boiling mess of knots.

"The Medic," he slurred eventually. Ned pushed himself back up, refusing his gorilla friend's help, and did as his mother had asked. He went in search of Lucy.

As he staggered towards them, the stunned children of St Clotilde's parted in silence. He fell through the bell tower's door and dragged himself up the narrow stairs. When he reached the top, his legs locked as the cold metal of a dagger connected with his throat, its pin-sharp tip pushing into his skin. The fingers on the blade handle smelt of soap and one of them was wearing a ring. A ring very much like his own.

"Who are you?" asked a girl's voice.

"I'm Ned. I'm… the Engineer."

The dagger at his throat was lowered. Ned's usurper,

the girl who'd lived half his childhood, had a short bob of blonde hair, piercing blue eyes and a proud, pretty face. She looked exactly as she had in his dream. On a chain round her neck she wore a second ring – the one her mother must have once worn. And suddenly she was hard to dislike.

Whatever she was feeling, Lucy Beaumont was obviously fiercely brave. Her only show of sorrow was a single hot tear rolling down her cheek.

"You took your time," she said, pausing to look him up and down. "I thought you'd be bigger."

CHAPTER 30

Farewell

His body felt brittle and empty, and his hand hurt. In a daze, Ned's memories of what had happened after he found Lucy were vague. He didn't see how her gift had saved his mum. How she'd laid her hands on the Mother Superior's brow, how the flow of blood had miraculously stopped, or how her heartbeat had begun to pulse with regularity once more. Lucy Beaumont was a healer. Ned's power could rearrange atoms, change one thing to another, bring parts together. Lucy's gift let her breathe life into dying cells. Gifted as Lucy was, it would be a day or two till Ned's mum was able to travel and the extent of her injury had left her in shock – she had not uttered a word or so much as moved an eyelid since her collapse on the roof. But Sister Agnes – the convent's second in command – had promised to send her on as soon as she was able.

In truth, Ned had been staggered by his explosion. He'd given himself completely to rage and in doing so had unleashed a terror so uncontrollable and pure that he wished he could tear the Amplification-Engine from his finger, undo its power and go back to being an average boy, with an average life. But it was the voice in the darkness that had really frightened him. "Yesssssss…" It had felt familiar, though he wasn't sure where from. It was something evil and it had spoken to him directly.

"She's not really a nun, you know. They made her the Mother Superior because she was our bravest. I don't think half the women here are really nuns."

Ned came out of his daze and looked at his now resting mother.

"What's she like?"

Lucy thought for a moment.

"She's like a lot of things… but mostly she's like you. She's, well, good inside."

They barely knew each other but he also knew the same thing of her.

"I know why you've been separated," Lucy went on. "I know it's my fault… but you should know how much she loves you, how much she wanted to be with you."

"I do, I mean I did. When I saw her on the roof."

"She'll be a great Mum to you when this is over, you'll see," smiled Lucy.

Ned looked at the girl beside him more closely. Every trace of jealousy had been burned out of him when he'd been reunited with his mother. He'd been so stupid. All it had taken was one loving look from Olivia Armstrong to know it.

In the tiny glimpse they'd had of each other's minds during the bonding, there'd been some sort of connection, a connection that was still there. It was too subtle to put into words, but Ned felt an overwhelming need to protect her. It was as though anything that could harm her would somehow harm him too.

The Sisters of St Clotilde had always known that Lucy was not theirs to keep, that her gift would one day be needed beyond their walls. A huddled group of women and children waved and cried as the airship took off. As for Lucy, her entire knowledge of the outside world had come from the stories of residents at St Clotilde's and the books she'd read in their library. In a single day, she had been torn from her safe cocoon and thrust into a struggle for a world she'd never really seen. As they rose into the clouds, she quietly shut the door of her cabin behind her. From outside, Ned heard a single sob; the kind of sob that brave girls do not like others to hear.

On his way back up to the airship top deck, Ned caught sight of Benissimo looking at him. It was a strange pensive look and the Ringmaster hurried away as soon as he realised Ned had seen him. Ned knew what it meant – Benissimo was as appalled by his explosion as he was. He kept remembering what the Ringmaster had said about some of the Engineers before him, how their use of the ring had driven them to corruption, or madness... or both.

Ned shuddered as he sat alone on deck, trying to gather his thoughts. The Engineer's Manual warned that excessive use of his abilities and the ring's could be draining but he had not been prepared for the complete exhaustion and confusion he now felt in his mind. The others were tending to their injuries, particularly Monsieur Couteau, who'd received his first bullet wound in over a decade. It was not the same circus as Ned had joined just a week ago, and today he was not the same boy. He had found his mum and a moment later been forced to leave her behind. Nothing in the world had ever felt more alien or more wrong.

A great black shape creaked along the deck's wooden boards towards him, armed only with a book and a bunch of his yellow favourites.

"Company?" rumbled George gently.

"I'm surprised you still want to talk to me, after what happened on the roof."

"Quite a show stopper, wasn't it?" grinned the ape toothily.

Using the Amplification-Engine with any kind of precision took an iron will. Ned now realised why there were so many detailed Engineer's blueprints and plans in his Manual. It wasn't just to help Ned learn, but to protect those around them. Even the slightest deviation could be disastrous, clearly. He had Felt too much and his Feelings were more dangerous than he could have ever imagined.

"It's really shaken me, George. I… I didn't have any control over it. I could have killed us, *all of us*."

"But you didn't, did you? The Engine can only amplify your thoughts, Ned. Your mind is the controlling factor, not the ring, and yours is as pure as any I know. What happened up there will go down in Veil history. You've been through the Manual as many times as I have. Not one Engineer has ever unleashed that kind of power, not even your father. You're unique, old chap."

Ned wasn't so sure. He wanted to tell George about the voice, how it had called to him when he'd been filled with rage, but he was too frightened of what George might think, or what it might mean if it happened again.

So instead Ned forced a small smile. "Thanks."

"'Nana?" said George, offering him the bunch.

"No thanks, I don't think my stomach's ready for food… We're in pretty bad shape, aren't we?"

"Well, I won't lie, we have taken a bit of a drumming. Benissimo is utterly furious; the spy must have tipped off Barba before we'd even left the circus and Miz will no doubt be on the warpath when we get back. I wouldn't be surprised if he turns over Bene's bunk next!" George ruffled Ned's hair with his huge fingers and smiled. "It's not all bad though, old chap. Your dear mother will be right as rain in no time and we may not look too pretty, but we have the girl now, and the boss has got us out of far hotter water than this."

Ned doubted that, but the mention of the Ringmaster reminded him of something.

"Earlier on, during the fight, I saw Benissimo get shot right through the heart, but he just got up and carried on as if nothing had happened. How is that even possible?"

The fur on George's neck and back visibly stiffened and he checked over his shoulder, before shuffling closer to Ned.

"The thing of it is, old bean, and please don't tell him I told you, but Benissimo can't be wounded. Or killed."

"What?! But what about the scar on his face?"

"Given to him by his bedevilled brother, before his power had fully matured. Benissimo walked away with a cut face, Barba a broken leg."

"Is he… are they immortal?"

"Well I don't know that I'd go as far as that, but they certainly don't seem to age," explained George.

"Wow…"

"Not, I'm afraid, as he sees it. To Benissimo it's a curse, something to do with his father. I don't know if the crime was his, his brother's or his father's, but I do know this: Benissimo and Barbarossa were not born the way they are today and only dark magic, Demon magic, could bestow such unnatural powers. Never ask him to talk about it, ever… I've seen him turn quite violent with those that have and he'd probably have my head for talking about it now."

"Is that why he's so, you know, obnoxious?"

George's face saddened.

"Imagine a world where you outgrow everyone you love, every friend, every ally. One by one you see them grow old and die. Now imagine that the only constant in your life is your war-mongering brother. That poor man has spent a hundred lifetimes trying to undo his sibling's wrongs – small or great. Blackmail, kidnap and torture are mere tools of the trade to Barbarossa. What he craves is power, though we've never seen him search it out so openly before. Every time Bene goes to battle against his brother, someone loses a husband, a mother, a son or daughter, and Benissimo feels personally responsible for them all. Now imagine doing that forever."

"There must be some way to stop Barba?"

"The only way to stop him for good would be to kill him and there's only one way to do that…"

"What?" urged Ned.

"Benissimo. He can kill him. But in doing so he would end his own life, such is the nature of their curse."

"So he can't do it because he'd die too?"

"Good lord no, to think that is to not know him. That man would gladly give up his life if it meant saving even one person."

"Then why?"

"Love," said the ape, his small dark eyes bright and sad. "Despite everything Barbarossa has done, he's still his brother. Bene could no sooner take his life than he could yours or mine, and because of that… people are dying.

Which of course makes him feel even more wretched."

Suddenly Ned saw the Ringmaster in a new light. Whatever the curse was, whatever it had made Benissimo, one thing was certain – beneath his obnoxious exterior was a man who had carried the weight of the world for more years than Ned could possibly imagine.

"Do you really think we can beat him, George? Do you think we can stop the Veil from falling and all that means?"

"At this moment in time that rather depends, old chap, on Theron Wormroot and what happens at his Keep. Fairies or 'Fey' are magic made flesh, and as wild as that implies. Our sense of right and wrong simply doesn't apply to their kind. They've waged war over a lock of hair, cursed whole bloodlines for mispronouncing their names and are prone to insane bouts of vanity."

"That doesn't sound great."

"It's not supposed to. But we must put ourselves into his care nonetheless. Just keep your eyes open when we get there; nothing is straightforward when dealing with the Fey."

CHAPTER 31

Theron's Keep

Theron's Keep was not within the safety of the Veil's protective shroud. Fairies do not abide by any law other than their own and have no need of it to stay hidden. They only exist because it amuses them to do so and no two fairies are exactly the same. Their size and form is defined by the kind of magic that flows through their veins. Theron Wormroot was unique.

He had built his Keep on the top of a hill, surrounded by a circular wall of giant hedgerows. Beyond the "bighouse" as the locals called it, stood the town of Fessler. Fessler was at least a hundred years behind the rest of Europe and its quiet cobbled streets knew nothing of the goings on behind the bighouse's impenetrable green wall, nor was there anyone old enough to remember actually seeing Squire Wormroot in the flesh.

As a young Fey, Wormroot's dominant emotion was greed. He had been more than happy to steal the gold from a sleeping man's filling, but it was not till his two hundredth year that he found his real fortune. The fairies' most mischievous spell is to make a person forget. On entering their realm you could be made to forget time or your loved ones, only emerging years later, if you were lucky enough to emerge at all. Theron Wormroot had found a way to bottle it. His tonic could make you forget anything. You simply had to think of the thing you wanted to forget as the liquid passed your lips, and it was gone forever.

Wormroot's tonic was especially popular with those suffering from broken hearts and had been in high demand till the Fey's Seelie Court got wind of it. Selling fairy magic was forbidden and Theron was stripped of both his wings and his powers, cursed to live in the confines of his Keep till the end of his days.

Because of his change in fortunes, he was always eager to add to his dwindling coffers and had embraced the Circus of Marvels with open and greedy arms. Following Sar-adin's attack, the troupe's arrival was the Keep's biggest visit from the outside world in eighty years and his bemused staff were doing their best to keep up with their needs. The troupe had half-driven, half-dragged themselves and their vehicles to the Fey's home. But with a good deal of their trailers and caravans burnt beyond liveable use, most of the troupe were effectively homeless. In Benissimo's absence, it had fallen to Mystero to ensure that everyone had shelter and medical attention. The top floor of the Keep had been turned into a makeshift infirmary and bulged with the wounded. The Glimmerman had been found whimpering in his hall of mirrors and was receiving treatment for multiple burns. Meanwhile Abigail had still not stirred from her strange coma. Below them, those without rooms made their beds on the floors of the corridors and only the Tinker remained outside. His trailer was still serviceable and had been set up on the Keep's grounds. Apparently there had been a major falling out between the minutian and Mystero, who had demanded to see his air-modulator to check on the messages that he'd been sending. The indignant head of R&D hadn't emerged from his van since, though he continued to work on an apparently vital gadget for the next leg of their mission.

Amongst all the chaos, Theron eagerly did his rounds whilst keeping a tally. He was overweight, red-cheeked and clammy-skinned, wearing clothes at least two centuries out of fashion and two sizes too small. He was also covered in jewellery and had the yellow slanting eyes of a cat. He was followed everywhere by Berthold, his 'pen and ink man', who kept a tally on the arriving troupe members. Berthold had many jobs on the Wormroot estate – butler, cook, handyman and, on rare occasions like this, scribe. He wore a faded long-tailed suit from a similar era to Theron's, and had a hard, bony head with a long beak-like nose. He looked to Ned almost exactly like a crow.

"Good afternoon, sirs, and welcome to my Keep," said Theron with a bow as Ned and his sortie alighted from their airship. "A terrible business these run-ins you've been having. Please feel free to stay as long as you need, or even longer."

Benissimo eyed Theron mistrustfully, but Ned noted that his tone was deliberately polite. With or without magic, the Fey were not to be taken lightly.

"Thank you, Squire Wormroot, we are most grateful for your hospitality. I believe my head of security has explained the delicate nature of our business?"

Wormroot's greedy gaze went to Ned and then Lucy.

"But of course. He has been most generous with his explanations. My silence is assured, your Eminence."

Benissimo smoothed his moustache and turned to

Lucy. "Make sure you get some rest; I'll visit you just as soon as I can."

Ned did not remember him saying anything even nearly as kind when he'd arrived at the circus, but then there had been no bloodshed.

"Theron. Please see to it that Lucy has a room of her own," continued the Ringmaster.

"I'm afraid the only room left is mine and—"

"That sounds perfect; your generosity is noted."

Theron's mouth dropped open but Benissimo was already at the stairs on his way to see Kitty.

"Whatever you desire," said Theron eventually, with another low bow. "Berthold! Don't just stand there, show the girl to her room!"

Ned took in his surroundings. All around them the circus's battered vehicles were in various states of repair and the air rang with the sound of hammers and drills.

George helped Monsieur Couteau and the rest of the injured to the makeshift infirmary, while Rocky – still one arm down but apparently unconcerned – went to check on his wife. Ned took Lucy's bag and followed her and Berthold up the stairs, the butler's crooked walk and the twitching of his head making him look even more crow-like than before. The ramshackle band of circus refugees all gawped and grinned in silence as they passed, knowing only too well who their latest recruit was and how important she was to their cause.

Waiting patiently at the top of the final flight of stairs sat Whiskers, who was doing an admirable job of looking excited, especially for a clockwork mouse. His head bobbed up and down and his little mouse eyes flashed white repeatedly.

"Whiskers! Hello, boy. How was Bene's surveillance mission? Spot anything good?" asked Ned happily.

Whiskers answered by shaking his head in a "lips sealed" gesture, before leaping off the landing and hopping down the stairs towards them at speed.

"I missed you too, Whiske—"

But the little Debussy Mark 12 had run straight through Ned's legs, grabbed on to the bottom of Lucy's skirt and clambered up to her shoulder.

"That's my, err… was my mouse."

Whiskers gave Ned a quick blink before nuzzling his nose into Lucy's neck.

Lucy smiled delightedly.

"Hello, Whiskers, you're a friendly little thing, aren't you?"

Berthold led the two of them to Lucy's room, before

excusing himself to rejoin the Squire on his rounds.

Theron's accommodation, though sumptuous, was of decidedly inhuman design. Bent cutlery and smashed watches were strewn about as ornaments and nearly every surface held some form of hand mirror, like a child's view of wealth, only turned on its head.

"Well, this is different," said Lucy.

She sat on the bed and sighed.

"Are you OK?" asked Ned, sitting beside her.

"I'm fine, it's just, everything's so, so… *much*."

"I know, it feels like that at first, but don't worry, you get used to it pretty quickly and they're the best troupe anywhere – you couldn't be in better hands." Ned was warmed by the realisation of just how strongly he meant it.

"You mean you're not from the circus either?" she asked excitedly, before catching herself. "Sorry, Mother Superior didn't tell me very much about you or her life before St Clotilde's. I… I think she found it too painful."

"No. I'm not from the other side of the Veil at all. I'm from Grittlesby."

"What's Grittlesby?"

Ned went quiet. Explaining a suburb to someone who'd never seen a city was not going to be easy.

"Ummm… Grittlesby is the opposite of this. It's boring, really, really boring."

"You should try living with nuns."

"They looked pretty cool to me."

"Yes, they are… pretty cool." Lucy's face darkened. Ned guessed she was remembering how many of them had died protecting their wards, protecting her. "Were you sad when you left Grottersbury?" she asked, quickly changing the subject.

"More in shock than anything else. I didn't know about Engineers and the Amplification-Engine, or about the Veil, till the day I left."

"I don't know what's worse. Not being told or always knowing. Did they tell you what I can do?"

Lucy looked around the room and fixed her eyes on a small bunch of flowers on the windowsill. They were old and withered.

"It's such a simple thing really, but it's caused so much grief."

She walked over to the vase and closed her eyes. The shrivelled flowers started to move. It was slow at first. Then their wrinkled leaves and petals began to unfurl and fatten. They flushed with colour. Bit by bit, their stems straightened, as though time was rewinding itself, till they stood in full bloom and as fresh as the day they were plucked. Of all the things he'd seen people do since leaving 'Grottersbury', this was the prettiest.

"Wow…"

"Yeah, it's pretty weird. The nuns helped me to learn how to do it, after I bonded with my ring."

Lucy looked as lost and alone as Ned remembered feeling when he'd first left Grittlesby. He had an idea. He was still recovering from his explosion in the convent, but he closed his eyes and thought of something he hoped might cheer her up while showing her what he could do. It wasn't anywhere in the Engineer's Manual, but Kitty had told him the only limits were those he gave himself – he could do this. Though there would be no Feeling involved this time. He wouldn't risk that again.

Ned picked up a collection of cogs, springs and wires from Wormroot's collection of broken watches and held them in the palm of his hand. He Saw the flower's edges, remembered its shape and began to plan. In front of them both, floating just above his fingers, were the beginnings of an Amplification. It was complex, far more so than anything he'd tried to make till now, but Ned was determined to show Lucy that they were in this together. Perhaps even more than that, he needed to prove to himself that he was capable. Because if he wasn't…? Well, there was no room for that.

The metal pieces rose into the air before Ned. They began to stretch and bend, then one by one they started to connect, a hinge here, a click there. His ring hummed. Ned thought his head was going to explode from concentration. But as the last flattened piece of metal melded with the bent wire stem, he opened his eyes and to his utter amazement, he saw a steel Edelweiss flower, perfect in almost every detail.

"Amazing," breathed a delighted Lucy.

"I didn't know I could do that till just now."

Feeling rather pleased with himself, his concentration slipped and the flower fell apart in his hand as a mess of separate pieces.

Ned blushed.

Lucy gave a sudden snort of laughter. In the end, Ned had to join in.

***

Being utterly exhausted, both Ned and Lucy had gone straight to bed. For some reason, and despite the ape's bulk, Ned and George had been given the smallest room in the house. Less of a room and more of a broom cupboard, their tiny quarters smelt of cleaning liquid and dust. Ned slept fitfully amidst George's snoring, his mind a jumble of worries about his dad, his newly-found mum, but more than anything about the task at hand. Would they find the Source in time, and even if they did, what then? What were Ned and Lucy actually supposed to do? Could he do it? And would the voice return again?

When he woke the next morning feeling extremely unrested, he found George was gone. He got out of bed and peeked round the door. Outside the corridors were empty and the Keep was almost completely silent.

It wasn't until he heard George's heavy footsteps padding across the floorboards towards him that he discovered where everyone was. As soon as Ned saw George's face, which had sagged into a mound of leathery wrinkles, he knew something was very wrong.

"What is it, George?" asked Ned.

"Kitty is... Kitty is..." The great ape could barely speak. "She's dying."

CHAPTER 32

Falling Star

"But... but when we left her in Italy I thought she was OK?" Ned stammered.

"Sar-adin's final outburst did more damage than she let on. The old bird was hiding her wound with every ounce of power left to her."

Ned felt his heart sink to the floor.

"But what about Lucy? I mean, that's what she does, right? She's the Medic. She fixed my mum, you were there – you saw her do it."

"That dear girl has been with Kitty all night. But she's beyond even Lucy's powers, Ned. We're going to lose her."

George walked with Ned in stunned silence to the top floor of the Keep. It was painfully quiet and a good portion of the troupe were huddled along its corridors, waiting for news. Mystero did not look up from his vigil at Kitty's door and the Tortellini boys had replaced their boisterous charm with a teary silence.

A hatless and haggard-looking Benissimo was waiting for Ned and led him wordlessly to Kitty's suite. It was a stark contrast to Theron's room and couldn't have been more fitting. Its walls were a faded pattern of soft greys and whites. Old laces and linens covered a four-poster bed and at its centre lay the tiny figure of Kitty. The old witch had never looked more peaceful or more frail. To see her sleeping like that, without her wicked banter, made her look like something from a picture book, an angel or a saint, albeit one dressed in pink.

"Kit-Kat, dear? It's Ned, he's come to see you," said Benissimo softly.

Very slowly, the old lady opened her eyes and joined them in the room.

"Bene…" Though too weak to move her head, her greyed-out eyes had lost none of their sparkle. "And I sense another… Ned, and that lovely girl, Lucy. Do you know, dear, I've been looking for her everywhere, and here she's been helping me… all night… helping…"

Lucy took Kitty's hand as though she'd known her all her life.

"We've managed to sort a few things out, haven't we, Kitty?" said Lucy.

"Yes, dearie, we certainly have. Why don't you and Bene wait outside and let me have a moment with Ned?"

Alone with the Farseer, Ned became completely tongue-tied. What do you say to a woman who could see the future and knew she was dying? But Kitty was having none of it.

"Now now, there's no time for all that. I've always known it would be today, and in this lovely old bed," she smiled. "Such is the way of it with Farseers."

"That must have been horrible."

"Actually it's been rather pleasant, like meeting an old friend."

"This is all my fault. We should have gone through the mirrors."

"Nonsense, my weeping-willow. This bed, in this Keep, has been waiting for me since the beginning. Mirror or not, this is where I would have wound up."

Ned felt a lump build in his throat.

"I'm going to miss you, you know, despite all your face-slapping!"

"Yes I do know rather, I've been in your head, dear, after all. The truth is, I've been inside a lot of heads, Ned, but yours is quite possibly my favourite, after my darling Benissimo, of course. He raised me, you know? Adopted me when I was a wee orphan. For all his blustering and chest-puffing, he's the best man I've ever met. He'll take my passing the worst."

Ned was stunned. Kitty was to all intents and purposes Benissimo's daughter. No wonder he'd looked so broken.

"Now, dearie," Kitty continued. "About the Source…"

"We still don't know where it is?"

"Actually we do, at least I do. The location was revealed in the pinstripes' note from Madame Oublier, the one no one but I read. The Prime of the Twelve has been passing down that secret for generations. We decided it was best to keep it from anyone till the very last minute. There is the matter of the spy, dearie, after all."

"But I still don't know what it is we actually have to do?"

"Do? You have to give it your all, Ned, without fear or hesitation."

Ned's anxious mind immediately went back to St Clotilde's, his fury, the dark voice that had called out to him. But all he said was, "I'll try."

She smiled at him gently with a hint of mischief. "You know, we do have time for a last reading."

Ned was only too happy to oblige. He took her hand and held it up to his face.

"Ahh, there you are… yes, just as I thought."

"What? What can you see?" said Ned nervously.

"Too much for my tired old lips to tell now, luvvie. But there is one thing… you're going to be the first."

"The first?"

"The first to realise the Engine's true potential."

"I don't understand. What potential?"

"Look in the Manual, Ned. There are pages missing. Don't worry, Lucy will show you the way, some day. Now, before you go, I have a little present for you. Gorrn? Show yourself, my love."

A shadow on the floor pulled itself together beside them. The great bulbous familiar that was Gorrn looked at Ned with the smallest of eyes and formed a sort of smile from his curving darkness.

"Roo?" said Gorrn.

Ned didn't know what to think.

"Err, hello Gorrn."

"Arr," said the creature.

"You should be flattered, dear. It was Gorrn's idea. Familiars almost never change their masters, but I think he's taken a shine to you. Look after him and he'll look after you. If you're ever in a pinch, '*famil-ra-sa*' will bring him to you. Oh and be polite – they're sticklers for a 'please' and a 'thank you'."

"So, where do I, er, keep him?"

"Ask him to hide, dear."

"Err, Gorrn, would you mind hiding, please?"

"Arr," said Gorrn.

And the creature dropped back down to floor level and joined with Ned's shadow.

"Thank you, Kitty, and not just for Gorrn, for everything. It's been an honour." Ned sniffed.

"No, dearie, the honour's been mine."

***

Outside, Ned took a seat by a withdrawn Benissimo. They sat in silence while they waited for Kitty and Lucy to have a final talk. Minutes later, Benissimo jumped from his seat and reached for Kitty's bedroom door, but by the time the Ringmaster's hand had reached the handle, the Circus of Marvels had become something else, something less. Their Farseer was no more.

Kitty's soul filled the room. It poured out of her like a tidal wave, rushing through walls, flowing down stairs and out into every corner of Theron's Keep. Every man, woman and child in the building felt it. It was a last farewell to Benissimo's merry band of oddities, a final goodbye from Kitty, their brightest star.

Some felt it as a happy memory, others as a warm whisper. To Ned it arrived as something between a hug and, rather weirdly, a slap to his face.

Lucy was sitting quietly by the witch's side, a steady stream of tears pouring from her eyes.

"The Source is in Annapurna," she said quietly as the Ringmaster stared down at his Kit-Kat's lifeless body.

"And there's something else. I don't know how he knows, but your brother is already on the way there."

CHAPTER 33

The Show Must Go On

Switzerland was no stranger to rain, but the little town of Fessler had never seen such a downpour. It was as if Kitty's passing had been felt in the sky. The Veil was almost out of time, but Benissimo, its most valiant protector, would go nowhere without his Kit-Kat being given the honours that she deserved. His troupe would just have to make up the time by not eating or sleeping until everything was ready. Besides, Barbarossa did not have Lucy – whom they now knew from the pinstripes' note was the Source's radar – so even if he knew roughly where to look, surely he would not find it before them. As the sun cast its final rays of the day, a magical shroud of black was created by the circus's various magic casters. It covered the Keep and its grounds. Every item of clothing, every doorway or brick, every blade of grass and every leaf on every tree turned to a lightless black. There wasn't a hint of colour anywhere.

It was customary for those that followed the wandering way to be buried where they'd drawn their last breath. Also in keeping with tradition, it was the Ringmaster who gave the service, and all of his troupe removed their glamours to mourn in their true form. Though all their clothes were black, Ned had never seen them look more colourful. Skins of every colour, adorned with feathers, scales or fur, some winged, some horned, some unfeasibly small or tall... the Circus of Marvels stood silent but proud in memory of its beloved Farseer. Lucy and Ned remained slightly apart as Rocky and George bore the hastily crafted coffin – adorned with Kitty's favourite pink scarves – to the outskirts of Theron's property. As they lowered her into the ground, the sobbing Guffstavson brothers unleashed a bolt of pure lightning that shot straight up into the clouds. Little splinters of electric blue light danced in the skies above their heads.

Beside Ned, Lucy was crying.

"You must think I'm ridiculous. I only met her last night," she managed. In response, Ned just took her hand, as a lump gathered in his throat, the kind of lump that never leaves you, even once it's gone.

***

Back at the Keep after the ceremony, nobody spoke. They were too heartbroken, and besides, there simply wasn't time. At the very first glimmers of sunrise, they would be headed for the Annapurna mountain range in Nepal, and there was work to be done.

Annapurna was famed for being the most dangerous and challenging climb in the world and the troupe had all been working round the clock to assemble the needed provisions. The Tinker was being particularly industrious, retreating back to his van and bolting the door shut, despite Ned's offer of help.

On the way up to his room, Ned passed Mrs Cottlecot and her team of seamstresses, who were frantically making the high-altitude clothing Benissimo had ordered. The air in the corridor was thick with both grief and desperate urgency, mixed with something else. Mystero looked even more tense than usual, something Ned hadn't thought possible. Anyone who crossed his path without a specific job or order was taken aside for questioning. Ned wished he could go and talk to Lucy or George, but the Engineer's Manual beckoned. If anyone needed to prepare for their journey, it was Ned.

Whiskers sat on his shoulder and watched as Ned pored over the Manual's complex notes, desperate to absorb as much as possible before their climb.

By now he'd practised Seeing and Telling a hundred times, and each creation he attempted was more complex than the next. Four pointed throwing stars attached themselves to spring-loaded daggers – created from only the atoms of air in the room and a handful of spoons – and at one point he forged himself a section of plate armour that moulded to his chest, but there was always something wrong, some detail overlooked or misinterpreted, and his frustration would then cause it all to fall apart. He HAD to be perfect – he had to follow the Manual to the letter; it was the only way to stop himself from being a liability to the others. But the harder he tried, the more he stumbled, till his concentration became undone and his hand burned. When his eyelids finally gave in, his mind was a jumble of muddled diagrams and half-remembered text.

As soon as he slept, and like so many nights before, he found himself in a wall of grey. But it was different to his other dreams. Gone were the acrid smells and menacing clouds. Here the grey fog was sweet scented and flowed peacefully around him. He walked through its layers till he saw a figure within a clearing.

"Hello, Ned," said Lucy with a smile.

"Lucy? How did you get in here?"

"I'm always here; this is my dream."

"How's that possible?"

"I don't know if I can explain it properly, I don't really understand it myself. Why don't you sit down?" she asked.

Ned sat himself down beside her.

"This is weird," he said.

"I think everything's been weird since you showed up," smiled Lucy.

"I know, I can't believe Kitty's gone… I'm going to miss her." He paused. "And I was hoping she'd be around to tell us exactly what we have to do when we get to the Source."

"I don't know that Kitty had all the answers, Ned. I think she just knew about people, and she seemed pretty sure about us working it out when the time comes."

Lucy seemed so sure of herself. So unflustered about the task before them. Maybe it was because she'd known about her role in things for longer. But it wasn't just the challenge ahead that worried Ned. Somewhere at the back of his mind lingered the worry that he might go mad – or bad – like the other Armstrongs had before him. He wanted to be an Armstrong, but the right sort. How he wished his dad was here – but there was still no news and deep down he wondered if there ever would be.

Just then he remembered what Kitty had told him about being the first and how Lucy would show him the way. He was about to ask her about this when, before he could say anything, Lucy's face dropped and she suddenly looked very, very afraid.

"Ned, quickly, there's something wrong, something really wrong!"

Her face was losing shape, what had been so full of light a second ago twisted to an oily black, spreading itself out to the dream around her. Everywhere Ned looked thunderous clouds began to form, till the dream had turned to a pitch-black nothing.

KABOOM.

Ned woke with a fright. The thunderbolt had broken just outside his window and it was still raining hard. He didn't remember what he'd dreamt, only that Lucy was in terrible danger. He leapt to his feet and kicked George in the gut as he did so.

"Ouch! What was that for, you rotter?"

"George, get up! It's Lucy, she's in trouble!"

They raced up the stairs, the ape's head sending

chandeliers swinging wildly, as they smashed into walls, jumped over sleeping troupe members and skidded along the wooden corridors, before finally bursting in through Lucy's door.

She was not alone. Standing over her sleeping body was a dark and crooked silhouette. It was Berthold, Theron's right-hand man. He was holding a dusty old bottle in his hands and looked like he was pouring its contents into a jug by Lucy's bedside. Before he could react a now raging George hurled himself across the room, knocking Berthold to the floor with a crash.

"Get your hands off me! *Kra!*" squawked Berthold indignantly.

George's face had lost its bookishness; now there was only the animal and its bellowing angry chest.

"What were you doing?" demanded Ned as the ape held Berthold in his giant fists.

"Nothing! I was just doing my – *Kra!* – rounds. I- I thought she might be – *Kra!*– thirsty."

With every sentence, the terrified Berthold managed to sound even more avian, till Ned realised that the man was actually crowing between words. Lucy was now very much awake and Whiskers had sprung into action, scrambling down from Ned's shoulder and inspecting the butler's fallen bottle. Seconds later a fuming Benissimo tore into the room, followed by his breathless head of security.

"What in the devil's name is going on here," Benissimo roared, "and why are there black feathers growing out of Berthold's face?"

CHAPTER 34

On Your Marks, Get Set...

Whiskers sniffed at the bottle Berthold had been carrying, then his eyes flashed repeatedly and he gave a squeak. Benissimo examined the evidence and his face darkened.

"Wormroot's tonic; he was putting it in her water."

Benissimo turned furiously on the now cowering servant, his whip coiled threateningly.

"Hades flames! Do you have any idea what this could have done to her?"

"It was the master, he ordered me to do it – *Kra!* – said it would be the end of our problems. They promised – *Kra!* – to give him back his magic. They told him if he could make you all forget your mission, then he could keep you, all of you. That is all he wants. He has so missed – *Kra!* – real people to keep him company."

"Who promised? Who is *they?*" yelled Benissimo.

But Berthold was no longer listening. He started to scrape the floor with his feet, as if they'd sprouted talons.

"He meant no harm – *Kra!* – not really. You see, his house is also his prison, and it is a lonely one."

Every inch of Berthold's skin was now black with feathers and he seemed to be shrinking in George's grip.

"The master's last spell – it is lifting – *Kra!* – he must be in trouble – *Kra!* Please find him! *Kra! Kra!*"

And with one last squawk and a flapping of his arms, Berthold broke free and took flight, now fully transformed into an aged black crow. Whatever spells Theron had used before his incarceration were coming away everywhere. Two floors below the serving girls had turned to geese and one of the boys who'd brought in the milk had changed back to a bleating lamb.

"George, find Wormroot before it's too late. Whoever has got to him must be our spy!"

But the ever anxious head of security was already half turned to mist and out the door before he could finish. George galloped after him at a pace.

Other than Ned and Lucy and George, only Mrs Cottlecot had at that time managed to retire for the night and fall asleep – the rest of the troupe still being hard at work – so hers was the only other water that Berthold had been able to tamper with. Mrs Cottlecot had woken some time later, turned on her light and taken a sip of water, and at the same time admired a blue scarf she'd made that lay by her bedside. As a result, she'd thankfully only forgotten one thing. Mrs Cottlecot had forgotten the colour blue. Not its name or its various shades, but the entire colour. As far as she was concerned, the sea was bright orange and the sky a pastel green.

***

Elsewhere, the spy had covered his or her tracks perfectly. Mystero and George found Theron's body in the cellars beneath the Keep, in much the same state that he'd found Abigail. Alone and frozen, with cheeks the colour of ash. As the Squire's body failed, so too did his last spell; his staff had all now gone back to their natural state, and farmyard animals would be no help with the investigations.

Despite their collective broken hearts over Kitty's passing, and the suspicion in the air, the troupe now banded together more tightly than ever. Any moment now the Veil would fall and their way of life, their very existence, rested in the hands of two children, brave enough, or fool enough, to try and save them. There were no rousing speeches, no cheers or clapping, just a rigorously wound troupe of men, women and oddities, frantic in their common goal – to get Ned and Lucy to the mountain.

Though the Glimmerman's gateway was still intact, and Ignatius making a recovery, the nearest mirror for which he possessed a key was somewhere in India. By the time they could have organised suitable transport at the other end, the Veil would most likely have fallen. How they would catch up with Barbarossa at all was still a mystery to Ned, till he heard the cacophony of blaring engine that was... the *Jenny*.

The *Jenny* was Madame Oublier's fastest airship, which she had sent along with a pilot and navigator. It was essentially an enormous engine, strapped to two thin, zeppelin-style balloons. It was a mass of brass tubing, exhaust pipes, pistons and fan belts and the kind of machine that Ned and his dad would have gawped at for hours. But today there was no time for gawping – there was only the mission and their rush to see it done.

The force was split into two expeditions. The first would travel in the high-speed *Jenny* the second would follow as quickly as they could in one of the bigger, repaired circus airships. Going ahead would be Ned, Lucy and the Ringmaster, along with George, Mystero, Finn and, rather oddly, the Tinker. The tiny minutian was almost never asked on missions, especially those involving any strenuous physical exercise. As they gathered by the *Jenny*, the first team's members were almost unrecognisable, covered as they were in high-altitude gear. Ned was already streaming with sweat in his thick, fur-lined jacket. His arms, like the others', were heavily laden with the boots, goggles, hats and scarves that Mrs Cottlecot had prepared, as well as their supplies and weaponry.

As they were about to set off, alarming news arrived from Madame Oublier. The Twelve's other circuses were still trying to quash sightings where the Veil had faltered and hold back the Demons that had already crossed over. But they were becoming increasingly overwhelmed. Fighting had broken out in London and New York, with a particularly violent attack near a Veil outpost in Beijing. A rare Chinese dragon had taken untold lives before finally being brought down by a squadron of circus-run griffons. Containing the news stories and implementing effective cover-ups was nigh impossible by now – there simply weren't enough pinstripes or troupes. People were beginning to see what used to be hidden. The end was quite clearly in sight and the Veil mere moments from a complete collapse.

"Lucy, it's cramped in there so find yourself a good spot; the others can make do," said Benissimo ushering her aboard. He'd managed to muster a fraction of his old self back, though the loss of Kitty was still visible in his eyes.

Ned stared.

"Go on, pup, spit it out."

"How come you're so... normal with her?"

The Ringmaster raised one of his bushy brows. "Perhaps I just like winding you up." But Ned knew it wasn't that – he was sure Benissimo still didn't believe in him and, rude as that was, Ned didn't blame him.

Inside the *Jenny*'s cockpit it was indeed cramped and Ned had to sandwich himself between a crate of supplies and George's broad, hairy back. He gripped the Engineer's Manual till his fingers physically hurt. He had precious little time now to learn from its pages.

The last member to join them was the Tinker. He looked positively malnourished, as if he hadn't eaten or slept for days. He hobbled up the gangway and almost barked at Mystero when the Mystral tried to help him with his precious cargo. The machine that Benissimo had ordered him to work on was strapped to his back.

Apparently it was some kind of monitoring device and might be able to help Lucy find the Source.

Their pilot was a Canadian named Billy. He had a well-groomed beard and an even bigger moustache than Benissimo. He was wearing a leather fighter pilot's helmet from World War II. By his side, cross-legged on the floor, was Chief Sitting-Bull. Not only was Sitting-Bull a genuine Sioux American Indian, but he was also a shaman of some fame behind the Veil. He sat barefoot in his jeans and baseball jacket, undisturbed by the new passengers and in a deep trance. The Chief would be using his skills to keep the *Jenny* hidden from the human world's eyes and radar. The last thing they needed now was interference from already paranoid army border patrols.

Billy fired up the *Jenny*'s engine with a deafening roar.

"That there's pure Canadian muscle at its finest. More horsepower than a stampede o' broncos!" he yelled proudly. "She chews a little heavy on the gas, but she'll get us there quicker than a bullet."

Ned hoped so. As the *Jenny* rose up into the air, Ned could see the villages and towns of Switzerland below getting up to start their day, unaware of the snarling mound of metal and balloon tearing across their sky, or the thirteen-year-old boy within it, his stomach churning with nerves.

Night had fallen again by the time they arrived. They had made the journey in a record twelve hours, which was fast even for the *Jenny*. As they sped across the Nepalese countryside, Ned watched out the window. They were in the Gandaki valley now, bordered on either side by the Dhaulagiri Massif and the Annapurna Massif, colossal mountain ranges that housed some of the highest peaks in the world. Lit up by the moon and stars, they were an eerie and intimidating sight.

The troupe's target was a treacherous mountain over twenty-six thousand feet high and named after Annapurna, the Hindu goddess of food. It was a fitting title for the provider of the Veil's source of power. The goddess was worshipped for being the giver of nourishment and protection, that which sustains all life. But whatever the great mountain's powers were, they were fiercely guarded by its walls of ice and heavy rock, and no mountain had taken more lives from those foolish enough to try and climb her.

They came in to land on the last remaining stretch of flat ground before their ascent up the mountain. As soon as Benissimo opened the hatch, a barrage of ice-cold wind howled into the *Jenny*'s cabin, almost knocking the Tinker to the floor.

Outside, amongst the jagged moonlit rocks and snow, they were met by a group of steely-faced shikari, the name given to the local hunters of the region. They had come on Madame Oublier's request from a remote Veil outpost in the neighbouring valley. These men had the blood of frost giants in their veins, though the height and features of their lumbering ancestors were now all but gone. Ned studied them in awe. Their eyes were of the lightest blue. They wore no shoes, very little clothing and were completely impervious to the cold. They also had more news, and it was not good.

"My brother arrived not more than an hour ago and he has explosives," explained Benissimo, passing on the news to his troupe. "He means to destroy the Source before we even get there."

Nobody replied. What had been a race against the falling Veil was now a race against something – someone – else too. If they didn't catch up with the butcher before he set his charges, everything would be lost.

The worried silence was broken when the shikari saw George. All at once they started to gabble excitedly in a language all of their own and it wasn't until Lucy pointed to their map that they explained why.

Lucy did indeed seem to know where the Source was hidden, it was as though something in the mountain was calling her. The place she had selected on their map was, according to their own legends, out of bounds to the shikari. The same legend had it that great apes guarded its boundaries; boundaries that no one had ever dared cross.

"Yeti... like him only white," explained their leader.

Both Billy and Sitting-Bull stayed behind to rendezvous with the second expedition. Meanwhile the rest of the troupe prepared for departure. Finn and his hawk forged ahead. They would be Benissimo's eyes and ears up the mountain; any hint of trouble and Aark would raise the alarm. George was loaded up with the bulk of their supplies and the rest of the expedition lined up behind him carrying what they could.

The Ringmaster took Ned to one side as he made his way to the front.

"Are you ready?" Benissimo asked, giving him a funny look.

It was not the first time he'd asked Ned the question.

"Ready? Oh yes," said Ned indicating his gear and his Manual.

"No, Ned, I mean are *YOU* ready?"

But before Ned could answer, Benissimo strode off again, taking his place at the lead and giving the troupe the signal to move out.

CHAPTER 35

Annapurna

Though hampered by the lack of daylight, the troupe attacked their goal with purpose, traversing the softer, rockier slopes at speed, and hitting the real mountainside within the hour. The cold bit hard. Ned's legs were soon covered with heavy snow and ice, and his eyes hurt from squinting. But they were making good progress. He glanced behind him and caught sight of Lucy who gave him a reassuring nod. It was a nod that said, "We can do this." For a moment, Ned dared to hope that she was right, which was when they were met by the first barrage.

Out of nowhere an angry wall of wind and snow flew at them from the top of the mountain. As the temperature plummeted even further, Ned felt the sweat under his clothing freeze on to his skin, despite all their protective gear. The Tinker started hammering on one of his instruments.

"A blizzard? This can't be right, boss. It said we'd have a clear run of it when we landed."

The Ringmaster peered at the roaring darkness.

"This is no ordinary storm. It's my brother; he's trying to slow us down."

The blizzard left them wading through knee-deep snow, unable to see, fighting against a wall of wind that buffeted them from top to toe. But Benissimo pushed them onwards mercilessly, until even the shikari started to raise their concerns.

"Safety be damned! We must get to the Source," insisted the Ringmaster.

Ned's muscles cried out with pain and he had to fight to breathe, though nothing was worse than the creeping cold, like ravenous pins biting at his fingers, toes and any small part of his face left exposed. Behind him, Lucy attacked the mountain in steely silence. He stifled his groans, and marched on.

Climbing, clawing, scratching and stumbling, they forged their way ever upwards. But with every foot gained in altitude, they lost a degree in heat, till they found themselves in a barrage of cold so deep, so unforgiving, that it penetrated the marrow of Ned's bones.

The expedition slowed to a crawl. They were still hours

from dawn and even under the powerful lamplight carried by a less-affected George, visibility had reached zero. As the storm worsened they stopped to tether themselves together by rope. Anyone lagging behind now would be lost in an instant and perish just as quickly. Ice formed on the fur of Ned's coat and the howling wind beat at his eardrums relentlessly. The only evidence of the others' existence was the occasional tug at the rope around Ned's waist from George ahead and Lucy behind him. His mind drifted in the darkness and he wasn't sure how long he'd been walking when something pulled him back to the real world... by not pulling at all. The ropes around his waist had gone slack.

Terror gripped him as he scanned the storm for any sign of George or the others ahead. If he couldn't catch up with them, he'd be finished. But that was only his second concern. Lucy was behind him and that rope had gone slack too.

"LUCY!" he screamed.

But his voice was a whisper to the blizzard's roar. Turning back down the mountain, he looked to the ground, barely making out his own footprints. In moments the blizzard would cover them up with fresh snow and his route to her would be lost forever. Panting and pushing, he stumbled back in her direction. He fell, got up, fell again, over and over as he searched. Each time he stumbled his clothes grew heavier and wetter with snow and the attempts to lift himself up again more exhausting. Finally he stopped trying.

Ned lay in the snow, his path to Lucy and his allies now gone forever. Ned would have cried out if he could, but there was nothing left of him. Somehow he didn't seem to mind. He wanted to rest, just a little rest, if only for a moment.

He let himself fall, roll back down the slope, a tumbling mess of exhausted boy in the grips of a cruel mountain and its unrelenting storm. He hit something hard, something made of flesh and bone. It was Lucy.

She was completely unconscious and half buried in snow, and Ned was not far behind. But Lucy needed him. Brave, uncomplaining Lucy, who lay there, horribly still. His mind went over the pages of the Manual. He could make fire from snow but what little heat his imagination could muster would be swallowed in an instant. What he really needed was… help.

"*Famil-ra-sa*," he breathed.

A colourless shape formed in front of him and waited for instruction.

"George, Gorrn… you've got to find George," whispered Ned.

"Unt," replied Gorrn.

His familiar didn't move. What was wrong with him? They had minutes at best before the cold took them, but Gorrn simply sat there staring, with his tiny unblinking eyes. Kitty had said something to him, what was it? Something about being polite…

"Please?" pleaded Ned.

"Arr," Gorrn replied, and disappeared.

Moments later George's snow-matted chest almost crushed them in its embrace, and a satisfied Gorrn returned to Ned's shadow. Ned shut his eyes tight, relishing the momentary feeling of safety.

George raced up the mountain, powering past the rest of the troupe, then the enormous ape deposited his two charges under the shelter of an overhanging shelf of ice before going back to help the others. The shikari arrived next, and began preparing them a restorative brew. Soon after George ushered in the rest of the team, before placing his massive body between them and the worst of the roaring blizzard beyond.

Even their guides had lost their place on the mountain, such was the strength of the storm. Benissimo threw down a fire rune to warm them, then hurriedly lit gas lamps to check on his maps, Mystero advising from his shoulder.

Ned knew they had minutes at best before Benissimo would urge them all on again, and he shivered beside a barely-conscious Lucy, waiting for Mrs Cottlecot's furs to dry and the fire to defrost the innards of his bones.

On the floor beside him, the frozen clockwork face of Whiskers blinked as the little rodent's gears started to thaw. Even tucked away in Ned's pocket, the mouse had suffered. The Tinker checked him over perfunctorily, while muttering to himself about fieldwork and missing his cosy lab. Dawn was by now close to breaking, though you couldn't tell through the impenetrable barrage of snow and wind.

"Five minutes," boomed Benissimo over the wind.

Lucy's teeth chattered as she spoke. "I th-think we're close, Ned, I can s-s-s-sense it." As she gulped back the shikari's brew, her shivering began to ease. "Thanks for c-coming back for me. Kitty's familiar came in pretty handy!" She paused. "Were you frightened?"

It was a good question.

Ned had spent almost every day since his birthday afraid of one thing or another; but he'd known since he'd first met Lucy at St Clotilde's that they had to protect one another.

"A little, but I'm more frightened of what's up there. Benissimo's been sure I'll fail as an Engineer since the beginning. And the thing is… I think he might be right."

"That's not why he treats you the way he does, Ned," Lucy whispered quietly.

"What about that glare he keeps giving me?"

She shook her head but didn't say any more, and for a moment they were quiet.

"Were you scared?" he asked eventually.

Lucy fingered the chain around her neck. "No, I've been preparing for this my whole life. So more angry than scared. Besides…"

"Besides?" he asked.

"I've got you, haven't I? I knew you'd find me. Again."

Ned nodded and managed a smile, through chapped lips and wind-battered skin.

"Yes Lucy, you've got me."

And at that precise moment she did. But as Ned was discovering, moments like these on either side of the Veil are often only ever that; an instant sandwiched between events that cannot be controlled.

"Two more minutes," urged Benissimo grimly.

George stood and shook the snow from his back like a wet dog.

And beyond their ice shelf the storm lessened, just enough for the sniper within it to fire his first shot.

CHAPTER 36

Cold-hearted

The loud crack of gunfire whistled through the air and one of the shikari staggered backwards, before looking down at his chest in bewilderment. A steady stream of blood poured out of him and he crumpled to his knees. Then everything moved quickly. George let out an angry roar, beating his chest in defiance at their hidden assailant. Then seemingly from all around them the mountain erupted in gunfire.

"Get down!" commanded Benissimo pulling the Tinker to the ground beside him.

Ned felt the blood rush to his ears as he and Lucy threw themselves behind a mound of snow, along with some of the other shikari. The only man left standing was Mystero, who calmly peered out through the storm, his body in its mist form oblivious to the bullets tearing through the air.

"I'm going in to find them," he called, and a second later was gone.

Off to one side, beyond the shelf they were sheltering under, they heard rage-filled roars bellowing back at another wave of gunfire.

"It's the yetis! They're fighting Barbarossa! He must have found the Source," yelled George, as every muscle in the great ape's body tensed, urging him to seek out and protect what he hoped might be his own kind.

"How in God's name…? He's got no blasted Medic!" said Benissimo. He grabbed on to George's backpack. "Hold still, George, we still don't know what we're up against."

As the Ringmaster pulled out his spyglass, a bullet tore across his cheek, leaving a crimson line in its wake, then, as Ned watched in wonder, his skin healed itself again almost instantly.

"Slim… it's got to be. Only a long-elf could see through this mire," muttered Benissimo. "We must be close. Lucy, do you sense anything?"

"To the side there, beyond the ledge, where the other shots and the roars are coming from… I… I think it's there."

Benissimo nodded.

Ned could vaguely make out a narrow ledge to their left. It was completely exposed and fell away to nothing. Any attempt to aid the yetis right now would be met by certain gunfire. George howled in animal frustration, pounding the ice with his fists. Slim and his men replied.

Crack. Crack. Crack.

Three more shots buried themselves into the ice shelf above their heads.

"He's trying to bring it down on us! Ned, how do you think you'd fare working your gift on a moving target?"

"What target?"

"His bullets, boy! I need you to stop his bullets."

A stationary target was one thing, but a bullet? How did you change something you couldn't even see?

"Err…"

There was a tug on his arm from Lucy, who looked him dead in the eye.

"Ned, you tore my six-hundred-year-old home in half and you weren't even trying. You can do this! I just know it."

Crack. Crack. Crack.

Another round was followed by another shard of splintered ice.

"No time for your nonsense now, boy, just get on with

it!" ordered Benissimo. Even without his top hat and jacket, the Ringmaster's words were not easily ignored.

Above them the ice shelf started to groan. As Lucy crawled over to the Tinker to use her gifts on the wounded shikari, Ned did as the Ringmaster suggested – he just got on with it.

He couldn't see the bullets, but maybe that was missing the point? The diagrams and schematics he'd pored over in the Manual were all aids; a way of training the mind in structures. But how close you were to the object in question or whether you could even see it was irrelevant. The key was visualising it, then Seeing it change in your mind's eye with crystal-clear focus.

Rifle fire sounded below and Ned shut his eyelids tight. Anything more complex would be hard to disassemble, but bullets were simple geometric shapes. He focused on the image of the lead shot, blowing it up in his mind till he imagined its microscopic ridges and curves changing to hardened ice. Metal to ice was one thing, now he just needed the ice to melt. The humming of energy crackled up his arm as his ring whirred into life. Opening his eyes, the world around him slowed and the next round of bullets speeding towards the ice shelf split into harmless droplets of water.

"That's it, Ned!" yelled Lucy.

And just then, there was a break in the storm as fingers of sunlight crept over the horizon. Whatever magic Barbarossa had used was clearly coming to its end. The violent winds changed course taking their barrage of snow with them. With their new-found visibility, they soon spotted the unmistakable figures of Slim and his gor-balin snipers positioned behind a bank of rocks.

"Don't stop, Ned!" shouted Benissimo.

The shikari launched a volley of arrows and the Ringmaster leapt to his feet, firing three consecutive shots from his rifle. Further down the mountain, two of the shadowy snipers fell backwards, a third narrowly escaping with his life.

The return fire came like a roll of thunder. As nine of the remaining snipers launched their cargo, Ned Engineered with everything he had.

Sweat started to pour down his strained face as he Saw the bullets in his mind, broke them down again and again, over and over, till water sprayed from the exploding bullets all around them.

But Ned was only one tiring boy and the snipers many. Eventually two of the bullets made it through, one lodging itself into one of the shikari, the other into the ice shelf above. There was an almighty crack and Lucy screamed as a pillar of ice broke free. George grabbed at it, his powerful arms using all their might to catch it before she was crushed, before spinning back to the battle in hand.

"It's no use – there's too many of them!" shouted Ned.

"Dig deep, boy! Dig deep!" roared back Benissimo.

And Ned would have done, had it not been for the sudden sight of Lucy's mouth open in terror. Following her line of sight to his right he heard the unmistakable whirring of gears grinding against gears and the spinning of two large gyroscopic hearts.

The tickers walked slowly into sight, making Ned catch his breath. They were copies of the tiger he'd seen outside Fidgit and Sons, only these didn't look like they were going to purr, and both sets of their glowing eyes were fixed firmly on Lucy.

"Don't make any sudden movements," he whispered.

"I couldn't move if I wanted to!" she shrilled back.

One of the tigers roared. It was a foul rusty noise, like metal being scraped against metal. With Ned's attention firmly on Lucy and the tickers, the snipers' bullets struck home again, two more shikari keeling over. Then one of the tigers started towards Lucy. Ned sprang into action, pounding across the ice in a race to reach her first. As

Lucy screamed in terror, Ned and the tiger both leapt, the tiger roaring, Ned shouting.

"DUCK!"

The ticker's claws cut through thin air as Ned hit Lucy's back, knocking her to the ground in a heap. As the two children tumbled together, Ned saw the tiger's metallic belly fly over them, landing harmlessly on the other side. The ticker skidded across the ice, before turning, ready to strike again. This time there was nowhere to run. They scrambled to their feet to find a metal monstrosity on either side of them. These creatures weren't like bullets. Even a seasoned Engineer would need an intimate knowledge of their entire structure to attempt any kind of really useful change. Their cogs, gears, pistons and casing were beyond complex and definitely beyond Ned. He was just wondering if he could at least reimagine some small part of them in a way that might help when somewhere at the closest one's feet there was a tiny metallic squeak. A now fully-thawed Whiskers stood facing the brute, a tiny speck of defiant metal. Ned couldn't help but smile – Whiskers, the most useful mechanical rodent in the world, had come to his rescue. Dear old—

Crunch.

The tiger dragged his foot through the metal entrails

of Ned's now flattened pet mouse and started pacing towards them once more. On the other side, the second tiger blocked their escape. The rest of their party was now completely pinned down by Slim and his snipers' gunfire.

"Ned, quickly, do something," breathed Lucy.

Ned looked at what was left of Whiskers and bit his lip. Now more than ever he needed focus... not Feeling. He struggled for a moment, fighting an inner urge to let rip with his power, scared of the damage it might do, or what he might become... But as the approaching monstrosity neared, a memory triggered in his brain. A frustrated afternoon of trying to fix a remote-controlled car, taking it apart and putting it back together repeatedly to no avail until he'd discovered the single missing screw that had rolled under his dad's toolbox. Ned didn't have to destroy the ticker – he just had to stop it working.

If he could change metal to water, then he could easily change the ice beneath the ticker to metal. The tiniest amount would do. He closed his eyes and focused hard. His ring hummed. And a slither of frost rose up from the ground and spun in the air, turning itself to a centimetre-wide metal ball bearing, perfectly round and hard.

"Hurry, Ned!" yelled Lucy again, as the tiger tensed to pounce.

Where there was one ball bearing, there were now a dozen. Ned Told them to rise up into the tiger-machine's ribcage, and the ball bearings answered. Almost instantly, there was a loud tearing sound of metal on metal as the balls found their way to the ticker's gyroscopic heart, lodging themselves like brakes in its rotating cogs.

"Screeee!"

It froze, convulsed, staggered forward and back, before falling to one side, in a crash of metal and ice. But Ned barely had a moment to celebrate his victory before the other ticker roared in clockwork fury and propelled itself forwards – only to be met by a bellowing George.

Ned's great-ape protector lolloped in front of the two children, leathery nostrils flared.

"I'll not have an oversized toaster hurting my friends!" he roared.

The ticker launched himself at the ape, and George swung his hammer of a fist. The sound of bone crunching on metal was sickening as they landed on the ground in a twisting pile. Ned called out a warning as above their heads the ice shelf shifted again, threatening to fall at any minute.

"Aaaaark!"

A piercing screech came down from the sky. High up in

the air, in the eye of a now visible sun, Ned saw the black silhouette of Aark's two heads and huge wings tearing towards the snipers. And Aark was not alone – beside her was another giant hawk, but with the body and head of a man and a wingspan as wide as two. The second hawk let off a shriek that pierced their ears and echoed down the mountain. As the two creatures dived, Ned yelled in excited disbelief.

"It's… it's Finn! Finn's got… *wings*?!"

The tracker had thrown off his long coat, revealing a bare, sinewy upper torso and two vast black and brown wings. With his true form revealed, Finn flew down at the enemy as a vision of raw fury. The gor-balins scattered as Finn's wings struck at them relentlessly and Aark clawed at their faces. Seeing their chance, the remaining shikari leapt up from their defences and charged at Slim.

"Bene, get them to the ledge, while you still can!" roared George as he wrestled with the tiger.

The great ape had managed to get the ticker in a headlock, but its metal casing was hard to grip and it was starting to claw itself free.

"The path's clear; we have to move," ordered Benissimo. Lucy nodded and moved towards the ledge.

"But what about George… the others… we can't leave

them like this!" argued Ned.

Beyond the narrow icy path there was a final volley of gunfire and a pained roar from one of the yetis. Then silence.

"Go, Ned, I don't know how much longer I can hold it…" yelled his furry protector, with his stupid, lovable, apeish grin, before returning his focus to the metal tiger clawing at his arms.

But as Benissimo dragged Ned and Lucy away, the Tinker following close behind, their eardrums erupted.

KAROOM!

The shockwave of the explosion knocked them all to the ground. It felt as though the mountain itself had cried out in anger. And the ice shelf above them groaned its reply, like some vast waking beast…

Clinging to the relative safety of the ledge, Ned, Lucy, the Tinker and Benissimo watched on in horror as George and the ticker were swept away by a crashing wave of ice and snow, the shikari hunters, Slim and his gor-balins tumbling after them. Only Aark, with her two heads for seeing and two wings for flying away, was able to break free. Her less agile master Finn had not been so lucky. He too was swept down the mountain on a roiling sea of snow.

"My brother," screamed Benissimo over the roar of the avalanche, "he must be blasting his way to the Source."

Ned felt his heart explode.

"NOOOO!" cried Lucy, as their friends disappeared down the mountain.

But there was no answer. The battle on the slopes had come to an end.

CHAPTER 37

The Source

In the wake of the explosion and with Barbarossa's storm gone, Annapurna was eerily quiet. They moved inch by careful inch along the narrow mountain ledge. Despite Grandpa Tortellini's training and his new-found ease with heights, Ned was well aware of what lay between their thin track of ice and the rocks below.

Nothing.

But nothing was not on his mind. All he could see was the image of his brave, banana-loving friend, being swept away by snow. Every step forward felt like a betrayal; George would never have left anyone behind. Benissimo on the other hand was a different creature entirely. There would be no going back.

When they reached the other side of the ledge, they came to a large flat shelf carved into the side of the mountainside, and barely visible from anywhere beyond the ledge.

"He's forced his way in," said Lucy. "This is where the Source lies. I can feel it."

At the far end of the ledge two perfectly carved doors of stone lay blasted and broken, the dust still settling around them. Behind them lay the entrance to an immense opening, at least a hundred storeys high and bordered by giant columns as wide as a house.

The doorway had been lovingly hewn from rock and was decorated with intricate carvings of gods mixed with gods, prophets with saints, angels with heroes, from every story, myth and legend imaginable. Amongst them, Ned spotted something else – intricate markings, one on top of the other, vaguely familiar yet somehow altered.

"Those symbols… they look like the ones on the front of my Manual."

"Similar, but not the same," replied Benissimo. "These are the primary signs of power, Ned. They were made by the First Ones – the same beings who made your rings also created the Source."

Remarkably, thick vines and flowers lined the Source's cavernous entrance. They were withered and weak, but not from the force of the blast or the mountain's cruel climate. To Ned the veins of black creeping along their foliage looked like some kind of disease, like they were dying from a sickness of their own. To one side of the rubble, they saw several motionless figures strewn on the ground. The butcher's explosives had killed both his enemies and, in equal numbers, the gor-balins he had led into battle. And the guardians of the Source too – the yetis – who were indeed identical to George, except for their white fur, now stained red with blood. Like the oversized gorilla they were born protectors, and had given their last to protect Annapurna's secret.

As Ned and his companions approached the collapsed doors, there was a kick of powdery snow. It twirled and twisted gracefully, growing thicker and more colourful, till the corkscrewing shape of Mystero took form. His eyes fixed intently on Ned and Lucy.

"Nothing will stop you will it, boy?"

"Huh?" Ned frowned. Mystero looked different. An altogether more menacing version of his usual, clammy-skinned self.

"I tried, you know, for your father's sake," went on the Mystral, while eyeing Benissimo warily. "I tried to frighten you away with the weir and collision course with the boeing, but you wouldn't take the hint, would you? You wouldn't be turned, and you wouldn't follow me through the mirrors. If you'd just come back to Barbarossa then, none of this would be necessary. I thought Wormroot's tonic would do the trick till your little dream ruined it all, and I nearly had you last night, but then I didn't know about Gorrn. Dear old Kitty got her last laugh there, didn't she? So much like your father, such stubborn Armstrong goodness, so wasted, so naive."

Ned couldn't process what he was saying. The man had saved his life more than once, had turned over every bunk and trailer the Circus of Marvels had, and all to find...

"Miz?" Was all Ned could muster.

"Yes, Miz... Miz the spy, Miz the traitor."

Lucy gasped and Benissimo's hand went to his whip, which had miraculously appeared at his hip.

"Now now, my friend, I wouldn't do anything hasty if I were you. I only need to take the children; your brother must be allowed to finish what he's doing, the laying of explosives is such delicate work," warned Mystero.

The Ringmaster looked saddened. But to Ned's surprise he did not look in the least bit shocked.

"I didn't want to believe it at first. Your Mystral mind was always just out of my Kit-Kat's reach, not that she'd ever have tried to read you. How could someone so trusted, so loved, turn so completely?"

"I've taken no pleasure in it, Bene, none at all. But we've been fighting a losing battle ever since Terrence and Olivia left us. The Demons, the Darklings, they're coming, whether you like it or not. Barba can control them, the fair-folk could rule the world with the Darkness at its side. It took years for me to see it, to really understand what your brother wants. Now I know he's right. It's time for the Hidden to come out of the shadows. We don't need to live in fear any more, not if we stand together. It's time for the rest of the world to fear us. I spared Abigail for old times' sake, and because I knew that she'd see the truth once the Veil falls, they all will. But you, Bene, you're a lost cause. No one can protect the world from itself, not even you."

"That's not for you to decide."

"Nor you, old man. A new day is dawning, my friend, all you need to do is step aside and let your brother bring it."

Benissimo cracked his whip straight at Mystero's face. It struck at his image with pinpoint accuracy, pushing him into inky clouds, before he drew himself back together.

"Really, Bene, is there any point?"

"I was just making sure, old friend."

"Making sure?"

"Making sure it would work. It took a while for the Tinker to figure it out. Riding the wind's messages in your mist form was inspired. It wasn't till Whiskers spied on you using our air-modulator that we were sure, sure that the very form you used to hurt us would be your undoing."

"I can't be undone, Bene, you of all people must know that by now?"

"You *couldn't* be undone, not until the Tinker had finished building his device. The poor man's been working his little fingers to the bone. It's been hard these past few days keeping you close and saying nothing – but it was a necessary evil. Tinker, I'm afraid now would be the time."

There was a loud whirring noise from behind Mystero, as the Tinker switched on the device strapped to his back. His precious cargo was, in fact, a converted vacuum cleaner, with added Hidden-made enhancements. The Mystral's face fell, but his realisation had come too late.

Ned watched Mystero as a funnel of mist was sucked out of his back and into the Tinker's machine. He clawed at the air frantically, like a spider being pulled down a plughole.

"Stop! Stop this, you can't do this to me! I am a Mystral! Nothing can hold me… NOTHIiiaaarrrghhh…"

It turned out that there was one thing that could hold him. The airtight crystal chamber in the Tinker's 'wind-wrangler' made a large shlupping noise and the last of Mystero the Magnificent, Benissimo's trusted friend and adviser, was sucked into his final prison. The sight of his twisted face being pulled into the chamber, along with his accompanying cries, made Ned's stomach heave. But justice had been served.

The Tinker stayed behind to message the reinforcements, while the other three pressed on through the great doorway. Benissimo didn't look back once at what was left of his old Mystral friend.

Inside they found a giant staircase that spiralled deep into the mountain. The walls of the great cavern were covered in detailed carvings. The deeper they went, the more angular the patterns. Ned started to see something in their grand design, the way the shapes and lines flowed and twisted, converging into one and leading them ever downwards. It was like a puzzle of complex circuitry, or the charted inner workings of some vast machine. The vines and plants that they'd seen outside were everywhere. They followed the carvings' curves and corners, entwined themselves around its spirals, as if somehow drawn to a power within the stone sketches. But the sickness the plants carried was in evidence also – in the withering black veins that crawled across the leaves and along the vines. It seemed to feed off the plants themselves.

As they continued their descent, it felt as if the walls were stirring, as if the carvings sensed Lucy and Ned, shifting almost imperceptibly towards them as they passed, till finally the walls started to glow. With their every step, pulses of light shot through the circuit of patterns, shimmering into the distance before fading away.

"Wow," said Lucy eventually. "This is so…"

"Weird?" offered Ned.

"No, it's beautiful."

Finally at the bottom, they came to the entrance of the main chamber. As they walked through the doorway, they stared around in awe. The sheer size of the space was breathtaking. The vast cavern's ceiling, that had been carved to a perfectly smooth cone, rose miles up into the mountain, ending what must be somewhere near its peak. Towards the top, Ned saw actual clouds hanging in the air.

"The whole mountain, it's… hollow," he said.

Calling it a cavern did not even begin to express its size. It seemed the First Ones had somehow managed to excavate an entire subterranean city within Annapurna itself. It was so large that it had its own ecosystem. Stepped plateaus to the old city's edges showed signs of once-healthy fields and a complex irrigation system supplied by waterfalls trickled down from the world above. From the extraordinary number of stone-carved temples converging at its centre and the ordered streets of houses that weaved beyond and between them, it looked as though the chamber had been both a place of worship and a home. Ned looked down streets and saw bridges and city squares. There were even walkways that spiralled up to the chamber's clouded heights. Ned had never seen architecture even remotely like it. It was grand and perfectly ordered, like the circuit patterns they'd seen decorating the walls on their approach.

But they didn't have time to waste – any moment there might be another explosion and it could be the Source's last. The butcher was up ahead and they needed to stop him.

"Now what?" asked Ned, looking at the Ringmaster.

But it was Lucy that answered. "The patterns in the stone. They've all been travelling in the same direction… to the centre."

There was another tremor, followed by a slab of rock falling from the chamber's roof. The scream of shattering stone was an angry reminder that the Source was running out of time.

"Let's go," the Ringmaster yelled.

They raced along the carved street that ran from the entrance past giant rectangular monoliths and rivers that poured through perfectly straight gorges. It was order carved from nature's jarring proportions, and it was breathtaking, even as they pounded through its streets at speed. There was another roar of falling rock and Benissimo urged them on, scanning wildly about for any sign of his brother. Exhausted, they finally approached a large, central square that seemed to lie in the middle of the cavern's abandoned city. There was no evidence of the butcher or his explosives, but Ned's ring suddenly started to hum. Loudly.

"Lucy, my…"

"I can feel it too," said Lucy.

The air was thick with energy, making the hairs on Ned's arms prickle. What had started as a familiar hum at his finger, now flowed all over his body.

"Look at the light," said Lucy.

In the centre of the square was a circle of towering stone pillars, where the carvings and plants of the great cavern were at their thickest, converging in a twisted knot of patterns.

Ned watched the glow in the stone circuitry pulse repeatedly around a circle. It was only then that he realised the light was pulsing in time to his frantic heartbeats. Judging by Lucy's face, he guessed she had realised the same of her own.

They moved through the pillars into the clearing at the centre, where they saw a giant, round metal structure, as reflective as chrome. It must have been twenty feet high and at least ten across its middle. It too was covered in curling arteries of metal, each feeding from the next and burrowing in and out of the metal shell, and like the walls, trails of light pulsed across its surface. The complexity of the tickers Ned had faced outside looked almost childish in comparison. There were no cogs in view, or pistons or joints, and yet it rippled one way then the next, constantly changing its shape as if the metal it was made of were actually breathing. Ned found it both wondrous and frightening, but there was also something about it that felt almost familiar.

As they got closer, a loud hum emanated from its surface before changing in pitch, as though it were altering its frequency to match theirs.

It was only when Ned got close enough that he could see the detail in its rippling surface – it was covered in writhing strands of living metal.

"It's like our rings. When I looked at mine under the

Tinker's lenses… its surface moved just like that."

But something was wrong. Large sections of the metal were dull and still, blackened with the same sickness that they had seen on the plants. Intermittently the whole structure juddered, almost to a complete halt, before stuttering back to life. There could be no doubt now that the Source was in its final moments.

Bensissimo remained silent. The Ringmaster's entire existence had revolved around protecting the Veil and the people on either side. Here right in front of him was the future of his fragile world and now it was no longer in his hands, but in the hands of two children.

Ned opened his Manual.

"I don't understand. If our rings were built by the same people, wouldn't the First Ones have told our ancestors exactly what they'd have to do? Why bother with a Manual, then leave out the most important part?"

"It's not biological, but it's not pure machine either. It's a… heart… it's the actual heart of the Source," said Lucy.

"Fascinating, isn't it?" said a deep voice from behind them. "I believe bio-mechanical is the term, both nature and science combined. Very clever, like those wee rings you wear at your fingers. Such a shame I have to break it."

CHAPTER 38

The Final Curtain

"Your timing could not be more irritating. Had the *Daedalus* had less distance to cover and the yetis been less stubborn, I would have already placed the charges by now, and… *BOOM*, there'd be nothing left to mend," said Barbarossa. "Still, given how late I've had to leave things, I decided a few more minutes wouldn't hurt – and I couldn't resist the opportunity to see your face, dear brother, when I destroyed the thing you care for most!"

His tone was enough to make the blood in Ned's body freeze. There was no spirit-knot in play, no potion-laden delicacies, and yet for just a second, Ned felt the butcher's words wrap around his mind. How could a voice, a single voice, drain his courage so quickly and so completely?

Benissimo's brother stood facing them, a case of dynamite at his side and his trusty cleaver, Bessy, in hand.

His snow-suit looked as though it had been skinned from a dozen furred beasts and his already heavy figure looked positively mountainous, like some great woolly mammoth risen from an icy tomb.

"Put it down, Barba, we both know how this will end if it comes to blows," warned Benissimo.

"Really, *fratello*? You mean our little curse? I don't need to fight you, brother, I only need to finish what I started. Explosives are so much more... final."

"What you started?"

"Yes, my dear sibling, what I started. How do you think I knew where to come? An amazing race, the Ifrits, their knowledge and interpretation of the world so different to ours, yet so easily shared with the right kind of offer. They know things that you couldn't begin to understand. You see, it was the Ifrits that brought me here, long before your little friends were even born. I spent months on this damnable mountain waiting for the chance to get inside... *months*. Those yetis are almost impervious to magic and I was very nearly found out. But once inside, the Ifrits' spell worked just as they said it would. Slow and steady enough to build my cabal of allies while the Veil crumbled. I wanted to let the world think that it had died of natural causes. But when you found the Engineer and the Medic

I was forced to show my hand ahead of schedule. You see, the Veil's falling is just the beginning. But fall it must – even if I have to blow this mountain off the face of the earth and let everyone know I did it."

"What in the name of Jupiter would make you do such a thing?"

"Why, our curse, of course, and the Demon who bestowed it. We were made ageless to help set them free, brother. Your shame forces you to fight it, when you should welcome them with open arms."

Ned watched Benissimo's face – it was a torn mixture of pain and rage. No wonder he hid his past – curse or not, he'd been made special by the very things he was trying to keep at bay.

"After hundreds of years of small evils, I finally understand my purpose," continued Barbarossa. "You choose to waste what you have – I choose to live as a God. The Demons have agreed to fight for me, brother, to give me the world."

"You're insane. They can't be controlled, by you or anyone."

"You're quite wrong. They will do exactly as they're told. You see, I have something they want, or will once this infernal machine curls up and dies. I'm going to bring back their Master. The Darkness is coming, brother, because I am going to bring it, and when it does, all of the world's creatures both light and dark will tremble at my feet."

A look of pure revulsion came over Benissimo. He spun to face Ned and Lucy.

"Whatever it is you need to do… DO IT!" he seethed, before leaping towards his brother.

Ned whipped his head back to the Source and pored over its tarnished metal in panic. Where should they start – he didn't have a blueprint for this, it was so… complex. What if Benissimo was right all along? All the trouble, the violence, the searching and running, and for what? So that he could let them all down? Never see his parents again? Let the world perish at the hands of a madman?

The surface of the metallic heart hummed like a tuning fork beneath his hands and the ceiling of the cavern tremored in reply. Lucy jumped as a small rock crashed at her feet.

"What do we do, Ned?" asked Lucy, her face a mirror of his own concern. She stroked one of the blackened vines hopefully, but nothing happened. "It's as if the sickness is too strong for me – I can feel it suffocating everything… but I can't shift it."

Behind them the two brothers fought, Benissimo wielding his whip and sword, Barbarossa his enormous blood-stained meat-cleaver. The Ringmaster's whip curled around fallen rocks and debris, hurling the pieces at his brother. But each time the butcher merely grimaced, before raising his cleaver to meet the rock and smashing it into dust. As Benissimo sought a bigger missile, Barba flung his cleaver through the air. It screamed like an angry bird, and the hilt connected, knocking the Ringmaster to the floor. Barbarossa charged. Benissimo calmly waited, and as his brother drew near he grabbed his arm and used his momentum to flip him on to his back, before righting himself and pinning him down with his knees. He grabbed at the butcher's fallen cleaver and raised it up ready to strike.

"Enough, brother!" the Ringmaster yelled.

Barbarossa spat the blood from his mouth and grinned.

"Enough or what? You'll kill me?"

"If I have to, yes, I'll end us both!"

"You don't have the stomach. You're too in love with your precious flock to say goodbye."

Benissimo cried out with rage, swinging the cleaver down towards his brother's throat; and then, just before it struck, he stopped.

"I knew it. You could have ended it all here and now. Just another inch or so and our curse would have come to an end."

In that moment, Barbarossa twisted an arm free, grabbed at a piece of fallen rock and, in a swift arc, he brought it up to Benissimo's head, knocking him to the floor with a cold *crack*.

"In my new world, *brother*, there'll be no room for love, fraternal or otherwise."

As indestructible as Benissimo was, a concussion to the head would take time to heal, time that his brother was only too happy to have. Barbarossa smirked at his unconscious sibling before turning his attentions to Lucy.

Both Medic and Engineer were oblivious to the approaching butcher. Ned was frantically flicking through his Manual, while Lucy was concentrating on the surrounding vines, eyes closed, arms outstretched, trying to banish their blackness, though still to no effect.

They were so lost in their efforts and the noise of falling stone from the crumbling mountain was so loud that they did not see or hear the butcher coming, nor the piece of rock – the one that had brought down his brother – still clutched in his hand. Until suddenly, to Ned's left, there was a hard crunch, and Lucy folded to the floor without so much as a whimper.

"NO!" Ned screamed, dropping to his knees.

While fearing to fail Ned had still dared to hope, even to the last, that they would somehow save the Source. But as he stared at Lucy's lifeless body, Ned realised that they had lost. Ned had failed them, every last one.

Huge slabs of stone now rained down all around them and the cavern was filled with the sound of screaming rock.

"I need you alive," Barbarossa yelled. "Once the heart dies, this whole place will come down. Quickly now!"

But even in this moment of utter defeat Ned would do anything other than obey the evil before him. A furious desperation filled Ned's heart and something inside of him took over – and this time he let it. What did it matter now if he lost control and destroyed everything around him? He had already failed. Better to take out Barbarossa too. With a pained roar Ned jumped to his feet, dropping the Manual. An idea was forming in his mind, his OWN idea. He was an Engineer by blood, maybe not the best one, but the only one here and now, and he would not give up. He Saw rock hewn into thin strands, weaving together, and a throng of snake-like chains exploded up from the stone around him, his ring thrumming at his finger. Hold him, he Told the chains, and in the blink of an eye they snaked through the air to wrap themselves tightly round Barbarossa. And as Ned Felt his anger, so did the chains, and they swallowed their own tails and tightened further, before their jaws snapped shut, into unbreakable stone locks. He'd done it. Perfectly.

"Unexpected but impressive," grimaced the butcher. Then his mouth turned to a smile. *"Demos-ra-sa,"* he spat, and from his sleeves poured dozens of small, dark, slithering creatures. Eyeless and scaled, with rows of black gnashing teeth. Perhaps they had once been familiars, but Barbarossa had turned them, to something new and cruel. They wrapped themselves around Barbarossa's chains and bit violently. But the chains held.

"Cortana-sar," seethed Barbarossa. And his creatures obeyed, their bodies thickening and teeth lengthening. They attacked once more, but again the chains held. The butcher bellowed furiously, *"ASCENS-SOR!"* and one of his blackened blobs swelled suddenly, its teeth now the size of swords. It clamped down and – crack – the first of the chains broke. Within a few short seconds Barbarossa had set himself free, and Ned's creation lay broken at his feet in a pile of useless stone.

Ned would not be beaten. The Veil was dying and his Medic no doubt already dead. He had nothing left to lose.

"*Famil-ra-sa*," he whispered, and the slow figure of Gorrn drew up from the ground.

Barbarossa's smile slid into darkness and his eyes filled with hate.

"Impudent boy!" He raised his hand and his creatures attacked. Gorrn fought valiantly, but there were too many. They circled him like a pack of eels, lashing with their tails and teeth, before chasing the outnumbered familiar into the chamber's stony shadows and disappearing from sight. All of them. Just as Ned had intended. Now he had Barbarossa alone again, Ned attacked one last time – channelling all his anger, fear and the last remnants of his courage into one final push.

His ring thrummed as piece after piece of the cavern's broken masonry bent to his will, flowing towards him in an ever-growing whirlwind of spinning rock. The stone turned to ice before blowing itself to fire. Melting, burning, freezing and warping, the air crackled like bottled lightning and Ned let his Feelings fly.

Barbarossa stood his ground, lashing at the stony missiles with nothing more than bare fists and Bessy. Ned was aware of nothing now but the atoms around him shifting to his will and roaring through the air, but eventually he began to tire – all Feeling fading, all Seeing blurred. Ned looked up, dazed, as the dust settled in silence around him. As it cleared, he saw the battered pirate, chest heaving and skin a mottled pattern of healing wounds. He was still standing.

Ned stared at him in disbelief. He'd used every ounce of power he had and still the butcher lived.

"You cannot beat me, boy. It's over. Come now, before this mountain falls down on both of our heads."

Ned knew the monster was right, the mountain would fall at any moment, but still he did not move.

Barbarossa fumed. "I have seen a thousand cities burn, helped wars engulf whole continents. I've made kings and destroyed them. How dare you stand up to me! You are… *nothing.*"

"You're wrong… about that… brother…"

Benissimo had crawled to where they now stood. He staggered painfully to his feet, his hand clasped around the grip of his blade.

Barbarossa sneered. "Why, Bene? Why do you fight for him when I've already won?"

"Because he can't see his own strength the way I do. Because he can't see how special he is, exactly as he is.

Because no matter how hard I've pushed him, he's never let me down. If a josser boy can come into our world and look its madness in the eye, with decency and courage… then I'll be damned if I won't do the same."

Ned could not believe the words he was hearing. But however much they meant, they had come too late.

"He's right, Benissimo… Lucy, she's… gone. I can't do it without her…"

"She's your Medic, boy, reach out to her. It's what you were born to do," the Ringmaster hissed, before throwing himself at his brother and driving his sword into his chest until its hilt touched bone. Barbarossa howled and dropped to the floor. Benissimo fell beside him. And as the butcher's life ebbed away, his brother gasped with him. The curse that had joined them in life was now dragging them both to their deaths.

CHAPTER 39

To Mend a Broken Heart

Ned fought the urge to run to Benissimo's side – he could not let the Ringmaster's sacrifice be in vain. He ran to Lucy and put his hand on hers, and as he did so their rings touched. And suddenly he saw her floating in his mind, in a darkness, cold and still. A great abyss making ready to take her.

"I've got you," he whispered, and the Medic stirred.

All around them the cavern echoed with the breaking of stone. The Source was coming to its end.

"Ned, how did you…?" she managed, still groggy from Barbarossa's blow.

"The same way we're going to mend the Source. We're the blueprints and the medicine, Lucy." He could see it all so clearly now. "When I asked Kitty what we needed to do she said – 'You have to give it your all'.

I thought she meant I had to learn it all, memorise the Manual exactly, follow the ways of all the Armstrongs that Engineered before me... but I'm not them. When I follow my heart – my Feeling – and not the Manual, that's when I Engineer best. That's how I made you that flower, how I ended the battle at the convent. And that's how we'll mend this heart, Lucy. With Feeling – together."

KAROOM.

There was another scream of exploding stone.

Lucy looked Ned straight in the eye and smiled.

And together they placed their hands on the Source's heart.

As they touched the metal, there was an almighty hum from all around them.

Under their skins, the tendrils of their rings coursed with power, running through their bodies like a howling wind, connecting with the Veil's heart. For the tiniest fraction of a second, Ned felt the many factions of the world's people, on both sides of the Veil. Their hopes, dreams and fears. The link he'd achieved with Kitty paled in comparison – this was a connection to the heart of everything. He felt the world's joy, the weight of its sorrow, and the Source's desire to protect it.

Magic, science, even nature, were all related. The Source's heart drew its power from them all.

Ned sent all that he was into the living metal heart – he Felt rather than Saw its many shattered chambers and dislocated components, and willed them back into order without really knowing what that order was, only knowing that it mattered more to him than anything ever had before. As he did so, he thought of his quietly heroic dad, of the mum that he had only just found but already couldn't bear to be without, of all his new friends – some of whom had given their lives FOR HIM; had believed in him even when he himself did not. He might never see any of them again, but right here, right now, he was where he was meant to be, doing what he was meant to do, and he wouldn't change it for anything in the world.

As Ned and Lucy mended and healed, Ned sensed something else, a retreating darkness. He felt it watching him, and only him, even as it fled.

"*Ned,*" it whispered.

And it was gone.

For the briefest of moments, everything was still and the great cavern lit up with a light so pure and bright that all that seemed to be left of the world was the beating hum of the Source and its now blooming chamber, resuscitated and alive once more.

Half delirious, half broken, Ned and Lucy pulled themselves up and staggered towards their dying Ringmaster, strewn out across the floor. His face was drained of colour, with no sign of his miraculous gift bringing him back to life. Beside him his brother twitched, and one of his fingers stirred.

"He could still make it, Ned," said Lucy, quickly checking the Ringmaster's pulse.

Ned nodded towards Barbarossa.

"So could he. Help me get Bene up; we've got to get out of here."

Despite their own exhaustion, they managed to raise the Ringmaster between them, half dragging his body along the street that led back to the cavern's entrance.

"I don't understand. We fixed the Source – why is the mountain still falling apart?" asked Ned, as he wrestled with his half of their burden, while dodging yet another falling boulder.

"I don't know, aftershocks maybe? Look over there – the rock ledge above the entrance – it's about to collapse. That's our only way out!"

"Hurry!"

They staggered their way up the last, long stretch of street, every step became more difficult, every breath harder to catch. Ahead of them cracks were starting to show in the great pillars either side of the city's entrance and the floor tremored. Benissimo stirred, his legs moved slightly, and his eyes opened.

"I… knew you could… do it," he managed, as they made it through the chamber's entrance and up the steps just in time, a wave of rocks shattering behind them.

"If you're healing then so is Barba! Hurry!" said Ned, pushing the Ringmaster ahead of him and turning to look behind.

But Benissimo's brother was already there, just behind them on the bottom step, cleaver in hand and murder written clear across his face.

A huge tremor threw Ned to the floor, but Lucy stepped forward, pulling out the dagger she'd kept from St Clotilde's and clenching it in her fist, she moved in front of the still weakened Benissimo.

"You don't scare me," she hissed through gritted teeth. And every inch of her face told Barba it was true.

"Really? WELL I SHOULD!" he roared.

This was the man that had killed her parents, Ned realised. Foolhardy as it was, she had probably been waiting for this moment ever since she'd been told about her past.

The butcher paced forwards and Lucy held her ground, her delicate hand wrapped around the dagger's handle and her arm tensing to strike.

Just then, from further up the stairs came the pounding of boots followed by the breathless arrival of a man in high-altitude gear, straight from the surface of the mountain and still covered in fresh snow.

The newcomer raised his hand in a sudden violent motion and the air in front of him crackled. Its atoms were thrust with such force, such incredible power, that they tore down the entrance tunnel's staircase, swerving past Ned, Lucy and Benissimo, before hitting the incredulous Barbarossa with the force of a rocket. He flew into the roof of the tunnel, cracking its stone surface in half. When he landed on the floor again, he did so with a thousand tonnes of stone fury collapsing about his ears, leaving the way back down the stairs to the Source's chamber sealed and Barbarossa lost from view. As Ned watched their newly-arrived saviour tear off his goggles, his mouth fell open. There could not – in all the world – have been anyone he wanted to see more.

Amazed by their sudden rescue, Lucy stared up at the welcome stranger. "Who are you?" she breathed.

It was Ned who answered.

"Lucy, I'd like you to meet Terrence Armstrong. My dad."

CHAPTER 40

Home

A moment later, both Ned and Lucy had collapsed with exhaustion, clearly more drained from the effort of healing the Source than they had realised.

When Ned woke again, it was in the shikari village of Mutu, to the beaming and slightly worn faces of Terrence and Olivia Armstrong. His mum, his actual mum, was sitting by his bedside. This time he was determined to do better.

But "I...I, um," was all he could muster.

"Just give her a hug, Ned," said his dad with a smile.

And that's exactly what he did. If a hug could talk, this one would have told Ned's mum everything he'd ever felt, everything he'd ever missed, or it might just have said thank you – for being alive.

"Ned, darling, I'm here now and I'm not leaving you.

Ever again," said Olivia Armstrong firmly.

Ned breathed a sigh of relief, but as the fog in his mind lifted, he remembered Benissimo's broken body and George and the others being swept away by the ice shelf.

"Where's everyone else?" he asked, already dreading the answer.

"Everyone's fine, Ned, at least they will be," answered his dad. "Thanks to the Tinker's calculations we managed to find your location on the mountain, quickly enough to dig everyone out of the ice before they froze too. It's a near miracle, but nothing worse than a few scrapes here and there, and all on the mend."

There was a fluttering by the tent's entrance, followed by a voice that Ned had been longing to hear.

"Hello, old bean."

"George!"

The king-sized ape was more bandages than fur, and had a noticeable limp, but nothing could mask his big toothy grin. Ned jumped out of bed and flung his arms around his friend.

"Ouch! I say, steady on, that toaster gave me a bit of a pummelling. Now then, who fancies one of my angel cakes?"

Gorrn, who had appeared by Ned's side the moment he'd stirred from his ordeal, now satisfied that his master was in good hands, slipped back into the shadows with an "Arr" and an angel cake of his own. Ned made a mental note to thank him later for his help inside the mountain.

As they ate their cakes, George and his parents filled Ned in on what had happened after he'd left the town of Fessler. Ned's dad had been leading a vicious pack of Darkling nightmongers on a goose chase around Hong Kong, when a newly recovered Olivia had finally got word to him of how things stood. He'd rushed immediately to the base of the mountain by every means possible to rendezvous with Ned's mum and the Circus of Marvels on what reinforcements the Twelve might be able to muster.

The shikari of Mutu had watched in awe, as ship after ship of the world's greatest circuses had arrived at their humble village. Oublier's second in command, Atticus Fife, had been the first on the scene, closely followed by other members of the council brave enough and fast enough to make the climb.

Both Abi and Squire Wormroot had miraculously come out of their enchantings when the Tinker's wind-wrangler had trapped Mystero. With his wife conscious once more, Rocky had been instrumental in leading the gathering reinforcements, including Ned's dad who had then left them to their search and rescue and raced on ahead.

The collapsing entrance to the Source's cavern had been the mountain's final tremor. With its heart fully functioning and protected once more, the mountain had settled quietly back into slumber. Search parties had scoured the area, but there'd been no sign of Barbarossa and they now unanimously agreed that the butcher must have been killed by the mountain's rocky embrace. How Benissimo was still alive if his brother wasn't was a mystery that not even the Ringmaster could answer.

Perhaps the greatest tragedy of the day had been the frozen bodies of the Source's shy guardians, the yetis. Not one of George's maybe-relatives had been found alive.

"I'm so sorry, George," said Ned.

"I'd have loved some answers. But now I know I'm not as alone as I thought I was, I can start looking afresh. Now, old bean, if you wouldn't mind accompanying us outside, there are some folk out there that would rather like to see you."

When Ned walked out of the infirmary, he was met

by the deafening cheers of the Circus of Marvels and all its allies. Horns, drums, cymbals – and of course, Alice – blasted out their welcome. With every sound and every holler, Ned's chest swelled. Josser, Engineer, Waddlesworth or Armstrong, whatever he was, he was most assuredly theirs, as much as they were his.

To his left, he saw Lucy was brought out of her tent at the same time, lifted high up on Rocky's shoulders, and was waving in his direction – and despite his aching limbs, George managed to lift Ned up on to his. Benissimo carved his way through the crowd towards them, top hat jauntily to one side, whip coiled excitedly in his hand.

"Ladies and Gentlemen," boomed the Ringmaster as he reached the front of the crowd, "from the mystic depths of faraway Grittlesby an Engineer arrived, and on the haunting slopes of the Val Lumnezia, our Medic was finally found. Two children of immeasurable talent and courage…" he continued as the crowd oohed and aahed, "…watch in awe, watch in wonder, prepare to have your ears blinded and your eyes deafened, MAY I PRESENT… NED AND LUCY, SAVIOURS OF THE VEIL AND THE REST OF THE WORLD WITH IT!"

The crowd went even wilder than before, if that was possible, and the party that ensued carried on till sunrise.

Jugglers with three sets of arms juggled, chameleon-skinned dancers changed colour as they pranced, and fire-sprites breathed their fire, in great arcs of orange light. Alice took to the skies in a flying race against a winged horse, a golden goose laid eggs for all the children, and the Ringmaster... well, he actually seemed to enjoy himself for the first time since Ned had met him. Everywhere Ned looked, his extended family of oddities and wonders celebrated and cheered as only the fair-folk could. While Daisy the Dagger presented him with a sword he'd most likely never use, the Guffstavson brothers filled the sky with great bolts of lightning, and the Tortellini boys spun dinner plates on their fingers atop a makeshift high wire, and all of course completely blindfolded, whilst Monsieur Couteau carved a vast roast into paper thin slices using his favourite rapier and a set of throwing knives.

But it was the sight of his parents that warmed Ned the most. It was the quiet way they looked at each other when they weren't laughing. The way they held each other's hands when they thought no one was watching. But above all, it was the fact that they were together. If anyone had told him on the morning of his thirteenth birthday that this was how his month would end, he would never have believed them. But then that was before he had found himself in the Circus of Marvels. That was before he became both an Armstrong and an Engineer – with a sprinkling of Waddlesworth thrown in for good measure.

EPILOGUE

A few days later, the 'Waddlesworth' family decided to return to Grittlesby.

Ned's parents were adamant they owed their son a childhood, and 'home' was the best place for it. Until he'd finished school, at least. Though Barbarossa was no longer a threat, he had mentioned a cabal of allies. After everything their family had done for the Veil, the Twelve had agreed to keep a protective eye on them, at least until Barbarossa's conspirators were found and apprehended. They were already on the trail of the Shar, who did not yet know that his coat of arms had been seen on Barbarossa's dreadnought.

With the Veil restored to full strength and the remaining Darklings and Demons who had crossed over having been rounded up by the frantic efforts of the circuses, the papers of the human world were now full of far-fetched explanations for the apparent hallucinations that seemed to have gripped its people. Experts laughed at eye-witness accounts of dragons in flight, fairy wickedness and whole magical worlds that had appeared overnight – in the desert, in a garden, and even in a kitchen cupboard! – only to disappear just as quickly a week later. The most commonly accepted explanation seemed to be a combination of infected drinking water and mass hysteria.

With the *Marilyn* still in need of extensive repairs, Benissimo was loaned one of the Twelve's airships to take them home. Landing on the green under the foginator's protective blanket, the airship's great engines were kept running as Ned said his goodbyes. Rocky and Abigail almost crushed the wind out of him and Alice had to be dragged away by Norman and at least ten other hands when she'd refused to let go of Ned's arm with her trunk. Even Finn managed a nod. And George was completely overcome.

"I shall miss having a roommate rather horribly I think. Here, a little bedtime reading," he said between sniffles, planting his enormous tome, *From Shalazaar to Karakoum*, into Ned's hands. "Now, do keep up your studies, old bean, make sure you eat a lot of fruit, and try and stay out of trouble, will you?"

"Thanks, George," said Ned with a teary smile, "I will. I wish you could come with us…"

But the heavy-hearted pile of fur had already turned and was skulking back to his trailer.

Back on his feet, the Glimmerman had presented Ned with a small hand mirror. It was a one-way key and would crack after a single use. If Ned ever found himself in trouble, this one-way journey would take him to an undisclosed safe house run by the Twelve.

"Thanks, Ignatius, but I don't think there'll be too much call for this where I'm going."

The Tinker also had a gift for him, which was by far his favourite.

"Well, sir, I know you're an Engineer and more than proficient when it comes to fixing, but I hoped you wouldn't mind me taking a look at this for you."

"Whiskers!" Ned shouted in delight as the Tinker presented his old pet to him.

After painstakingly collecting up what he could of the robot mouse's parts from the avalanche's trail of destruction, the Tinker had locked himself away for days, and in that time he had finally managed to get Whiskers operational again. Apparently, with a few custom-made enhancements. Ned's shadow rippled with approval –

Gorrn had taken rather a liking to his pet.

"You better look after him, I'll miss that little mouse," said Lucy, walking up to him at last.

"You do know he's not real, don't you?" said Ned with a smile.

"After everything we've been through, I'm not sure I'll ever know what's real again."

"Have you decided what you're going to do?" asked Ned.

"I don't think I can go back to the Order now. Not just because of the convent, I'm sure they'll have found somewhere else by now. There's just too much to see in the world; and I wouldn't fit in on your side of the Veil. So I think I'll stay on with Bene and the others, if they'll have me."

The ring on Ned's finger hummed and his chest hurt at the thought of Lucy leaving.

"They'd be lucky to," he said, looking at his feet. "It's been an adventure, Lucy. I hope I see you again some day."

Lucy gave him a knowing smile.

"Don't worry, Ned, I'll be seeing you soon enough."

"You sound very… sure."

She leant in closer and kissed him on the cheek.

As he looked at her, he noticed something different

about her eyes. They had a mischievous twinkle he'd seen before, but on someone else, someone older. In her hair there was something new too – a plastic pink and white cat on a pink hair slide, was it… was it Kitty's? But before he could ask her about it, they were joined by Benissimo, and Lucy slipped away.

"So this is him and here he is," said the Ringmaster gruffly, while doffing his top hat.

Benissimo looked as strong and able as the day Ned had met him. It made no sense, not if his brother were really dead. Unless they had somehow broken the curse.

Seeing the inquisitive look in Ned's eyes, the Ringmaster shrugged his shoulders.

"I don't have all the answers, pup, but I do know this. Curses can be broken. A princess doomed to sleep forever can be woken by a handsome prince. You and Lucy reversed whatever evil lay in that mountain. I should have died when my blade struck my brother, but I didn't. Whatever it was that joined us is gone. Whether it's you or the mountain I have to thank for it, I'll never know."

"You're welcome," smiled Ned.

"Veil-bound and right secure!" roared one of the Tortellinis behind them.

"Wind's about to change, Ned. We need to get a move

on, there's a level twenty-two in Athens that we've been asked to take a look at. An ordinary incursion – a cyclops, if the intel's right. The troupe could do with a more regular mission; all this saving the world stuff's been most unsettling."

"Can't say I'll miss you," grinned Ned.

"And there's no doubt my circus will fly higher without you along to mess things up," quipped back Benissimo.

"Goat face."

"I thought I was a rat?" laughed the Ringmaster. Then he did the most extraordinary thing – he gave Ned a hug.

"You, Ned, are a surprisingly exceptional young man."

Once Ned and his parents were safely aboard, the airship lifted off dreamily, through swirling clouds of fog. And with a roar of the engines and a final trumpet from Alice, the Circus of Marvels – the greatest show on earth – was gone.

Someone had once told him, that your home is where your heart beats the loudest. Ned's heart had never beaten more loudly or more proudly, even as he waved them goodbye.

THE END...
(or is it?)

ACKNOWLEDGEMENTS

The Circus of Marvels would have never happened without the encouragement, sage advice, and above all unbelievable patience of Paul Moreton. Paul is a Prince among agents and a King among men. I will never truly understand why he puts up with me but will always remain grateful.

A gigantic and heartfelt thank you to Ruth Alltimes and her team at HarperCollins, for knowing my story far better than I, for never having anything but unbounded enthusiasm and for not letting me get away with anything. Above all, I'd like to thank them for making it fun, whilst always making it better.

J FISHER

The next

NED'S
CIRCUS
OF
MARVELS

Coming soon!
Read on for a sneak preview…

United States Bullion Depository, Fort Knox, Kentucky. Three thirty-two AM.

Heavy boots pound the tarmac, as officers bark their orders and sniffer dogs whine, blinded by the rows of steaming halogen floodlights. More and more arrive by the second. A never-ending procession of armoured cars and trucks loaded with soldiers. More men, with more eyes to see. Above them, a dozen gunships and their ground-shaking propellers scan for signs. But there is nothing, only the appalling certainty that this is not a drill.

Beyond their fences and walls and barricades, a president

is being woken and powerful men in charge of a nation's numbers, its digits and its dollar bills, are meeting and shouting and blaming.

Underneath the chaos and the panic of the search, Shwartz and Greer sit in a bare cement room. Private Marvin L Shwartz, is in considerable trouble.

The Bullion Depository at Fort Knox was protected by both the United States mint police and the army, along with their tanks, attack helicopters and artillery. A force totalling well over thirty thousand men. The actual gold, all four-and-a-half-thousand metric tons, lay behind a one-of-a-kind, twenty-one inch, drill-, laser- and blast-proof door, designed by the Mosler safe company. It was monitored by twenty-four hour orbital satellite and ground-sweeping radar. Automated machine guns covered every possible entry point, and it was rumoured that the entire surrounding grasslands were carpeted with land-mines.

It was, to all intents and purposes, completely impregnable. That was of course until this morning on Private Shwartz's watch.

Greer's earpiece blinked: there was news from outside.

"They're here! Already? Are you serious?"

It was at this point that Private Shwartz started to perspire.

The door behind Greer slid open quietly and two men

dressed in light grey suits entered the room. One of the men had dark red-blond hair and introduced himself as Mr Fox. His greying accomplice, a Mr Badger, was built like a house and stood by the door without uttering a word. The Staff Sergeant was excused, leaving Shwartz with the two woodland animals that were Fox and Badger.

"Marvin, I represent the BBB. I hope you don't mind me using your first name Marvin, I find it helps enormously in these situations," said Mr Fox.

"No Sir," Shwartz paused. "Sir the BBB, I'm sorry, is that a part of Homeland Security? Am I going to prison?"

"No and maybe. Bagshot Bingley and Burke is not connected to the US or any other government body. We are insurance underwriters and the United States gold reserve is one of our contracts. As I'm sure you can appreciate, a claim of this magnitude presents logistical problems, even for an outfit with as much reach as ours. When something of this value goes missing, it is my job to get it back and rest assured Marvin, I will get it ALL back."

"All sir? But we only had half here, the rest is..."

"I'm afraid the other half was taken earlier this week. Now please, Marvin, if you wouldn't mind, let's start with the issue of 'access'. You were the last guard Marvin, between the intruder and the vault. Is there anything you can tell me?"

"No Sir. Like I told Staff Sergeant Greer, one minute I'm walkin' my route, and I hear these footsteps. The next thang I know, I am on my back, and the vault doors are wide open."

"Marvin, there are over fourteen retinal eye scanners, over twelve hundred security cameras and countless laser trip wires in this building. If your statement is true, then the intruders managed to waltz through the entire compound undetected. Which is almost as unlikely as the removal of thousands of tons of gold… in less than an hour. Do you have any idea who could have done that?"

"No, no I don't Mr Fox."

"Is there anything you DO know Marvin?"

"There is… one thang, kinda weird. Just after I heard the footsteps there was this music playin', with no notes."

Fox leant in a little closer and smiled.

"Music with no notes. That sounds… familiar."

Before he had even raised his hand, Badger produced a phone from his briefcase, only it wasn't a brand that Private Shwartz had ever seen and there were no keys or touchpad to dial any numbers.

"Owl? Yes it's Fox. I'm afraid there's been a development. It's happened again…"